Touch
of
Death

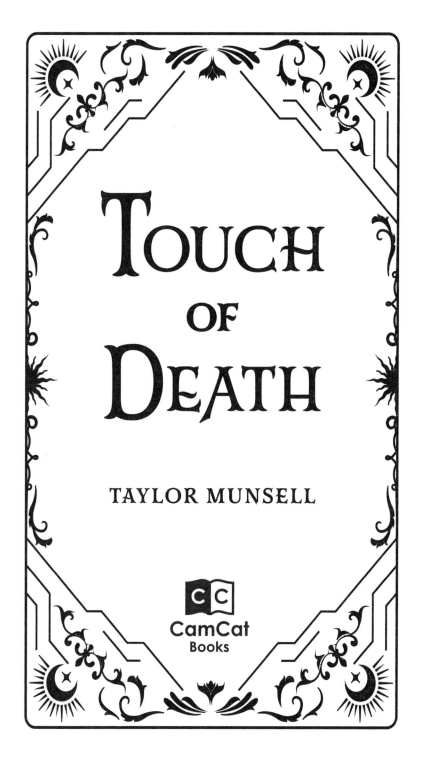

TOUCH
OF
DEATH

TAYLOR MUNSELL

CamCat Books

CamCat Publishing, LLC
Fort Collins, Colorado 80524
camcatpublishing.com

Hardcover ISBN 9780744310238
Paperback ISBN 9780744310245
Large-Print Paperback ISBN 9780744310290
eBook ISBN 9780744310252
Audiobook ISBN 9780744310306

Library of Congress Control Number: 2024931200

Book and cover design by Maryann Appel
Interior artwork by ArtVector, Lazarev, Lyubov Ovsyannikova

5   3   1   2   4

FOR CHARLOTTE & OLIVIA

ALWAYS FOLLOW YOUR DREAMS

CHAPTER

1

BLOOD DOESN'T SCARE ME. That's not the reason for the tremor in my hands.

There are things far worse than a little blood.

"I can't believe you're making me do this," I grumble, kicking the toe of my boot against the gym floor.

"I'm not making you do anything." Felix bumps me with his broad shoulder. "I simply suggested you should go through the blood drive. It's expected."

My snort earns a narrowing of his brown eyes. Expected. I don't know how a blood drive honors the memory of a student, but he's right: every person in the school is "doing their part."

"But that doesn't mean I have to like it." I reach up to fiddle with the peridot crystal pendant at my neck. If nothing else, maybe it'll actually shield my emotions today. "I should have asked Gran to make me a draft to calm my nerves."

Though, I'm not sure even Gran, the most powerful witch in the coven, could make a draft strong enough for that. She wouldn't try if she knew I was only doing this to say I need to go to bed earlier to recover and get out of the coven meeting tonight.

Felix lowers his voice. "We can leave."

I shake my head. "We've already been seen. Time to be a big girl." And we're next. The line of students waiting to donate blood still stretches behind us, but any second now Felix and I will be whisked away to one of the portable beds lining the school gymnasium.

"Your call." Felix shrugs. "Anyway, no harm can really come from it."

Not true.

I glance around the gym. Every light is on, but they aren't really bright enough. The stench of stale sweat hangs in the air, mingling with the too-strong smell of antiseptic.

A shudder courses through me as I try, and fail, not to think about what that antiseptic smell is covering up. Blood might not scare me, but it's still not my favorite.

At least there are no unwelcome guests so far. Although they aren't visible, I feel them pressing in on me, trying to make me see them.

I tug on the hem of my glove, more out of habit than anything. They're one of my favorite pairs: the black lace is almost as smooth as the silk that lines them. If I have to wear gloves, might as well make a statement.

"They'll be wearing gloves, too," Felix says gently. "They won't touch you."

Nodding, I hope I seem more confident than I feel.

"Felix Davies," another junior girl calls. Her sleek black ponytail falls to her mid-back. She's dressed in scrubs, so she must be in the school's nursing program. Her dark eyes move to find Felix grinning at her. Color floods her beige skin.

Felix has that effect on most girls—and boys—to be honest. Between his warm brown skin, easy smile, and dark, inviting eyes, he can charm anyone.

Except me. Just thinking about it gives me the creeps. He's basically the big brother I never had.

"Come w-with me," she stammers. Poor girl.

"Georgiana Colburn?" an unfamiliar voice calls.

"George," I say reflexively. Felix glances back and gives me a thumbs-up.

The nurse and owner of the unfamiliar voice smiles at me, her eyes only momentarily snagging on my blue hair.

"Right this way, young lady," the nurse says as she escorts me down the row of beds. I glance back, trying to catch Felix's eyes, but he's busy charming his student nurse while she gets him settled.

I follow my nurse to an empty bed, palms slick with sweat inside my gloves as I sit down. The crinkling of the paper lining the bed as I adjust makes me cringe.

As the nurse works, my mind races, trying to think of any spell or incantation, anything that would make this situation less daunting, but I come up with nothing. For being a witch in a coven so connected to death, an event with this much blood should send power coursing through me, especially considering my specific gifts. But I've got nothing. Maybe I should actually pay attention in my magic lessons.

I hear the snap of gloves, a tear, and then the smell of alcohol burns my nose. In a few swift movements, she is tapping on my wrapped arm, looking for a vein. The nurse notices the way my whole body tenses as she touches me.

"Take a deep breath," she says, probably thinking I'm nervous about the needle, not that her skin might touch mine, and I'll wind up experiencing her death. Even with her gloves on, I don't feel safe.

A hiss escapes my lips as the needle slides in.

"Good girl." She adjusts the blood bag before pulling off her gloves and tossing them in one of the bins along the center of the room. The blood drains from my face at the sight of her bare skin. "You're all set. I'll be back to check on you in a little while."

She heads to another student down the row, leaving me alone. After almost a lifetime of dealing with it, I've gotten quite good at avoiding touching. Gloves, covered skin, even the attitude is another way to keep me safe.

Still, the occasional slip happens. Someone will pat my cheek or catch my arm, their fingers grazing the skin between my glove and sleeve, and I'll slip into experiencing their death. Just the thought makes me shudder.

The bed to my left is empty, but the poor kid in the bed to my right looks like he's trying to scoot as far away from me as possible. My attitude might work a little too well in keeping people away.

It still hurts my feelings, even after all these years. I wish I could tell my classmates that I don't want to get near them either. The encounter is always worse for me than it is for them.

My eyes find Felix, and he flashes me a grin, just as cool as ever. His poor student nurse is still standing by him, black ponytail bouncing as she talks.

I scan the rest of the gym. My gaze catches on a girl with dark skin and tight curls. She smiles and gives a little wave. I stare back at her as my brain tries to process if she meant the wave for me.

It's possible. She's a witch, too, and with Gran as the coven's Supreme, she'd know who I am. She's new, only moving here a couple of weeks ago for the beginning of the school year. I rack my brain trying to remember why she moved here. Something about a divorce, I think. Intercoven marriages can be tricky, especially when the spouses have two different magics. Almost every witch ends up in the coven that's not ours. Death witches make other witches kind of jumpy. Ridiculous, but true.

I realize I've let my mind wander too long, but the boy on her left catches her attention before I can decide to wave back.

Closing my eyes, I lean against the headrest, trying not to think of ways to kill Felix for talking me into this. I know he meant well, but still. It's not like he has to worry about the risks. Ghosts don't appear to him if he lets his guard down. My breathing and the squeaking of shoes on the gym floor fill my ears. A heavy feeling settles on me, raising the hairs on my arms. Someone's watching me.

"Why hasn't anyone come to see me yet?" an all-too-familiar voice asks from beside me.

Shit.

Guess the crystal isn't going to work today. With the way my magic has been acting up as my ascension closes in, I shouldn't be surprised. I squeeze my eyes shut tighter, but I can still feel her beside me.

Of all the gifts the Goddess could bless us with, being a medium isn't a common one among magic wielders, but it's not unheard of, especially among death witches. Gran would always spew something about embracing the cycle of life and how their presence is an honor. But she never had a ghost appear behind her in the mirror when she was brushing her teeth. When I was little, it would terrify me when the occasional ghost showed up. As I got older, it became more of a nuisance than anything else.

"Hey, are you okay? You look a little pale. Well, paler than usual."

I'm sure she does, too. Maybe if I don't respond, she'll go away.

"Isn't your name Georgia or something?"

Guess not. "Georgiana—but my friends call me George." Well, friend.

"Whatever. Why did that nurse help you first? I was here before you."

I peel one eye open. Sure enough, Jen's lounging on the empty bed, bubblegum-pink bicycle helmet in her lap. Her complexion is more translucent than golden now, but there's no mistaking her. I've put a lot of time into trying to decide what would make this less weird. At least they never look gruesome, just a slightly less corporeal version of themselves.

I think I would have died the first time I saw one if they were the horrific-looking ghosts from horror movies. I can't think of a way ghosts could be normal, but it always creeps me out when they're carrying the items they died with. If there's a reason some do and some don't, I'm not aware of it. Though, I've never been inclined to ask one.

"I don't know, Jen. Maybe she likes me better." Not the nicest thing to say.

But Jen wasn't the nicest either.

She eyes me, sucking her teeth before speaking. "You know my name?"

"Obviously."

Everyone knows her name. If they didn't before, they sure do by now. In the three weeks since the accident, she's become more popular than ever. This is the Jennifer Monroe Memorial Blood Drive after all.

She preens and shifts on the bed.

"Makes sense." She looks at me again. "You look a little sweaty."

Brushing my damp bangs from my forehead, I mumble a yes before glancing back at Felix. The grin is gone, and concern now creases his brow.

"I'm fine," I mouth to him. He nods, looking unconvinced. I can't blame him. While I've been dealing with this most of my life, he's only seen me interact a few times. Normally, I can ignore them. Unless I'm under duress, like when blood is flowing from a needle in my arm into a bag.

Jen follows my gaze. "You're always hanging around him. Are you two, like, a thing?"

I snort, forgetting I'm trying not to look like I'm talking to myself. The boy on the bed to my right scoots a little farther away. "No."

"Dumb question. You aren't his type." She scoffs, dragging her eyes from my blue hair to my Doc Martens.

"I'm sure that's it," I say through gritted teeth. I have to remind myself that she's been through a lot.

Jen pulls her long blond hair over her shoulder before leaning back, the paper remaining smooth beneath her. "I hope they hurry up soon. I'm supposed to meet Jason tonight."

I don't respond. I'd prefer to avoid being the one to tell her she won't be meeting Jason tonight. Or any other night.

"Hey," Jen says as the nurse comes to check my bag.

"You okay, sweetie?" the nurse asks as I cringe. I nod. "Hmm. Well, you should be done soon. Yell if you need anything." She smiles before turning away.

"Um, I need something!" Jen calls after her. The nurse doesn't turn around. "Unbelievable! She just completely ignored me."

As much as I don't want to be the one to tell her what's happening, I can never bear when they're in this state of confusion.

"Jen?" Might as well get this over with. "What's in your lap?"

Jen watches the nurse another moment before looking at the helmet. "My bike helmet." She runs a finger along the large crack on the side. "How'd this get here?" she breathes.

Don't make me be the one to say it.

"Weird. I don't know why I have this. I don't ride my bike to school."

Only to her boyfriend's house at night. She's still looking at her helmet, confusion crinkling her perfect skin.

I hate this part. I hate when they don't know. I hate having to be the one to tell them.

"Hey Jen." I dig into my back pocket for the flyer and awkwardly unfold it with one hand. "Can you come here and read this for me?"

"Can you not read?" she snarks, not looking at me.

I take a deep breath and remind myself, again, that she's been through a lot. "I'm a little woozy. Please?" The last word grates along my nerves.

"Fine." She hops up from the bed. Her hands grip her helmet as she comes up beside me.

"Why do you have a flyer with my picture on it?" Her pert nose wrinkles in disgust.

"Just read the paper." I sigh, bracing myself.

So many emotions flit across her beautiful face: confusion, anger, grief, before settling on denial. Her emotions clang through me.

"This can't be for me." She glances around the gymnasium at our classmates gathered there.

"It is."

Hazel eyes lift to meet mine. It's not lost on me that I may be the only one to ever look into those eyes again.

"But why am I here then?" Her words are barely a whisper. I tense as realization dawns and her gaze drops to the cracked helmet in her hand.

Her jaw slackens as her wave of despair crashes into me.

And then she's gone, unable to hold on to her form in her anguish. It's always the same.

She didn't even know my name before today, but a tear still rolls down my cheek. And then Felix is interrupting his bubbly young nurse, trying to get up and come to me. He knows something's wrong now. I won't be able to convince him otherwise.

My eyes find them, the others lurking on the outskirts of the gym. The ones who have been with me since the beginning and the ones who have joined along the way. I feel them—their grief and rage and despair—as they linger in my peripherals. They're a part of me.

I wonder if Jen will join them.

CHAPTER

2

AS SOON AS THE NURSE pulls the needle from my arm, I'm off the bed and leaving the blood drive, completely ignoring her as she scolds me about needing to take it easy.

Felix is hot on my heels as I try to put distance between myself and the gym. Maybe if I walk fast enough, the ghosts will stay in there for now. Not likely, but a girl can dream.

"What happened?" Felix calls after me.

"Nothing." I don't look back as I stomp down the hallway.

"Did someone touch you?"

"No." Thank the Goddess for that. "I told you, it was nothing."

"It didn't look like nothing." Felix's long legs help him easily keep up with me. The hallways are empty since most students are in the courtyard before school starts or at the blood drive.

"What do you know? You couldn't see her." I mean it like a joke, but my words sound brittle even to my ears.

"George, the comedian." Felix grabs my elbow to stop me. He lets go when I wince and nods at my arm, at the bandage under my sleeve. "I'm sorry, I forgot."

"It's fine."

I take a deep breath through my nose.

"It was Jen," I say with a whoosh.

"Monroe?"

"One and the same."

"Is she still here?" Felix glances around.

"No, she couldn't hold on to her form." I don't tell him that there are still spirits lurking on the outskirts of my vision. My hope that they would stay in the gym was obviously in vain.

His lips pull into a thin line. "I'm sorry. I shouldn't have made you do that."

"You didn't force me to do it. Just suggested. Besides, you didn't know that would happen."

"You told me it was a possibility."

"I did."

"I should have listened."

"Yes, you should have." There's jest in my voice this time, but the pain doesn't leave Felix's face. "Oh, come on, Felix. I'm used to it."

He flinches. I can't blame him. No sixteen-year-old should be used to seeing ghosts. Even ones who are death witches.

"Buy you an ice cream after practice?" he asks.

"Trying to assuage your guilt with bribes?"

"Maybe." His shoulder lifts in a lopsided shrug.

"I accept."

"Hoped you would. Don't be late." Felix is already turning down the hall. Most of us would use giving blood as a reason to skip class. Felix, on the other hand, insisted we do it before school so we didn't miss anything. At least Gran won't suspect anything when I tell her I need to rest instead of going to the coven meeting.

"I never am," I say, watching him go before heading to my first class of the day.

-◦◦◦◦◦◦◦◦◦◦◦◦-

THE AP HISTORY classroom is humming with excitement as I slide into my desk. The desk next to me is still empty, the other witch from my coven—I remember now her name is Trixie—still at the blood drive. I feel a twinge of guilt that she's been sitting next to me for a week, and today was the first time I noticed her. I'd like to say it's because she never made an effort, but that's not exactly true either. My eyes flick to the empty desk as I try to convince myself I'm not a total asshole for ignoring someone less than three feet away from me.

My phone vibrates, stirring me from my self-loathing.

FELIX: im starving.

GEORGE: big baby.

GEORGE: you should have eaten. class hasn't even started.

I can picture him sitting in his AP Physics class, acting like the world is ending because he hasn't had second breakfast yet.

The final bell rings. Mr. Whitaker's desk is empty; the sub is probably running late for the day.

I'm watching the three bubbles as Felix types when a voice startles me. I jump and the phone almost slips from my gloved fingers.

"You look like you don't sleep at all." Jen leans forward, propping her chin in her hands. She's sitting in Trixie's empty desk.

The seat in front of me is empty, but Steve, the senior two seats up, turns around to see what startled me. When he sees nothing, he rolls his eyes before turning around. I refuse to engage. No one else can see her, so no one will know I'm ignoring her.

"I know you can hear me." Jen leans over to wave a hand in front of my face. "Yoo-hoo, earth to George."

I don't know why I continue wearing this peridot. It obviously has no impact on the ghosts of high school girls.

"Go away." It comes out as a mumbled growl since I'm trying not to move my lips.

"Huh?" Steve turns around again.

"Nothing. I didn't say anything," I blurt.

"Of course you didn't." He turns back around.

The seconds tick by, the class growing more anxious as no one enters the room.

"Where's the old guy who's usually in here?" Jen asks.

I shoot her a glare from the corner of my eye. She doesn't notice. Of course Jen wouldn't know who Mr. Whitaker is. She wasn't in his class, so he wasn't important enough to be on her radar.

I'm just texting Felix to ask what happens if the teacher doesn't show, when the door opens.

"Oh, he's—" Jen starts. I pop my head up, glancing at the now empty seat. She's gone. That was abrupt.

I turn to see what she was looking at.

My mouth drops open.

A young man strolls in. His shiny black hair is swept to one side of his inviting face. Thick, black-rimmed glasses are perched on his nose and a tan satchel is tucked under his arm.

The room is instantly silent at his presence.

He glances at the still empty desk before turning to look at us, a smile spreading across his face. I swear I hear sighs throughout the classroom.

He's almost painfully handsome.

"Holy shit," Krista mutters behind me. She was Jen's best friend and is one of the most popular girls in school. If even she is starstruck, he must be as good-looking as I think he is.

"Is Mr. Whitaker not here?" he asks, voice smooth.

No one answers him.

His smile doesn't falter as he spots one of the only open desks in the room: the one in front of me. He walks toward it with confidence, sliding into the seat as every set of eyes in the room watches him.

If he's thrown off by the amount of attention he's getting, he doesn't let on. He's only saved from the stares of the class by the door opening and the second shock for the day.

Mr. Whitaker shuffles into the room, not glancing at the class until he plops into the chair behind his desk.

"I thought he died," Krista mumbles behind me.

I would have too if I didn't see the people who have actually died on the reg.

Mr. Whitaker lets out a hacking cough that hurts my chest just listening to it before he finally looks up. He scans the room, his gaze landing on the now occupied seat in front of me.

"Class, we have a new addition. Some of you may remember my grandson, Silas. He'll be staying with me this school year."

"There's no way," Krista says. She leans forward to whisper at me. Normally she ignores my existence, but apparently she can't keep her revelation to herself. "That's Snotty Silas. I don't know what he did, but he got hot."

I squint at the back of his head as if that would help me see any kind of resemblance to the skinny kid with oversized glasses and a constantly running nose to the boy who even I can admit is attractive, now sitting in front of me. He moved with his parents when we were all still in elementary school, never to be heard from again. Until now, it seems.

Mr. Whitaker soldiers on, oblivious to the whispers spreading like wildfire in the room. "I was out retrieving him from his parents' house in Seattle. But now I am back. Where did you leave off?"

No one else is paying attention, too busy trying to check out Silas without openly staring. Mr. Whitaker spreads the papers around on his desk, still waiting for an answer. I shift in my seat before clearing my throat. Might as well be the scapegoat. "The Civil War."

Mr. Whitaker harrumphs. I guess that's his version of thank you. "As George said, let's open our textbooks to page forty-seven." That's it. No other introduction, no other explanation as to his absence or the arrival of his grandson. He just dives into the lesson as the rest of us sit and blink at him.

My phone buzzes.

FELIX: whitaker is back? a new student? what is today?!?

GEORGE: a thursday.

GEORGE: wait, how do you know? you're not even in this class.

Three dots pop up as I wait for his response. I look up to find Mr. Whitaker writing on the whiteboard. Silas watches him. Although his hair is still in that *I just woke up like this* style, the hairline on the back of his neck is cut with precision.

Gooseflesh prickles my skin.

FELIX: krista texted me. apparently he's beautiful.

Turning around, I see Krista has her phone in her hand and is typing away furiously.

"What?" she mouths as I turn back around.

GEORGE: news spreads fast.

FELIX: we've got to stay entertained somehow.

FELIX: what's his story? where's he from? why's he here?

I flick my eyes to Mr. Whitaker, but he's just reading from the textbook page. His voice is so calm and soothing, I'm sure the class would be falling asleep if it weren't for the excitement of a new student.

Trixie's arrival already got the town whispering. In a small town, one new student is an event. Two, especially in the same grade, is unheard of.

Silas looks fully alert, like he's hanging on every word Mr. Whitaker is saying. I didn't know anyone could be that interested in his lectures. The old man seems to barely register that students are in the room.

His clothes, though stylish, almost look like he popped out of the wrong decade. It could be purposeful, but his pants are just a little too high and his cardigan looks like something Felix's grandpa would have worn.

But the more I look at him, the less sure I am about my feeling. Maybe I'm just overreacting, still on edge after the blood drive.

FELIX: ???

GEORGE: idk. he didn't say much.

FELIX: weird.

It certainly is.

FELIX: wait, snotty silas?

It's been a decade since he left, but he still hasn't been able to shake the nickname.

GEORGE: one and the same.

FELIX: now I'm really curious.

GEORGE: what's new? we'll talk later.

The rest of the class continues in the same way, with Mr. Whitaker reading the remainder of the chapter out loud before assigning the short response questions at the end of the chapter for homework. He gives us the rest of the class to work on the responses, and the sound of pencils scribbling is mixed with the whispers of students.

And for whatever reason, Jen never reappears.

CHAPTER

3

THE HALLWAYS ARE EMPTY SINCE everyone is still in class as I exit the bathroom. I usually only go to the bathroom during class. No nosey glances or gossip that way. And no one to bump into, literally. My black lace gloves are tucked into my back pocket. I've never much liked wearing gloves; it's more of a necessary evil than a comfort. Still, I feel naked without them, too exposed. But I refuse to put them on before my hands are fully dry.

Unfortunately, the bathroom was out of paper towels again, so I'm stuck wiping my damp hands on my pants as I leave.

As the bathroom door swings shut behind me, I take a step forward and my foot slips out from under me. My arms fling out, intent on stopping my tumble.

A hand reaches out, catching mine on the descent. The heat of bare skin soaks into mine and there's only a moment of panic, my brain trying to find a way out of this, before I fall in a new way . . .

-««•»»--««•»»--««•»»-

SHE LOOKS OUT of place in this too bright room, the blue of her hair like a shining halo. Her teeth are bared, those emerald eyes shining with a feral rage.

"Big mistake," she growls.

I can't help but smile. I love a girl with spunk.

A scream erupts from her throat as she launches at me in a tear of blue. She slams into me, the full weight of her slight frame toppling us to the floor. I barely have time to draw a breath before her knife sinks into my shoulder.

I didn't even see her grab one. She moved so fast.

Pain erupts as the blade slices deeper, black dots flooding my vision.

Now I'm the one screaming.

Is this it? Is this how I go?

At the hand of a seventeen-year-old girl?

I try to shove her off, but she's like a woman possessed. She rips the knife from my shoulder. She straddles me as she raises the knife again, this time with both hands gripping the handle, and sinks it in.

Again.

And again.

The pain is unbearable, muddying my thoughts. There are so many explanations I have, but now, all I can think about is getting her off, making her stop.

I try to push again, but my arm fails me. I'm just so tired.

My struggles don't faze her.

She's coated in my blood. A vision in crimson. It spatters her face, coats her stomach, slicks her hands, but still, she keeps stabbing.

She's screaming words, my blood flinging into her mouth with reckless abandon.

Is this what it feels like? Is this death?

Is it finally my time?

I try to cough, but a wheezing sound escapes as something warm drips down my chin.

She sinks the knife in again. I feel it as it pierces my lungs, my heart. Pain pounds through my chest.

Tears are tracking down her beautiful bloodstained face. Clean streaks between the gore.

"Go. To. Hell," she says through clenched teeth.

Darkness seeps around my vision, so I can only see her face as I—

⸻⸻⸻

MY EYES FLY open, my breath coming in heaving gasps. I can't get enough air into my lungs. My throat squeezes tighter.

His face is above me, concern furrowing his brow.

Blood thrums through my body, thundering in my ears.

"It's George, isn't it? Are you all right?" Silas asks. I barely hear him through the buzzing. He reaches for my elbow.

It all comes back to me: my fall, his hand reaching out to catch me. He must have lowered me to the ground when I slipped into his death, because that's where I find myself. I scurry back, shoving my hands behind me to scoot away. Sweat coats my palms, and they slip out from under me. My elbow slams into the tile. I keep pushing.

I can't touch him again. I won't go through that again.

Whatever that was, I never want it to happen again.

As if I'm back in the vision, I feel the slide of the knife through my ribs. Hot blood sliding down my side, filling my lungs. The taste of copper.

Not real. Not real. Not real.

I close my eyes, but the image of my blood-slicked form is seared into the back of my eyelids. My eyes fly open.

"Are you okay? You passed out." His tone is concerned, but there's something in his face, almost like he's assessing me.

❋ 18 ❋

Tears flood my lashes. My head is shaking. He moves forward again.

"Fine," I choke out, pushing away from him again. My whole body trembles, adrenaline, fear, and confusion sparking too many connections in my brain. I need to leave. Now. I can't stay here.

"You don't look fine. We should get you to the nurse." Silas reaches for me again.

The sound that comes out of me sounds more animal than human. He pauses.

"I'm fine. Really. Happens all the time." I've repeated this so many times it actually feels natural.

Silas is still eyeing me. He doesn't seem afraid like most people are. There's concern etched into his features, which makes this whole thing worse. My stomach rolls as I feel his blood on my skin again. I need to get out of here. I need to find Felix.

Desperately, I try to remember how to walk. I can't think of anything but his blood slicking my hands.

I choke on a sob.

Anything. I need to think of anything other than the knife sinking deeper. Anything other than the feel of the blade as it split my— his—chest.

"I don't think you are." His gaze is piercing. "You look pale."

"I'm fine." I start to stand, and he reaches for me again when I stumble. I dance from his grip, almost collapsing to the ground again. "Fine," I say, backing away from him. I mutter one more "fine" before turning on a heel and sprinting from him.

⫷⫸ ⫷⫸ ⫷⫸

THE CHILL OF the day rips through my lungs in heaving gasps. I texted Felix as soon as I burst from the hallway. My fingers were shaking so much that I could barely type out the three letters.

GEORGE: SOS.

He knew what that meant and was already rushing across the parking lot before I had even made it to his car, probably using his Felix charm to get a hall pass. Felix has me propped against his Jeep, another item in a long string of "forgive me for not being around" gifts from his parents, his face inches from mine.

"George, look at me. Take a breath," Felix says, gripping my shoulders.

My hair spills from my ponytail, sticking to the wet streaks on my face as I continue to shake my head.

"No, no, no, no, no, no," I hear myself muttering, but it's like someone very far away is speaking.

The dead coalesce all around us, their curiosity barely overpowered by my emotions. They're crowding the deserted parking lot. I see them through my tears. Jen's in front, but she doesn't come any closer. None of them do.

But since Felix arrived, I haven't been able to say the words, to tell him what I saw.

What I felt myself do.

"George!" I can hear the panic in his voice now.

"No, no, no, no, no," I keep muttering, mascara tears tracking down my cheeks. There's a ringing in my ears, drowning him out so the only other thing I hear is the sound of the knife as it broke through bone, the splattering of blood as I lifted my hand again.

Felix's fingers dig into my arms over my sleeves. I'm drowning in the memory, the blood that filled my lungs, Silas's lungs. Felix shakes me. I can't stop crying. My breath comes in short bursts. I can't take a full breath. Black spots speckle my vision.

Warmth spreads through my skin as Felix's hands touch either side of my face . . .

-◄◄◄•►►►--◄◄◄•►►►--◄◄◄•►►►-

"GOODNIGHT, MY DEAR," I hear as I close my eyes, sleep calling to me. My breath evens, slowing to a steady rhythm. I wonder . . .

-«‹•›»- -«‹•›»- -«‹•›»-

EASE FLOODS THROUGH my body as I open my eyes, but pure rage quickly follows it. My hands collide with Felix's chest, and I shove him away from me with all of my strength. Despite our considerable height difference and blood loss, my anger must bolster me because he lets out an *oomph* as he stumbles backward.

"What. The. Hell. Felix!" I yell.

He's never touched me without permission before. Never. It is a violation of everything that makes us, us.

"I'm sorry!" He's rubbing his chest.

Good. I hope it hurts.

"I didn't know what to do. I've never seen you like that. You were hyperventilating." When I say nothing, he continues. "I panicked. George, I'm sorry."

My eyes search his face, rage draining as quickly as it flooded me. "Don't do it again," I mutter, a sudden exhaustion weighing on me. I slide down the side of the Jeep to sit leaning against the tire.

He crouches in front of me. "I won't. Why are you out here?"

I'm not sure how to answer that.

The sun's shifted behind the clouds, and I shiver, not just from the cold.

My jacket's still inside. And my backpack. Both still next to my desk in class. I don't think I can bring myself to go in, so I just rub my arms for warmth.

I suck in one shaky breath. Exhale. Another less shaky breath. "I touched Silas."

Felix sighs, moving to sit next to me. He brings up his knees, resting his forearms on them.

"I'm sorry," he says. And it's empathy, not pity, in his words. "I can't imagine how hard it is."

I take a shuddering breath. Hard doesn't begin to describe it. I usually have an . . . adverse reaction when I experience a death. But I've never had anything like this.

"Is it soon?" Felix asks, sympathy slipping into his words. Of course that's the most logical reason for how upset I am. The real reason is so much worse.

I lift my glasses on top of my head and swipe the tears from my cheeks. My fingers come away black and my mind registers that my hands are still bare. My gloves are still tucked into my back pocket. I pull them out and tug them on. My carelessness with them today has already cost me too much.

"No," I say. "Well, I don't know." The thought makes my stomach churn. Figuring out when it happens would mean reliving the vision. I can't do that. My hair was still blue, and the fury in my eyes is something I hope to never see again. Whatever led up to this, it wasn't premeditated. It was out of anger.

"Then what happened, George?" Felix's voice wavers, his concern deepening into fear. "I have never seen you this shook up."

A part of me doesn't want to tell him. He's my best friend and one of the only people who looks at me with no judgment. He'll never look at me that way again. There's no sensible way to say what I'm about to say that doesn't make me sound like a monster.

Maybe I am the monster.

"It was me," I whisper.

"What was you? Wait, it was your death?" Felix's brown skin turns ashen.

I shake my head. "It's worse than that." Inhale. Exhale. Another tear slips free. "It was me," I say again. "I—" Another breath. "I killed him." My eyes fall to the asphalt. I watch Felix's shoes, unable to look him in the eyes.

When the silence stretches on, I finally look up. Felix's lips are pulled into a thin line, the charm that usually oozes from him replaced with something that feels like pain.

"Felix?" I say when I can't take his silence any longer.

"It must be a mistake."

"You know it isn't." Felix knows, better than most, what these visions mean. Once a death is written, it cannot be changed.

"When?"

"I don't know. Soon? I was a little overwhelmed by what was actually happening, but I looked the same, I think."

"Why?" he asks.

I'm grateful he doesn't ask how I saw myself in the vision. I'm definitely not ready to explain that.

He pushes up, pacing in front of me. I watch him for a bit, grateful for the distraction of his movement before I clamber to my feet.

"What are you thinking?" I'm flooded with the fear that he'll want nothing to do with me. I am a murderer, after all.

Murderess? Soon-to-be murderess? Murderess in training?

Shut up, brain.

"We have to tell your gran," he says, still pacing.

It was my first thought too, but as I try to put distance between myself and what I saw, I realize I don't want anyone else to know. Even Gran. "Absolutely not."

"Who else will know what to do?"

"There's nothing to do, Felix. It can't be changed." It's the mantra I've lived my whole life by. There was a time, when I was younger, when I would try to stop the deaths by telling people they were coming. It didn't matter though. Death always came.

"That's bullshit and you know it."

His words startle me. Felix almost never curses. As much as I'd like him to be right in this moment, I think the alternative might be worse.

"Felix, if it could be changed, I would know that by now. And if this is how we find out . . ." I can't bring myself to say the rest. If this is how we find out death can be changed, then how many deaths have I been responsible for by just letting them happen?

He cuts me off. "You've done nothing yet. No one can be convicted before a crime has been committed." His fists are clenched, knuckles shining white, as he keeps pacing.

"Felix—"

"Are you accepting it?" He whirls to me, stopping his pacing. The look on his face is wild, frantic.

"No, of course not, I just—" I try to take a deep breath, but the tightness in my chest hasn't eased. Instead, I pull my hair into a messy bun. Felix watches me the entire time, eyes searching my face for answers I can't give him. "I just don't want to think about it."

"Ignoring it is your plan?" Felix presses. He's tense, muscles poised to move. He may be about to run away, or throw me over his shoulder and spirit me from here. It could go either way.

"Ignoring it is one hundred percent my plan." Anything to never have to think about my face covered in blood or the scent of iron in the air. A shudder runs through me. I look down to my hands, then up at the ghosts hanging around the edge of my vision. My magic, it's been acting up with my coming ascension. I've been seeing more ghosts than usual, maybe I'll see irregular visions too.

Felix opens his mouth to speak, but I hold up my hand to stop him. "For now. I can't think past what just happened."

"I still think you need something more substantial," Felix mutters.

I sigh. "Fine. I'll avoid him and hope I never am in that place, wherever it was, to kill him." As the words leave my lips, I hear how ridiculous that sounds. I don't know when or where that . . . event . . . took place, so there's no way I can stop it. What's more terrifying though, is I don't know the *why*. I would imagine it would have to be something truly terrible to make me consider killing someone, especially in the brutal way I felt. There must be a reason, but I'm not sure I want to find out the answer to that question.

Prison. I'm going to prison. They aren't going to let me wear gloves in there, and there is no personal space. That's where I'll die, surrounded by criminals and drowning in living their deaths.

"We're telling your gran. Now. Get in the truck." Felix's voice pulls me from my thoughts. This is the side of Felix I never see. The commanding, take-charge Felix who gets things done. It's why he's the captain of the football team, not the quarterback, even as a junior. But he doesn't use that voice with me.

"What? You can't miss class. We have a quiz in English." The fact he's suggesting skipping class is somehow scarier than what I just saw.

"And we both know our grades will be none the worse for a missing quiz. Mr. Edwards will forgive us. Get in the truck, Georgiana."

I narrow my now swollen eyes. He knows I hate when he calls me that. "You're a bully."

"And you're a bull," he says, opening the door for me. "Let's go. Gran will write me a note. No one will question it. Even outside the coven, that woman is terrifying."

Rolling my shoulders back, I plant my feet.

"No."

"Stop being stubborn."

"I'm not being stubborn. I don't think telling Gran right now is the right thing. It just happened. Maybe I overreacted."

"What? Do you think there's a better reaction to seeing yourself murder someone?"

I rub my chest, the slide of the knife too fresh in my brain. Felix knows I see death when I touch someone, but he doesn't know I also experience it as the person dying, that I feel their pain as it happens. That's a little tidbit I've chosen to keep to myself.

"No, but you know how Gran is. She worries enough about my magic and the ghosts that trail me." I swing my arm to motion to the ghosts. Although Felix can't see them, at least now he'll know they're there. They're still pressing in around me, but I'm too tired to push them away. Jen's here too, her despair weighing on me more than the others. "And with everything going on in the coven, I don't want to worry her."

"What's going on in the coven?" Felix asks.

Shit. Separation of witch and Felix is the motto I've lived by for years—I'm not muddying those waters now. Explaining my theory about my magic wouldn't be worth it yet. I need to think more.

"Nothing, just drama, nothing to worry about. Felix, let's go back inside, finish the day, and forget this ever happened." He opens his mouth to speak, but I cut him off. "Fine, not forget it ever happened, but drop it for now."

"Avoidance isn't always the solution."

"Here, we disagree. Look, I'm not avoiding it, I just don't know what that was, and I would like to lean into the hope that I'm not a murderer by taking a step back."

"I'm not letting this go," he says, but he steps away from the Jeep.

"I know you're not. We can talk about it again after school." Or never would be my preference, but I keep that bit to myself.

Felix hesitates. He doesn't want to let the subject drop. He also knows if he pushes me too much, he'll get nowhere. Finally, he nods. "Meet me right here after practice."

"Fine."

CHAPTER

4

STUFFING THE WRAPPER IN MY pocket, I pop the lollipop into my mouth as I wait. I can't taste the sugar, but it's just another thing to keep my mind occupied and off the events of the day.

The rest of the day was blessedly uneventful, with even the spirits staying away from me. Although it took me literally seeing myself murder someone to get a break, I'll take what I can get.

My mind has been spinning, and I'm convinced the rogue vision was a consequence of my coming ascension. I just need to get into Gran's library after the coven meeting and verify . . . somehow.

Most of the cars have left the student parking lot; only the ones belonging to the football team remain. They all gave blood today, so it was just a day of memorizing plays.

Glancing up, I see Felix and a few of his teammates heading this way, Windrop Central High School emblazoned across the front of their team shirts.

Using the designation of Central has always seemed silly to me. Windrop is barely big enough for the one high school here, so we could have been simply Windrop High School. At least the school is actually in the center of town.

There's a reason Windrop doesn't appear on maps, why it's so hard to find. Back when the coven settled here, a couple of centuries ago, the reigning Supreme hid the town, shrouding it so only those who stumbled upon it could find it. As roads were built and the area grew, Windrop remained off the beaten path. No major roads come here, but occasionally someone will take a wrong turn, or a job will need to be filled and someone from Boston will appear. Mr. Whitaker's continued presence in town is the only explanation for how Silas made it back.

The thought reactivates the searing pain in my chest, and I rub my sternum, trying to think about anything else.

A light breeze ruffles my hair. It's chilly but doesn't have the cold bite of autumn just yet. The trees sprinkled throughout the parking lot are still green, but if I look close enough, I can see the first hints of gold and red along the edges of some of the leaves.

I want to enjoy the beautiful day. But the vision is darkening everything, sucking the joy out of fall.

Felix and his teammates stop far enough away that I can't hear what they're saying, but based on their glances, I can guess.

Why are you hanging out with her?

Doesn't she freak you out?

I heard she sacrificed a cat last week.

That's the worst one. I would never hurt a cat.

Felix laughs at something the quarterback says before strolling toward me.

"You look much cooler than you are," he says as he approaches.

"I see you're the one making jokes now," I say, twirling my lollipop.

Felix drops his bag in the back of the Jeep and hops in the driver's seat. It's one of the last days he can have the top and doors off until spring. "I'm just saying, you look so aloof leaning against this sleek beast with your obscure band T-shirt and oversized glasses on like you're too cool for the rest of us."

"First of all," I start, climbing into the passenger seat. I send the Goddess a prayer of thanks that he installed the step rail so I could get into this thing with at least some dignity. "I am too cool for the rest of you. Second, Blink-182 is not an obscure band. They're popular."

"They were popular. When my parents were teenagers. Now they're obscure."

"Whatever. You're just jealous that I have such superior music taste." I wave my hand at him. I won't let him make fun of my dad's favorite band.

I expect Felix to start the truck, but the smile falls from his face the moment I put on my seat belt.

"How are you?"

"Oh, you know, my usual cheery self." My attempt at humor does nothing for Felix. His mouth is still tight with worry. "I'm fine. Shaken, tired, and my face hurts, but I'm fine, really. I'm just hungry. Probably the blood loss." My stomach turns as the memory of the taste of blood coats my mouth.

"I will feed you, but I expect you to talk."

-꙰꙰꙰-

THE PARKING LOT at Matt's is packed, every car that was previously at Windrop Central now seeming to have found its way here. As the only actual restaurant in town, it's not surprising.

It looks exactly like how they depict small-town burger joints in TV shows: booths lining both walls, the red vinyl on the benches having seen better days; a counter and barstools; a little bell ringing when an order is up. The only difference is that this really is a small-town burger joint, with no cameras or overpaid actors.

Felix and I find our way to our usual booth, the only empty one in the building. Our classmates are squeezed into every other booth, practically overflowing into the aisles between them, yet this one always remains open. No one else ever sits in it.

"Why do they think weird is contagious?" I slide into the seat. Coming in contact with me won't cause them any harm, contrary to popular belief. I am the only one who has to deal with the true ramifications of skin-to-skin contact.

"They're idiots." He takes the seat across from me. "And don't complain. It means we always have a seat."

My responding eye roll just earns a chuckle.

"What can I get you kids?" Suzy, the waitress, asks as she walks up. "Let me guess, the usual?"

"Yup," Felix and I respond in sync.

Suzy's been at the diner as long as it's been open. Her father was the original owner, then her brother, and now her after her brother's passing. She very well might be near eighty, but she doesn't look a day over fifty.

"Be right back." Suzy disappears behind the counter and back into the kitchen. My gaze drifts out the dingy window of the diner. The breeze outside is picking up, probably a front moving in, as clouds start to fill the sky. The equinox is tonight, and the coven will be meeting. I banish the thought, refusing to dwell on it. It's bad enough to endure the whispers at school—I shouldn't have to endure them at night, in my own home.

"It's my favorite season," I say.

"Why's that?"

"Because it's finally cool enough that I don't get weird looks for always wearing long sleeves and gloves."

"Well, if you really wanted to blend in, I don't think the blue hair helps."

My hand lifts instinctively to my hair, currently piled on my head in a topknot. "I like my hair." The vision of my blue hair plastered to my face with blood might change that though.

Felix holds up his hands in mock surrender. "I like your hair too. I was just stating it's not the look most choose when they want to be inconspicuous."

"True, but it was a lot of work to get it this color, and I don't want to put in the time to figure out how to make it another color."

"Reason number four hundred seventy-two why not to spell your hair a random color."

"Coming from the boy who has not a drop of magic in his blood." My voice is hushed, but no one's listening to us. Even if they were, something else would get their attention and they'd lose interest. I have to give it to Gran: of all the brilliant things she's done in her time as Supreme, shielding the coven from the townspeople this way is definitely her best work.

"Doesn't mean I don't have any sense." He lifts a brow.

Suzy comes with a Coke, mint malt, two large orders of fries, and enough ranch to drown a rat.

"Thanks, Suzy," Felix says, flashing her his winning smile.

I pull the malt toward me and take a sip as Suzy walks away.

"I don't know how you drink that." Felix does an exaggerated gag. I just take a long pull. "Disgusting," he says as he dips a fry into the ranch.

Within minutes, most of the fries and my shake are gone. Felix points a fry at me.

"So, wanna talk about what happened today?"

I throw my head back and close my eyes. "Do I have to?"

"You never have to do anything."

Lowering my head, I meet Felix's eyes.

There's never been anything romantic between us. Just a girl desperate for any kind of friendship, and a boy who didn't run away after one of her "episodes." But my favorite thing about him is that everything is always my choice, my decision about what to say, what to tell him, what I don't. He may push me, but he'd never force it.

Today was the first time Felix has ever done anything without explicit permission.

The hairs on my neck rise, and I shake my head. "I don't have any answers. I've never experienced anything like that. I've seen violent deaths before, but never at the hand of someone else. It's always a slip and fall or a car accident. It's never been"—I drop my voice to a whisper for the next word—"murder, before. And I've never been involved." I rub my chest again, still unable to shake the feel of the knife.

"What are you going to do about it?"

"I've thought about that all day. I've decided to chalk it up to being woozy after having my blood drawn and leave it at that." And hope it was my magic continuing to slip from my control. That's at least fixable.

Felix glares at me. "You know you can't avoid everything that's difficult in your life, right?"

"I can if I try really hard."

"George."

"Felix." I scrub my hand over my face. "I just don't know that I'm ready to focus on it. It could have been a fluke. I've never donated blood before; maybe it messed with my gift."

And I only did it to try to get out of the equinox meeting tonight. At this point, I don't think it was worth it. As if she can sense I'm avoiding her, I feel that tug in my stomach Gran uses when she tries to contact me. The clock on my phone says it's getting close to six. Gran wants to know where I am. I ignore it, focusing on Felix.

"And talking about murder," I say in a whisper again, "is not something I can handle right now."

Whatever Felix sees in my face causes him to soften. He gives me an exaggerated sigh before leaning back in the booth. "Fine, but I expect you to tell me if anything weird happens."

"Aye-aye, captain," I say, giving him a salute.

"Smart-ass," he grumbles, but at least the concern in his eyes is lessening. He looks at his phone. I may want to avoid the coven, but Felix won't risk Gran's wrath. "It's getting late. Let's get you home."

⊰⊱⋅⊰⊱⋅⊰⊱

IT'S WELL PAST six by the time Felix's Jeep comes to a stop in front of my house. Gran is standing on the wraparound porch, arms crossed over her chest.

Her tiny frame would spike fear into the heart of even the most seasoned opponent. The white of her dress and hair stands out in stark contrast to the dark green of our home.

Felix narrows his eyes at me when he notices her. "You didn't tell your gran we'd be late?"

"I forgot."

"George!" he hisses. "She's going to hex me!"

"I forgot!" I growl back. It's not the truth, but I won't tell Felix that. I didn't want him to make me come home. "And no, she won't. She loves you, and you know it," I say as I hop from the truck.

"Why are you late?"

"I'm sorry, Mrs.—" Felix starts, but a raised hand from Gran silences him. The silver of her broach catches in the porch light as she turns to him.

Her talisman is set into a ring of diamonds rimmed with an elaborate sunburst shape. The rune isn't clear in the dim, but I can picture it, anyway.

I always thought it looked like a slanted *n*, but that doesn't make its meaning any less important. Uruz, the rune of power. An uncommon rune among all covens, but especially so among those with power so entwined with death. It's not the only reason that Gran intimidates most she meets, but it certainly helps.

She may be in her seventies, but her age only makes her look regal. I can't remember her any other way, but she always says her hair turned white the day I was born, a foretelling of how much trouble I would be.

She's always been a small woman, but the last few years have seemed to shrink her under their weight, with the coven pressuring her about me. She's not any less imposing though. I'm at least three inches taller than her, but she still manages to look down her nose at me.

"I know this is not your fault," she says gently, placing a hand on Felix's arm. He visibly relaxes with the confirmation she's not mad at him. She turns narrowed eyes to me. "It is hers. Head inside, Felix. Your plate is on the table." She drops her hand from Felix's arm, a silent dismissal.

I glare after Felix as he disappears into the house without another word. He may stick up for me in public, but he's too scared of Gran to speak against her, even for me.

"I've been calling." Gran blocks my path as I try to climb the stairs to the porch. Wisps of white hair escape her braid and flutter around her face.

"I don't have any missed calls." I shrug.

"Not that stupid phone—*here*." She jabs a finger at my belly.

"Ow," I say, rubbing the spot. It still hurt, even though she didn't actually touch me. "Gran, I told you to use the phone."

"I don't like the phone."

"Well, I don't like being tugged at."

Her emerald eyes narrow—my eyes, my mother's eyes. "The autumn equinox is tonight."

Which is why I was avoiding coming home.

"Um—" I grasp for my excuse to avoid the meeting. "I gave blood today." *And saw myself become a murderer.* "I'm not feeling up to it."

"You seem to have felt well enough to go to Matt's."

"Come on, Gran. Don't make me go. I already have to deal with people calling me a freak at school. Don't make me have to go through it with the coven too."

Her face softens an almost inscrutable amount, but I notice. "No one would dare call you a freak."

"Not to my face."

"You've already missed too many meetings." Gran reaches for my hand, careful to only touch the glove. "We have to go. It's expected."

My life is a series of expectations. It's expected because Gran is the Supreme, the leader of our coven, charged with the safety and secrecy of the death witches in the Northeast. And since my parents died, much to the coven's chagrin, I'm to be the Supreme after her.

"Fine." I won't argue with her. I know there's no use. Gran isn't being cruel, but she will not abide breaking traditions.

"Good girl," she says as she drops my hand. "Go on in and eat. I'll be in shortly."

I leave her on the porch and slip into the house to join Felix. Gran pretends like she is enjoying the evening, or just needs a minute alone, but I know what she's really doing. She's been doing it since the first one appeared at my bedside at four years old.

The protection spells are one way I know Gran loves me. She's giving me a sanctuary, a place where the spirits can't reach me, and that gift is something I will never stop being grateful for.

CHAPTER

5

THE COVEN ALWAYS MEETS IN our basement. Well, calling it a basement is an understatement. The library is larger than the school gymnasium. Gran has the most extensive collection of magical tomes in the country, but I'm pretty sure her collection could compete with some of the ancient collections of Romania or Egypt. Shelves of books line every wall from floor to ceiling. Heavy mahogany tables, surrounded by ornately cut yet surprisingly comfortable chairs, are scattered throughout the space. Oversized leather armchairs and couches, usually tucked into the alcoves of the library, are arranged near the center of the room, which we use for meetings. The dark-blue carpet muffles my footsteps as I move to the back of the room, looking for an open seat.

Wielders, or witches if they prefer, stand and chat among themselves. Their attire ranges from the casual, dressed in jeans and some form of shirt, to the more traditional, wearing the robes of our ancestors. The only way to pick them out would be if their talisman was visible. Even then, it would take a trained eye to find them in a crowd. This might as well be a hodgepodge book club meeting.

When I first explained how magic worked to Felix, he was convinced our link to death made us akin to the dark witches in *Harry Potter*. I tried, and failed, for years to explain the link to death has more to do with a respect for the cycle of life and our ancestors. Yes, we technically draw the energy we use for magic from death in various forms, but usually not in a malicious way. And we definitely don't mess with zombies.

Necromancy is a no-no even among death witches. It wasn't until he saw our bedraggled fourth grade teacher—a man so nice it hurt—arriving for a coven meeting that he began to accept my explanation.

"I bet she isn't going to show," a middle-aged witch with mousy brown hair and an upturned nose says. I don't know her name. "It's not like she ever does."

"She"—the owner of the town bookstore, a redheaded witch in her early twenties, lowers her voice as I approach—"is right behind you."

I ignore them—or I try to, at least—as I head toward the non-ascended coven members. The younger wielders huddle in cliques based on age. Only a few of us haven't ascended yet, so most stick together. A bond forms in ascension groups through all the late nights studying and practicing before our eventual ascensions. It's true for most wielders, except for me. I weave past a group of new dedicants just out of elementary school to sink into one of the solitary oversized armchairs.

We're not the only coven in the area, but we're certainly the largest. Many come from all over the Northeast just because of our basement. Witches from other covens will ignore the fact that we're death witches if they're in need of obscure information.

Usually the dim lighting and smell of old books are comforting, but all the candles are lit tonight, the light filling the room.

Jack hops into my lap, and I focus on his weight, my only comfort at the moment. My hand absently runs along Jack's body as he lazily purrs. Familiars generally aren't encouraged to be a part of the coven gatherings, but as Gran and I are the Supreme and Rising Supreme, I guess exceptions are made. I glance at Bennington, Gran's raven familiar perched on her shoulder. Even just sitting there, he looks haughty.

Glancing down at the cat, I say a silent prayer, thanking the Goddess that my familiar wasn't some bird, especially a rude one. Though I'm not sure how much better a grumpy calico tomcat with a lame ear and stub tail is, I will not complain.

We only gather as a complete group four times a year, midnight on each of the seasonal solstices and equinoxes, but it's still miserable each time.

I can feel their eyes—the accusations and questions—as they pretend to listen to Gran. They resent me, both for my disinterest in magic and for the role I have in the coven.

Magic is . . . complicated. Covens usually gather based on the way they draw energy, and the energy naturally lends to different strengths. As death witches, our strengths tend to lie in the more mystical arts; mediums, seers, and other spiritualists are common among our coven.

At our ascension, we learn what strengths our magic will lean toward. Again, those can align with how a witch draws energy, but they're more flexible. There are the common signatures, like leaves or flame. Then there are the rarer signatures, like Gran's rune of power.

I pull my lips between my teeth and bite down. Not hard enough to break the skin, but hopefully hard enough to keep away the vision of my face covered in blood. The rune is probably the biggest reason

I've avoided controlling my magic. If I don't ascend, I don't get my rune, and I don't find out I have some other kind of dark magic.

Like my gifts. Gifts are coveted specialties that only certain witches are blessed with, like being an empath or animal scrying. Not gifted in scrying? Then a witch can't do it. Not gifted with experiencing the death of anyone you touch? Then you won't see yourself killing your classmate.

Bile sears my throat. I swallow, trying to maintain control. Jack yowls in my lap, and I loosen my grip on his fur.

That little gift is still unheard of among wielders, even in this coven. No one wants to know their death, especially since it's almost always terrible and even more so when the death can't be changed. Now, more than ever, I wish it could.

Wait until the coven finds out I'm a would-be murderer. Another wave of nausea rolls over me at the thought.

"We have quite a few young witches coming of age this season," Gran says, her words pulling me from my thoughts. She turns to smile at me and the other three teenage wielders who will turn seventeen before the winter solstice. I look for Trixie. She's with the others ascending this year, nerves radiating from her as she's introduced to the coven.

Sinking my hands into Jack's fur, I wonder what's going on in her head. What does she think of the coven? What does she think of me? Jack just snuggles in deeper.

Trixie turns and offers me what looks like a genuine smile. With a start, I remember the wave from the blood drive earlier today and try to return the smile. It might be a grimace.

If I could get up and leave right now, I would. If I could leave my magic, I'd do that too. Technically, it's possible to separate a wielder from their magic, but the wielder risks bodily harm, death even, during the process. I haven't reached that level of desperation.

Yet.

"Trixie will have her birthday before we gather for the solstice," Gran explains to the coven.

I startle. I thought I was the only one; my seventeenth birthday is exactly four weeks from today. Trixie sits up a little straighter. Interesting. If her ascension is so close, maybe her magic is going haywire too. Hopefully not as grotesquely as mine.

"But for now, she will continue her studies until her individual trials and ascensions. The Quarterly exams will be in the next two weeks. I suggest you remind your dedicant to practice before then." Gran gives me a pointed look. She hasn't pushed me much regarding my magic. She may be obligated to do what's best for the coven as Supreme, and maybe she sees taking care of me as part of that. Still, the whispers in the coven have gotten louder as my ascension nears.

"These tests are important, as they prepare the dedicants for any new gifts that might arise during ascension."

I shift in my seat. That's just what I need: more gifts.

⠀-⟨⟨⟨◆⟩⟩⟩--⟨⟨⟨◆⟩⟩⟩--⟨⟨⟨◆⟩⟩⟩-

I TUNE OUT the rest of the meeting as Gran drones on about grievances between members and expectations of the winter solstice. It's always the same. I'm out of my chair and disappearing up the basement steps before she finishes concluding the meeting.

There's a chill in the air, the night wet and heavy with the first front of autumn. I slip between the cars in our driveway and head for the oak tree in the side yard. Jack's on my heels, eager to get out into the night to prowl for mice.

It's always better to disappear for a little bit when the meeting concludes. Best to let everyone mingle and dissipate without having me around to make them uncomfortable. I sink to the base of the tree and dig my phone out of my back pocket. Gran makes me leave it in the kitchen for meetings, but it's always the first thing I snatch when we're set free.

Seven messages.

FELIX: how are the crones?

FELIX: did you put a hex on any of them yet?

FELIX: actually, can you figure out how to make my physics homework do itself?

FELIX: i forgot to tell you i have a date tomorrow night. i know you'll have questions, but i'm just telling you now because you'll have to drive yourself.

Dammit.

FELIX: i know you're probably cursing me right now. but it's reagan. and you know how i feel about reagan.

I almost roll my eyes. Yes, I know how he feels about Reagan. Though, I don't see the appeal.

FELIX: i will cancel if you need me though.

Randomly appearing ghosts make it hard for me to drive, not to mention unsafe. Plus, I just don't like it. While the thought of having to drive myself to work makes my skin crawl, I would never make him miss a date. Especially not because he's worried about me after today.

FELIX: anyway, i'll pick you up and drop you off at home, but you'll have to take the car to and from work. try not to let them get to you. see you in the morning, if i don't die under the weight of high school expectations.

I can't help but laugh at the last part. He always acts like he can't handle his workload, but he puts those expectations on himself.

A twig snaps and I whip my head to the sound. Trixie stands a few feet away. Her tight curls are pulled into space buns on the top of her head, making her look both cool and much younger than I know she is. She smooths her hands down her skirt, the brown of her skin almost glowing in the moonlight.

"I had to get out of there," she says with a nervous chuckle. "Too stuffy with all of those wielders in one place."

I say nothing, nerves stealing my words. She takes another step forward.

"I'm Trixie. I'm in your AP US History class. And we'll be in the ascension class together. Tomorrow will be my first one."

"I know." The words tumble from my mouth. I've grown so accustomed to people keeping their distance from me, it's become a habit to be an ass. "I mean, I've seen you at school."

She takes another hesitant step forward, emboldened by my response. "I'm almost sorry I missed AP History this morning. I heard the new kid made a splash. I'm kind of glad I'm not the only new student this year."

The mention of Silas is like a punch to the gut, nerves forgotten. "Yeah, it was quite the news," I say.

Trixie hesitates. She tries a new tactic. "I heard Mr. Whitaker wasn't coming back, so I bet that was a surprise too."

The tension in my shoulders loosens a bit as we change subjects. "Yeah. It was a shock. What made you think he wasn't coming back?"

She smiles. It's open and inviting, like she's never had a reason to dim her light. Maybe she hasn't. "Because I heard he's about four hundred years old."

Mr. Whitaker fell asleep during one of our classes on the first day of school two weeks ago, and we hadn't seen him since. There were running bets he died, but since I never saw him, I knew that wasn't true. No one guessed he'd come back with a long-lost grandson.

A smile pulls at my lips. "He is definitely older than four hundred."

Trixie stands a few feet in front of me, looking unsure. Jack steps around the oak at my back. I wait for his hiss, his distaste for most people instant, but instead he weaves in between Trixie's legs. His purrs could crumble the house. Huh. Even the grump likes her.

"You can sit," I offer. I'm surprised when she does just that, tucking her black-stockinged legs underneath her. Jack crawls into her lap.

"Are you prepared for the Quarterly?" she asks.

"No," I say, finding a fallen leaf to pick apart. "I never pass those."

"Do you have study groups here? We did in my old coven." When I glance up, her face is open, inviting. It makes me want to keep talking to her.

"Yeah, we have them," I say, waiting for her to figure out she doesn't want to talk to me.

Trixie frowns. "You haven't joined?"

I shake my head. "Haven't you heard? I'm the coven pariah." I laugh, but it's choked, unnatural. I don't know why I suddenly care about someone's opinion, especially someone I just officially met.

I see no hint of disgust on her face as she responds, just mild interest. "I thought that was just because of the touch of death thing?"

"Touch of death?" That's new. I realize I'm leaning toward her, my subconscious wanting me closer as something about her draws me in.

"You know, because you can see how people die with a touch."

"I experience it." Gran's the only one I've told that tidbit to. I don't know why I'm telling this girl whom I barely know.

"What?" She leans closer too, curiosity sparkling in her dark eyes.

"I don't see it. I experience it." The last word comes out a croak as the image of Silas's death pops into my head.

She shrugs. "Weird."

"Yes?" I say. Her response catches me off guard.

"Sorry. I don't always choose my words carefully. Doesn't make making friends any easier."

"Neither do these," I say, lifting my hands to wiggle my gloved fingers at her.

"Fair enough," she says, relaxing back to rest her weight on her hands. "How long have you been able to do that?"

"Um, since sometime around my fourth birthday."

"That's weird too. Usually, gifts manifest in a wielder's early teens, if at all."

"Yup. Lucky me."

She bites her lip, and I can almost see the wheels in her mind turning. "And there's no changing what you've seen?"

I let the verb slide. "Nope. I've tried." I suppress the urge to shudder with the thought of what that means after today. I'm a murderer, even if it hasn't happened yet. "Besides, I don't always know when it'll happen. I've never seen time markers."

"That's a heavy burden to carry."

"I guess."

Silence descends, but it's not uncomfortable. I clear my throat, shifting. "You're going to be shunned for talking to me."

"Pretty silly reason to shun someone, for trying to make a new friend. Besides, the other two in our ascension class have known each other since diapers. Let them be their own clique, and we'll be ours."

My cheeks heat as a full smile spreads across my face. "I like how you think."

"Beatrix!" a woman calls from the porch.

Trixie wrinkles her nose. "That's my mom," she explains. She carefully plucks Jack from her lap, to which he lets out a pathetic meow of protest.

Whiner.

Standing, Trixie brushes the grass from her skirt. "I gotta go."

"Totally," I say, getting to my feet too.

"See you at school?"

"Definitely."

As I watch her walk away, I'm struck by the strangeness of the feeling in my chest. It's not something I've felt often. After everything that's happened today, I thought a cloud of darkness would hang over me forever. But still, this new feeling is there, rising up in my chest to block out the ache of future wounds.

Hope.

CHAPTER

6

I ALMOST MISS MISTRESS ROWINA'S narrowed eyes as I scribble down what she just said at ascension lessons the next night. She's probably wondering why I'm taking notes for the first time ever.

Whoever's idea it was to have the ascension lessons on Friday nights is a cruel and spiteful person. Not only do these lessons ruin any enjoyment I may feel that it is Friday, but they also make looking forward to the end of the week impossible.

And with the equinox meeting last night, having witch stuff two nights in a row is basically my worst nightmare. Well, second to worst nightmare.

My blood-slicked face will always win.

In the last twenty-four hours, I have dodged at least fifteen worried looks from Felix, barely gotten any sleep, and committed to remedying my lack of magical control, especially with my imminent ascension. I thought the run-in with Silas in the hallway would be the worst thing that happened, but his presence in my AP US History class is a close second. Having the person I'm going to murder sitting in the seat in front of me for an hour every day is my definition of torture.

I'm so far behind in my studies; catching up feels impossible. It's hard enough to pay attention. Especially on a night when Mistress Rowina is lecturing. I might need help.

I didn't get a chance to talk to Trixie before class started. Though maybe that's not such a bad thing. She might not want to be friends with a soon-to-be murderer. It would be smart not to let her get close to me. Absently, I wipe my gloved hands on my pants like that will erase the blood on them.

"Dedicant Georgiana?"

I suck in a breath through my nose, flicking my eyes up to Mistress Rowina. She looks crooked; her cane is the only thing holding her up as she drones on from the center of the library. But I know better.

She likes to remind us that appearances can be deceiving, and that we can find strength in magic. I think she overdoes the little old lady look for that reason. Her gems surrounding her talisman wink in the light as she adjusts her hand on her cane. I'm not sure what rune she has, but I know it's not Uruz. Gran's the only one with that distinction, and I think Mistress Rowina has always resented her for that.

"Yes, Mistress Rowina," I say through gritted teeth. I've asked her not to call me that, but as a Third-Degree Witch, she thinks the requests of dedicants insignificant, even if I am slated to be the next Supreme and will one day outrank her.

"I asked you a question." She places her other bony hand over the one on her cane and locks her cat eyes with me.

Shit. Although I've decided to try to learn about my magic, old habits die hard.

"I didn't hear it," I mutter. She knew that already. It's probably the reason she called on me. Mistress Rowina will consider this insolence. And tell Gran.

"Of course you didn't. You may not take your lessons seriously, but the future of the coven is important to the rest of us."

My cheeks burn as seven sets of eyes turn their attention to me.

I've never wanted to embrace my magic. But I can feel it growing low in my gut. It's almost like an animal trapped in a cage, testing the walls for a way out. As my ascension nears, I know it will only get worse, both the testiness of my magic before and the strength after.

That's part of what makes the possibility that my vision might have been my magic going haywire make sense. But if my gifts are only at partial strength now, I don't really want to know what they will look like when my full power is realized.

"Can you repeat the question?" My voice is a squeak.

"Young lady, if—"

"Mistress Rowina?" Trixie calls, interrupting the tongue-lashing I'm sure Mistress Rowina is about to give me.

Rowina drags her eyes from me. "Yes, Dedicant Beatrix?"

"May I answer the question?"

"I suppose, since our Rising Supreme can't be bothered to pay attention."

Someone lets out a snicker. I make a note to make the first magic I actually try to learn be a way to curse the wielder who snickered.

"Morels can be used in that situation," Trixie says.

Mistress Rowina nods before resuming her droning.

I catch Trixie's eyes across the room. "Thank you," I mouth.

Trixie flicks her eyes to Mistress Rowina and inclines her head. "Focus," she mouths back.

I nod and turn my attention to Mistress Rowina. It's not terribly boring information, so maybe paying attention might distract me from thoughts of blood. The lesson tonight focuses on the uses of mushrooms, particularly in poisons and drafts, but I tend to ignore Mistress Rowina on principle.

Adjusting in my seat, I try to focus. At this point, it's the only idea I have in order to keep blood off my hands.

-«•»--«•»--«•»-

"YOU REALLY SHOULD pay attention," Trixie says. We're sitting at one of the three tables arranged in the magical history section of Gran's library, scribbling out the notes for the assignment due next week. It's my usual place to sit, among the only books I've ever bothered to take off the shelves. If I had to pick a favorite subject, both magical and otherwise, it'd be history. The rest of the dedicants have already left for the night, but Trixie asked if she could stay late to use the library.

I couldn't say no. Besides, I found I wanted her to stay. Tonight is only the second time we've spoken, but I think, maybe even hope, she might enjoy my company. Maybe we could be friends.

Jack lies sprawled across an open tome, his stub of a tail flicking in contentment. He thinks he's taken control of the book. Little does he know, we opened it so he would lie on that instead of the ones we need.

"I was trying," I say. This time it's not a lie. Panic tries to claw its way up my spine as I realize just how much work is actually ahead of me. Trixie deadpans.

"It's just so hard." I sound like a whiny child as I drop my forehead to the tome in front of me. The assignment focuses on making a restorative draft out of the mushrooms provided. Other ingredients are allowed, but the mushrooms must be used.

And we have to identify them first.

"I don't think that's it."

Lifting my head from the tome, I find Trixie's dark brown eyes watching me. I didn't notice it at first, but her eyes are stunning. My stomach does a weird flipping thing. There's a hint of mischief in them, like she knows a secret she'll never tell. Her stare drops to the book on the desk.

I tug on the edge of my glove, struck by the need to do something with my hands.

"Are you scared of your power?" Trixie asks quietly.

That fluttering disappears as my stomach plummets. Does she know what I saw? My eyes drop to my hands, but there's no blood there. She can't possibly know about my vision. Still, my hands are shaking as I lift my eyes.

"Maybe," I say. Here's the moment of truth. I could deflect her question like I often do, but I decide against it. Sucking in a deep breath, I go for honesty. "I guess part of me always thought that if I tried to actually learn more about my magic, it would only get worse."

Trixie cocks her head. "What would get worse?"

"My gifts," I say, drawing out the last word. I've never actually admitted why I don't try in lessons, but now that I've said it, it's kind of freeing.

Trixie wrinkles her nose. "Ah. The touch of death stuff?"

"The touch of death stuff."

"Well, you are a death witch, so . . ." Mischief sparks in her eyes.

"As are you, but your magic is nothing like mine."

"Eh, that's debatable," Trixie says with a shrug.

"How so?"

"All our magic revolves around death. Hence the coven of death witches. Mine reacts to the life force in others. Yours is just more in tune with the actual death piece of the life cycle."

For once, I'm lost for words. It takes me a moment to figure out what to say. "I've never thought of it like that."

"You know, sometimes witches find better control after their ascension."

"Gran has mentioned that."

Trixie is unfazed by the slight bite to my tone. "And you don't believe her?"

"I don't want to get my hopes up."

"Hmm. Well, I don't see how avoiding lessons would make your gift any better. And I think you have a slim chance of making it worse." Trixie's fingers drum on the desk. I cling to her words. "You do, however, have a chance of losing your coven."

The words land like a slap, although I don't think she means them to. "I don't think they're much invested in me as it is." Deflect, deflect, deflect.

Trixie's eyes meet mine. "Are you invested in them?"

Her question catches me off guard. "Well, no? I don't know."

She goes back to her work. "I think, in your hatred of your own magic, you assume everyone else hates it too. That might be true of some, but not all. I think it's kind of neat."

"You don't have to deal with it."

"You're right, I don't. But you also don't have to isolate yourself from the group because you do hate it."

Words dry up in my throat. There's nothing to say to that. She's right. I start arranging the mushrooms, trying to get them in the right order, even though I can barely identify them. "Thank you again, though, for answering in there."

"I'd say anytime, but I'm thinking you won't need me to next time?" Trixie raises both brows.

I hold up my hand. "I promise to pay attention if you'll help me catch up before our Quarterly?"

Though I do want to learn to control my magic to potentially not become a murderer, I can't pretend like wanting to hang out with Trixie isn't part of it.

"One, I'm pretty sure that's the sign for 'live long and prosper' from *Star Trek*, but I'll let it slide. Two, that's a near impossible task." Trixie smirks. "But, deal. Magic is intent, you know that, right?"

"Of course," I say, though it's perfectly valid that she thinks I wouldn't.

Trixie smiles, like I've checked off a box of skills learned. "Tell me," she continues. "What do you know about flora and fauna?"

"Flora means flower?" I shrug.

"Good Goddess, this is worse than I thought." Trixie's eyes are alight with humor. "We'll start at the beginning then."

-≪◆≫- -≪◆≫- -≪◆≫-

THE SKY IS just hinting at morning when Trixie and I finally climb from the library. Light shines through the stained glass surrounding the front door, bathing the foyer in warm red light.

"I'd offer to drive you," I say. "But I don't really drive."

"It's cool, my mom should be here in a minute anyway." Trixie's last word sinks into a yawn.

I yawn in return. Future murderer I may be, but, if nothing else, at least I'm not a sociopath.

"The schedule of a witch doesn't work well with the schedule of a high school student." Trixie holds the screen door so I can step out onto the front porch.

"Not at all." I rarely sleep much as it is, but I can feel the ache of exhaustion already setting into my limbs.

"Thank the Goddess it's Saturday."

"At least there's that."

I don't mention that I have a shift at the town library in less than four hours.

A car pulls up, the gravel drive crunching under the tires.

"This was fun," I say tentatively.

Trixie smiles. "I'm glad you think so. You'll need lots of extra sessions if you want to have a chance at passing your Quarterly, not to mention your ascension trials. Those are brutal."

"Don't remind me." I groan. As Rising Supreme, I've been forced to not only attend every ascension in the past few years, but also the trials leading up to them. Suddenly, being a slacker again doesn't sound like such a bad idea.

"You have sixth period study hall, right?" Trixie asks as her mom's car stops in front of the house.

"I do."

"Want to blow off mortal homework for witchy homework with me?"

"I think I have to." Though I'll take any excuse to blow off homework.

"You do. Remember, magic is intent. And study this weekend. I'll be quizzing you." Trixie adjusts the strap of her backpack before heading to her mom's car. She pauses halfway there and turns around. "I do have one request."

"What's that?"

"I saw a flyer for an art class at the school tomorrow night. Come with me?"

Whatever I thought she was going to ask, it isn't that. "An art class? I'm not really artistic."

She shrugs. "I think that's the point of taking a class."

There's a very large part of me that wants to say no to this, but there's also a part that wants to say yes to whatever gives me more time around her. I lean into it. "Yes."

Trixie turns with a smile, a dimple denting her left cheek. "Great. I'll text you the details."

CHAPTER

7

AS A RULE, I AVOID being at school any more than I have to, but true to her word, Trixie texted me the details for an art class on campus today.

TRIXIE: I signed us up. Class is at 6:00 p.m. I'll be at the front steps at 5:45 p.m. Don't be late.

"Why are you at school?" Jen's voice from behind startles me, and my phone slips from my gloved hand. Cursing, I pick it up and thank the Goddess nothing broke.

"I think the better question is why are you here?" I ask, peering at her from the corner of my eye.

"I'm here because you're here. So, why have you brought us here?"

Us. Like we're a set already. "I'm meeting someone for an art class if you must know."

Jen perks up, flipping her ghostly blond hair over her shoulder.

"Like a date?"

"No," I splutter, though now I'm not entirely sure. I glance down at my outfit: the same beat-up Docs I wear every day, dark-wash jeans, and a long-sleeve shirt. At least I decided to do my hair today. If this is a date, maybe I should have dressed up more.

"Definitely feels like a date," she teases. "Look how red your face is."

A car pulls up in front of me and Trixie climbs out, waving to her mom before coming to me.

"Go away, Jen," I say through clenched teeth. I hear her chuckling as I cut her off from me.

"You're early," Trixie says as she climbs the steps.

"You sound surprised," I say, shoving my hands in my pockets to keep them from fidgeting. I will my cheeks to cool, but I don't think it's working.

"Maybe a little. Come on." Trixie leads me into the building and to the left. There's an art studio at the end of this hall. I've never actually had a reason to go in it. "I'm glad you said yes. I didn't want to come by myself."

"I'm sure someone would have said yes. I've seen you talking to other people at school," I say as Trixie opens the door.

"I could've, but I wanted to come with you."

I try not to look too closely at that statement as I head into the classroom. The room has about twenty easels, with a stool in front of each easel spread out in the space.

A small table with a tray, a cup of water, and a selection of brushes stands next to each one. Each easel is set with a fresh white canvas. The smell of paint clings to the air, covering something else I can't quite place.

"Oh," I say. "So, this really is an arty art class." A variety of watercolors lean against the wall in the front of the room. They're all skillfully done, but there's almost something cold about them.

"What other kind of class would it be?" Trixie laughs as she heads to two easels next to each other. "Don't you like art?"

"Sure," I say. "In the theoretical sense. I'm more of a writer than a painter."

Trixie looks back over her shoulder. "A writer, huh? You'll have to let me read something sometime." Luckily, she turns back around before she sees the heat creep up my neck into my cheeks. As we get closer, I see each table has a small picture of a landscape on it. Both mine and Trixie's seem to be of the river at different times of the year, hers fall and mine winter.

"Inspiration?" I ask, picking the picture up and showing it to Trixie.

"I guess so," she says, settling in across from me.

"You never said what kind of class this is. I'm assuming painting?"

"Watercolor."

"Why did you want to take a watercolor class?" I glance around the room. We're definitely the only high schoolers here, let alone the only ones under fifty.

"I don't know. I've never taken one before and I like art, so when I saw the flyer, I figured why not. Plus, it's free."

"Free? Who paid for all the paints and canvases?" I don't know how much painting supplies cost, but I can't imagine they're cheap.

"No idea, but you can't beat free."

"Who's the teacher?" I ask, looking around for someone authoritative. "Maybe she's paying for it."

"The teacher is a he." Trixie nods toward something behind me. The sense of something else creeps in, raising the hairs on the back of my neck. Slowly, I turn to look as she continues. "Silas. Apparently he's going to run one once a month."

As if on cue, Silas walks into the classroom, an easy smile on his face. I whip my head back around, panic gripping my chest. "He just got here, and he's already running painting classes?" I say, hoping my voice sounds natural. My palms are already sweating in my gloves.

Trixie shrugs. "He must like it, especially since he's doing it for free."

"And probably paying for the canvases." I pull my gloves up my wrists a little higher. I never should have come here. I'm going to have to leave. "I will warn you: I am terrible at painting. Maybe we should do something else."

Trixie holds up her hand. "I swear not to judge and just to enjoy your company."

I want to bolt, but I hesitate, the promise of a night with Trixie the only thing keeping my butt in the seat. It might be worth an uncomfortable evening. Besides, I doubt I kill him here, in a room full of people.

Though I never saw myself as a killer to begin with, so what do I know.

Rolling my shoulders, I try to relax a bit. I can do this. Just enjoy the night and don't touch him. The death was a weird fluke anyway, I have nothing to worry about.

Either way, self-preservation has never been my strength.

⋘◆⟫⟫ ⋘◆⟫⟫ ⋘◆⟫⟫

BY HALFWAY THROUGH the class, my canvas just looks like a blurry mess of colors. The tremor in my hand whenever Silas walks near has made it almost impossible to make anything resembling a clean brushstroke. "I don't think it looks like the picture."

Trixie walks around to look at my canvas. She tilts her head to the side. "Well, no, but you can just say it's abstract."

"I told you I am terrible at art," I grumble. I may not try at a lot of things, but I hate failing when I do.

"You did. And I said I wouldn't judge."

I get up and follow Trixie around to her canvas. If someone told me this was the work of a famous artist, I would believe them. The landscape depicted on her canvas is a thing of pure beauty. She's painted the river that runs through town, the oranges and reds of the fall leaves juxtaposed against the swirling blue of the water.

"You're joking."

Trixie looks panicked. "What? Is it bad?"

"It's beautiful." I wave my arm at the paintings lining the walls. "It's almost as good as the pieces Silas brought in." That's not quite true though. Although Trixie's painting depicts fall, when things are dying, it has more warmth than any that Silas brought.

"Almost?"

"Trix," I deadpan.

She looks around at the paintings. "Yeah, those really are museum quality."

"They are, but this is close."

I don't notice him until he speaks from behind us. "George is right," Silas says. I take a step back, adding more space between us. "You're very good, Trixie."

Trixie looks almost bashful. "Not as good as you."

I'm struck by a pang of something I just can't place.

"Ah," Silas says with a smile. It's wide, showing all his perfect white teeth, but doesn't quite reach his eyes. There's something guarded about them, almost like they're shuttered. "Don't be disheartened. I've been doing this a very long time."

Looking at him again, I wonder if maybe our definitions of a very long time are different. He can't have been doing it that long if he's only just barely older than us. He might pass for a senior, but he still looks like a high school student.

He notices my attention and turns to me. "What about your work, George? Let's see it."

Nervously, I lead him around to my easel. He's quiet a long moment before he speaks. "I see painting isn't one of your gifts."

"It doesn't appear so." I have to swallow past the lump in my throat. Luckily, he doesn't know anything about my actual gifts.

"To really give life to a painting, treat each color like its own living, breathing thing." He runs his fingers down the canvas. A shiver creeps down my spine as I remember those fingers trying to push at my arms as I brought the knife down again. "Think of the color like it's an individual, intermingling with the others, to become a complete work. They do always say that art is a work of the soul, do they not?"

"Work of the soul" certainly isn't something anyone would say about my monstrosity. Still, his voice held such sincerity, I can't help but answer. "Sure."

He turns to look at me. This is the most attention he's given me since he and I bumped into each other outside the bathroom Thursday, and I had a full-blown meltdown.

Come to think of it, this is the most attention I've seen him give anything since he got here. In class, he's completely focused on the lesson, entirely ignoring the looks and whispers that follow him. He's warm and friendly, but seeing him with his art, it's clear this is where his passion lies.

The weight of his attention is suffocating but intoxicating. It's easy to see why everyone is enamored with him. He cocks his head to the side like he can hear my thundering heart, then turns back to my canvas. "I don't know you can do much to save this painting. I can give you a fresh canvas if you'd like?"

"No, thanks. I'll just watch Trixie until class is over."

"Suit yourself," he says, sliding his hands into his pockets and strolling away.

"It should be illegal how good-looking he is," Trixie says from around her canvas.

I snort, trying to mask the second pang of jealousy. If I kill someone because Trixie finds them attractive, I'm going to be very disappointed in myself.

"Gross. Are you hot for teacher?"

"Absolutely not." Trixie wrinkles her nose in disgust. "I'm just saying you should have to be at least a little ugly to teach anything. He's distracting students from their studies."

"I say again, gross. Besides, this is just an art class."

"Maybe, but he's still distracting."

Trixie doesn't notice the roll of my eyes as I drag my stool around to watch her keep working. Silas continues to circle the room, offering tips to other students.

He may be younger than most of his students, but everyone gives Silas just as much respect as they would if he were their senior. "He looks much more relaxed here. Maybe he'll become the next art teacher."

Trixie laughs. "That position will never be open. From what I've seen of Ms. Witte, if she dies, she'll be teaching the class as a ghost." I give Trixie a pointed look. She takes a second to catch on, and then she's laughing. "I didn't mean that when I said it, but I guess she could teach the class to you as a ghost at least."

I look around instinctively, but no one is close enough to hear her. "Hilarious," I say, but I have to admit, it is kind of funny.

TRIXIE OPTS TO take her painting home with her. I, on the other hand, leave my sad canvas on the easel. Silas can dispose of it.

The temperature has dropped by the time we get outside. Trixie stands by me as I pull my bike from the rack. There's no lock; this is Windrop, after all.

"So," Trixie starts tentatively. "I'll see you at school tomorrow?"

"Bright and early." I'm surprised by how much I actually want to see her in the morning. I swing my leg over the bike as Trixie's mom pulls up.

"Thanks again for coming."

"I had fun."

"Did you?" Trixie lifts a brow.

I smile. "I really did," I say.

"Good. Well tomorrow, study hall. All things witchy?"

"Yup. I'll be there." Even though I just met her, this secret between us feels like a chasm. If anyone could help me figure out what happened, I'm pretty sure it would be Trixie. I'm also sure that telling her would change what she thinks of me, and I can't handle that. "And Felix, he's cool." I hope she understands what I mean when I say that.

"I thought he might know, but I wasn't going to assume. That's good then. We won't have to be that sneaky." Trixie's mom beeps her horn. "All right!" she yells. "Gotta go." She waves her hand before bounding down the stairs to the car.

CHAPTER

8

NO PART OF THE SLEEP I got last night could be considered restful. Between tossing in my bed trying to fall asleep and the nightmares that met me when I managed to sleep, tired would be too light a word to describe how I feel.

I think I've slipped into paranoia, driving myself crazy with all the what-ifs surrounding my vision. I spent all first period trying to ignore Silas. Luckily, he didn't so much as look at me. But every time I looked at him, I could feel the knife sinking into my chest, the first tear of skin, and the blood seeping out.

My blood-soaked face leaning over him.

The entire period, I kept my fists clenched so tight I cut half-moon circles into both palms, even through my gloves. But I couldn't help watching him, hoping for the hint of something sinister under his skin. At least then I would have a logical reason for me to suddenly become a killer.

All I've learned so far is that he's a bit shy, his smile is infectious, and based on his performance in class, he's probably one of the smartest people I've ever met.

When the final bell rang, every muscle in my body ached, and I all but ran from the class. By sixth period, I'm ready to collapse from exhaustion. The tension in my shoulders just won't ebb.

Felix sits at my table, his books spread in front of him. He's been watching me all day like he's afraid I'll bolt if he looks away. Trixie's with us, too, helping me catch up on magical studies, but for the moment, she's out on a restroom pass.

My face breaks into a yawn.

"Didn't sleep much last night?" Felix hasn't asked me about Silas and the art class all day. It's been a blessing, but with Trixie out of earshot, he must have decided he didn't want to wait anymore.

"No." I lift my glasses to scrub my face. I didn't bother with makeup today. I knew I would just rub it off anyway. "And the whole day has just been awkward."

"Want to talk about it?"

"No. Yes. I don't know. I'm not sleeping well," I say.

Felix nods solemnly. He understands what I'm saying, what's keeping me up at night. "Have you asked Gran for something to help you sleep? You said she does that for you sometimes."

I shake my head. "I haven't. I don't know if there's any way I won't feel uncomfortable. I feel . . . slimy." Even that isn't a correct description of how I feel. It's almost as if the blood is already coating my skin. It feels like a brand of my crime, although technically I've done nothing wrong.

"Have you thought any more about your next steps?" He asks the question like I'm planning a renovation, not trying to stop a murder.

"Actually, I have," I say, sitting up straighter.

"Is it more avoidance?" Felix asks with narrowed eyes.

"No, it's a legit plan," I say. "Untrained magic can act up as we near our seventeenth birthdays, so that's probably what it was. Trixie's helping me get it under control."

"Did you tell her?" Felix's eyes widen.

"Well, no," I admit. And I still feel guilty about that. She's been nothing but kind and open to me, yet I'm keeping this huge secret from her. Who knows if she'll still be so kind to me when she finds out what I maybe-hopefully-don't do.

"Maybe you should. You said she's smart. She could help."

I shake my head before he's finished speaking. "She's helping me with my magic, that's enough." I hope.

A muscle in Felix's jaw twitches. "Has anything like this happened before, the magic acting up?"

"Probably," I say, although I'm not entirely sure. "But it's all I've got to go on at this point, other than just accepting the future."

"I still think you should tell Gran," Felix says with a frown.

I hesitate, wondering if I can explain Gran's precarious situation in the coven—all due to me—without getting into too much detail. Trixie slides into the chair next to me, saving me from my indecision.

"Tell Gran what?" she asks.

My heartbeat kicks up, and I can't tell if it's from my secret or her presence. "That I'm having you help me with magic." The lie tastes like vinegar on my tongue.

Felix watches me a moment longer before returning to his work.

"I'm sure she's realized," Trixie says with a laugh. She has realized. In fact, I think Gran did a little jig when she first saw me studying with Trixie. "Back to flora and fauna today?"

Trixie hasn't mentioned the art class yesterday other than to say it was fun. Jen's declaration that it was a date has been gnawing at me all night. I'm not sure if I want it to be a date. Making a new friend is anxiety-ridden enough.

"Probably for the best," I say, opening one of the books in front of me. Felix is glaring daggers at me across the table, I can feel it. I make sure not to look directly at him.

Trixie takes a deep breath, like she's savoring the scent of the book in front of her. Can't say that I blame her. She darts a glance at me. "I figured we'd finish with mushrooms. Then move on to healing flora. They're my specialty."

"From what George has said, I thought everything was your specialty." He's finally stopped glaring at me, but he still has the look about him that means he's going to press me about this later.

Trixie was a little wary of Felix at first, or at least before she realized the full extent of what he knows, and why he knows it. Her eyes drop, a slight smile lifting her lips. "I wouldn't put it that way."

"I would," I say, heat climbing my cheeks. The words came out of my mouth so fast. "You're much better than me at, well, everything."

Trixie fidgets under my attention, but there's a smile on her lips. "That's because I try." She drags the last word out.

Felix gives me a pointed look. He more than anyone knows how much trying matters now. I look away, unable to hold his gaze. "Yeah, yeah, yeah. Let's get started."

⋘●⋙ ⋘●⋙ ⋘●⋙

I FIND MYSELF walking home from school after seventh period. The homecoming game is Friday, so Felix has to stay late at school for extra practices this week. It's fine by me though. He's been on edge ever since the incident with Silas, and I just need a minute.

I tilt my head to the side to crack my neck and maybe release some of the tension. It doesn't work.

The school was filled with streamers and decorations and the student body was buzzing, packing the halls and bumping into one another. Besides the game Friday, the dance is Saturday. And everyone is going. Except me. It's the last thing my nerves need.

Jack saunters in front of me. He's never come to school with me, but he was waiting on the sidewalk when I left the grounds. I'm not sure what made him do that—it's not like I told him what I saw, but he's here anyway. Part of me is grateful. Though I don't know what I'd do if Gran saw him. Some witches keep their familiars with them all the time, but Jack and I don't have that kind of relationship. Gran would know something was up the moment she saw him being clingy.

I left my jacket hanging on the back of my chair at breakfast in my attempt to get out of the house as soon as I could. I wrap my arms around myself, rubbing them to generate some inkling of warmth. It seems the sunshine is gone for the season.

"You should stop doing that with your face. You're actually kind of pretty when it's not all scrunched up like that." The appearance of Jen startles me so much I almost stumble from the sidewalk.

Glancing to my left, I see Jen gliding along beside me.

I'm a little relieved to see her, but her comment still rankles me. "You're always so sweet when you appear."

"I do my best."

"Where have you been?" I ask, glancing sidelong at her.

"What do you mean?"

"I haven't seen you since yesterday. Normally you're hanging around the edges."

Jen's face crumples before she shakes her head. "I guess time moves differently when you're dead. I don't know. It feels like I just left you at the beginning of your date. How was it, anyway?"

"That's personal," I say, my voice pitched higher than usual. If Jen notices how much her question rankles me, she doesn't say.

"Fine, keep your secrets." Jen's expression doesn't change, but I could swear I feel a twinge of hurt behind her words.

"What do you want, Jen?"

"Can't a girl just want someone to talk to?" she says with a half shrug.

She's trying to look casual, but her anxiety is coursing through me. "I guess so. But does it have to be me?" I regret the words as soon as they leave my mouth.

"It's not like I have a lot of options." Jen drops her voice. "The others are just so sad."

I fight the urge to look around. Sometimes, if I acknowledge them, they see it as an invitation to talk to me. Jen apparently doesn't feel she needs me to actually want her around.

"Well, they're dead, so."

She purses her lips. "I mean, you're right. But they all just keep muttering about justice and it's really tiring."

"Justice?" I can't help but look around now. There aren't any other spirits with us. I turn back to Jen, too thrown by what she's saying to care if I look like I'm talking to myself. "Justice for what?"

"Their deaths," she says, shrugging again. She's so casual about it, like an unjust death is the least of her concerns.

I rack my brain, going through every spirit I've seen. None of them were murdered, not one.

"Every death has been accidental. Or illness. There aren't murders in Windrop. Who do they want justice from? Me?" My mouth goes dry.

That's just what I need: a hoard of vengeful ghosts.

Jen gives me a sidelong glance, brow raised. "What? Don't be ridiculous," she says, brushing it off. "Look, I don't want to talk about them. I'm just saying what I heard."

Her form fades a fraction. She's lost interest in me.

"Wait," I say, grasping at something to make her stay. I want to know more about the justice thing, but I don't want to push her. "What did you want to talk about?"

She solidifies again, her hope blooming in my chest. "Jason. Does he miss me a lot?"

I breathe a sigh of relief. At least I don't have to lie about this. "He's devastated, actually. Blames himself for your death."

"That's so romantic." I can feel her swoon.

"I guess so." Such a weird thing to say.

Jen's eyes focus on Jack strutting along in front of us. "Are you following that cat?"

"Technically, I suppose. We're both heading to the same place."

"Where are you going that you need a cat?"

"He's not actually a cat, he's a familiar." The nice thing about ghosts is they're great listeners. The best-kept secrets are the ones taken to the grave.

"A what?"

"A familiar." When the crease in her brow doesn't abate, I continue. "Basically, they're like a spirit. They inhabit the form of an animal and offer protection and guidance as young wielders come into their powers. After that, they become companions but still try to protect when possible."

"You're a witch? I thought that was just a rumor." Jen looks intrigued now, her form almost buzzing. "It's creepy," she says with an exaggerated shudder. "I love it. Makes you so much cooler."

My brow furrows. "Jen, why do you think I can see you?" I've only talked to Jen a few times, but I don't think she's the brightest crayon in the box.

"I don't know. Because you're weird?"

"Great observation." I change tactics. "The other spirits, are they being nice to you?"

Jen looks revolted. "Nice to me? This isn't kindergarten."

"I'm just asking."

She sighs. "Yeah, sure. No one really talks to each other much. We're all just stuck here, together."

"Huh?"

It occurs to me I've never actually asked them anything. At least, nothing of substance. Sure, I had normal little kid questions in the beginning, but after my parents died and wouldn't show themselves to me, I just refused any contact. I've spent so much time avoiding them that I never stopped to think they may have something to say. I always just assumed I only saw them because that's my gift, but I never thought there may be something more.

"You can just ask them."

"You're the only one I interact with."

Jen gives me a sidelong look. "Really? Why?"

"I can usually keep them away, but I can't seem to get rid of you."

"Rude," she says with a pointed look. Jen sighs. "Well, we're stuck here. You know, unable to move on. Maybe it's some unfinished business stuff, but who knows."

"What do you mean? Do you have unfinished business?" The thought of Jen with some grand plan to right the wrongs in her life is almost funny. Almost.

She glares at me. "I died tragically at sixteen. My life was certainly unfinished." Silence stretches between us. I have no good response to that. "Anyway, now that the rest of them are hissing about justice, I don't think I'll talk to them again."

Gooseflesh prickles my skin.

"Jen, I—" I start. The space she was in just a moment before is now empty. No goodbye or slowly fading from my view.

She's just gone.

CHAPTER

9

BY THE TIME JACK AND I climb the steps to the house, my nerves are raw. I just keep replaying Jen's words, the look on her face before she disappeared. I'm beginning to feel like my distaste for my magic might have larger consequences than just visions of me murdering a classmate.

If the ghosts really are seeking justice, what are they seeking justice for? If they've been following me because they wanted revenge this entire time and I've been ignoring them, maybe they're angry with me. And maybe they're the ones I should fear. The screen door slams shut behind me, startling me from my thoughts.

The staircase calls, beckoning me to climb it and sink into a hot bath. Sighing, I ignore it. I head into the brightly lit living room to find Gran sitting on the floor, tarot cards laid out before her. Jack hops into his favorite chair in front of the fireplace while Bennington glares from his perch behind Gran.

"What's going on, Benny?" I call. Bennington lets out an irritated caw. He ruffles his feathers at me in a distinctly haughty fashion. He hates the nickname.

"You shouldn't goad him like that," Gran mutters.

"But it's so easy. And so much fun," I say, crouching down to sit next to her. After the eventful last few days, I'll take any enjoyment I can find.

"Whatcha doing?" I ask, even though the cards laid out in front of her make it obvious. I tuck my Doc Martens under my legs, careful not to catch them on the tights beneath my shorts. Tights under shorts always, including in the heat of summer, because even when I feel that my skin may melt from my body, exposed skin is never okay. I tug on the hem of my glove, just in case. Gran notes my nervous habit before shifting.

"Just looking for variances," she mumbles, flipping another card. Gran always leans on her magic when something happens, trusting the Goddess to provide, to lead, to answer. Lately, she's been reading often.

Something must have happened with the coven, something other than just an unruly granddaughter, but I don't have the guts to ask her what.

"Anything interesting?" My eyes run along the cards, looking to see if there's any mention of me being a would-be murderer, but it's all gibberish to me.

"Hmm, it's a little too murky to tell." Gran gathers all the cards and begins shuffling the deck.

"Can I try?" I ask.

Gran lifts her head, surprise coating her expression. "You want to read the cards?"

"Yes?"

"Trixie must have really sparked something in you."

I try, and fail, to ignore the flip my stomach does at her name.

"Partly." I certainly won't add that seeing myself as a killer is what actually sparked my sudden interest in magic.

Gran doesn't push but hands over the cards. "Gloves off."

"I know," I say, laying the gloves on my knee and picking the cards back up. I run my thumb along the worn edges, the gold foiling catching the light from the fireplace.

"Your mother was a gifted reader," Gran says quietly. "These were her cards, and mine before, and my mother's before me."

I know that, but it still hurts to hear. I shuffle the cards, fingers clumsy from disuse.

"Do you know the question you wish to ask?"

"Not really." Well, I don't know if I'm ready to hear the answer to what I really want to ask.

"Stay broad, then. Ask what your next few months look like, and let the ancestors guide you. You have a major change in three weeks."

She means my birthday and ascension, and though she's not referring to my impending murder of my classmate, I shudder all the same. Clutching the cards to my chest, I pour my question into them. The next part is almost automatic. I might not remember all the meanings, but I've watched Gran lay the cards my entire life. The spread is a simple one: the Four Powers.

I pull the first card and lay it between us, top pointing to the left corner.

The Tower.

I glance at Gran.

"It's too early to speculate. Lay the rest of the cards."

I lay the second card across the first.

Death.

Swallowing, I lay the last four cards quicker.

Ten of Swords to the right. Five of Pentacles on the bottom. Four of Swords to the left. Six of Cups at the top.

I remember very little about the cards, but as the color drains from Gran's face, it's easy to tell that it can't be good.

"What does it mean?" I ask, searching Gran's face for clues and tucking my trembling hands under my legs.

"The cards in the middle show your path and the obstacles." Gran taps on The Tower and Death.

I clear my tightening throat to speak. "The Tower indicates change, right?"

"Simply, yes. Which is to be expected with your ascension."

I'm really hoping that's the change the cards are referring to. "And Death lies in the way?" I'm going to guess that card is the death of Silas.

"More or less. But not necessarily death the way you're thinking," she adds at whatever she sees in my expression. "Often it can indicate a period of rebirth."

Leave it to a death witch to put a positive spin on death. So far, that's true.

The vision of death changed my interaction with magic.

But even as Gran says it, she looks like there's something she's not saying.

Silence grows between us, secrets lingering in the air.

"Okay . . . and the rest?" I press.

"This placement," she says, tapping the Ten of Swords, "is supposed to show what you will learn or the knowledge you'll need. The Ten of Swords indicates a period of pain and struggling. While this placement," she taps on the Five of Pentacles, "is how you'll need to go beyond yourself."

"What does the Five of Pentacles mean?"

"Ask for help."

"Definitely not my style," I joke, but it falls flat. It's another card hitting true, since Trixie is helping me with my magic. I scan the cards again, a wave of unease washing over me. The reading is so accurate, yet there are so many interpretations, so many variables, that it's hard to find its exact meaning.

Gran doesn't laugh. "This one," she taps the card to the left, "indicates your determination."

"Four of Swords?"

"A time of great struggle."

"Great."

"And this," she taps the top card, "is for an area of restraint. The Six of Cups is for the past."

"I need to show restraint about the past?"

Gran looks over the cards again, lips pressed. "Maybe."

"What does it mean?" I ask, looking over the cards again.

"Something is coming, something big for you. It might break you, or you might come out better on the other side."

"Fantastic, that's not vague at all." Sarcasm drips from my words.

"Tarot can't tell you what will happen in the future, it just helps direct your path." Gran stands. Bennington swoops from his perch to her shoulder. "You should keep practicing, learn your cards. You have the gift to pull, but you need to learn to read them for yourself."

"Where are you going?" I ask, gathering the cards.

"To make some peppermint tea and heat up something for dinner. It's later than I realized." Gran only drinks peppermint tea when something's bothering her. I look at the cards in my hands.

"I'll come help."

"No, stay in here. I'll be back in just a few minutes." She pauses before she leaves the room, turning back to me. "Georgiana?"

"Yes?"

Her lips pull into a thin line. "Your life was never meant to be one of ease. I knew that the moment your mother told me she was carrying you. You caused her trouble the whole pregnancy. And then when you were born, screaming and red-faced—you were so defiant, right from the beginning. I knew my assumption about you was right." My shoulders slump as she pauses. I'm not sure if this is meant to be encouraging or not, but Gran sighs before going on.

"But I truly believe the Goddess would not give you anything more than you can handle. I hope you remember that, whatever the future holds."

Gran hurries toward the kitchen, and I'm left with only the cards in front of me and the sound of the crackling fire. Gran was shaken by the cards, that much I'm sure of. Bennington is still shifting uncomfortably on his perch. Gran may hide her thoughts better than most, but Bennington is always a dead giveaway.

Jack is sound asleep in the chair. If he senses my mood, he doesn't show it. Maybe we're not as in tune as Gran and Bennington.

I run my finger along the edge of the cards, my mother's cards. If I had ever shown any genuine interest, they'd be my cards, too. Tears flood my lashes for the first time since after my vision. I wish she were here. She wouldn't have the answer, but just her presence would help.

At least, I think it would. It's been so long now, I'm forgetting what she felt like. Holding her cards, I can almost pretend like she's in the room with me. Trixie may be helping me prepare for the Quarterly, but it's not clear whether I should focus on something that is a strength or a weakness. Though I'm far enough behind that everything seems like a weakness. I make a mental note to add tarot to the subjects to catch up on, not just for me, but because some part of me thinks my mother would be proud.

CHAPTER

10

SILAS'S PRESENCE AT MATT'S IS overwhelming. He's too close, infiltrating all areas of my life. One wrong move, and I could be right back in that vision, his blood on my hands. Matt's is supposed to be my safe space, yet here he is, eating a cheeseburger and talking to two of the guys from the swim team.

It's been one week since what I'm now referring to as "the incident" and nothing else has happened. Still, I don't want to risk it.

"Earth to George!" Trixie says, waving her hand in front of my face.

"What? Sorry," I say, shaking my head a little.

"I can't believe they're still going on with the game tonight and dance tomorrow," Trixie says, dipping her fry into ranch. Her love for ranch is just another way she's perfect for our little group. For me.

I drop my eyes, embarrassed by the thought.

Principal Hawkins had a heart attack while running along the river yesterday morning. She was pronounced dead before she even got to the hospital. The town has been in a state of shock ever since, as Principal Hawkins was barely in her forties. With her death hanging over the school, even the Homecoming preparations are more subdued than they normally would be.

"Just spacing out. I agree, you would think they would cancel out of respect."

Trixie gives me a suspicious look before speaking. "Vice Principal Stevens this morning: 'We need to maintain a sense of normalcy.' It's just a bit morbid if you ask me."

"Agreed," I say, trying not to look over Trixie's shoulder at Silas. Felix slides into the booth on Trixie's other side, blessedly blocking my sightline.

"What'd I miss?" he asks.

"Just talking about the fact that they should have canceled the football game and dance, in light of recent events," I say. Movement catches out the corner of my eye. Even without looking, I know it's Principal Hawkins trying to make me notice her.

"'Windrop carries on,'" Felix says, imitating Vice Principal Stevens. "I'll still be at both."

"With Reagan," I say, waggling my eyebrows at Trixie. She giggles.

Felix scrunches his face. "Reagan said she doesn't want to see me anymore."

"What?" I say. "Since when?"

"Two nights ago." Felix flinches at the irritation in my face. "You've had a lot going on," he says by way of explanation. "She says she can't be with someone who's preoccupied with someone else."

"Who would you be preoccupied with? You've been into her for forever," I say, brows furrowed.

"You," he says quietly as his eyes meet my own.

The silence in our booth is total.

Our laughter shatters through it.

I'm still wiping tears from my eyes when Trixie speaks. "Lucky you got out now. She sounds like an idiot."

"Obviously," I say.

"I'm pretty sure either of you would have more sexual tension with a rock than with each other," Trixie says, making me snort. She turns to me. "What do you want to focus on today? I figured I'd come over after this." We have a reprieve from ascension lessons this week, as the Homecoming game is just as big of an event for the town as it is for the high school, so even the coven leaders will be attending. This is probably the only time I'm not grateful for that.

"And miss my game?" Felix says in mock horror. I never go to the games—there are too many people—but I always watch the recordings, cheering him on in my own way. Trixie just rolls her eyes before waiting for a response.

My heart skips a beat. "I was wondering if we could start with tarot? And maybe spend a little time on pendulums and other reading magic?"

Trixie looks surprised. "Sure. Any particular reason? I don't think they'll be on the Quarterly."

"I've had some weird readings lately, and I'd like to be able to better understand their implications."

Felix's fry freezes mid ranch-dip. I didn't tell him about the reading, and I know he's registering that I must also be keeping something from him. But the more I think about it, the more I see the connection between the reading with Gran and my vision.

Trixie notices Felix's reaction too, but Jack decides now is the time to hop on the ledge just outside the window. He paws at the window once, letting me know just how displeased he is to be kept away from where the snacks are.

"You brought your familiar to the diner?" Trixie says, watching Jack through the window.

"Not really. He's been following me everywhere—" I clamp my lips together. I realize my mistake as soon as the words leave my mouth.

Trixie's eyes narrow. There's only one reason my familiar would be following me: trouble.

"You know, he's just been needy lately." I let out a chuckle, but it stutters in my throat. Felix looks up, noticing the tension.

"George, what's going on?" Trixie demands.

"Nothing," I say with a half-hearted shrug, but I can't help but slide my eyes to Felix.

"Goddess below, you're both in on it!"

"I don't know what you're talking about," I try.

"George, I think maybe we should tell her—" Felix adds.

"Felix!" I hiss.

"See! There is something!" Trixie slams her hand on the table. She seems to remember where we are and lowers her voice. "What is going on?"

I look at Felix, but he only shrugs. He gave me his opinion, but this is my secret, my decision. I think back to the cards with Gran. The Five of Pentacles meant to ask for help. My eyes search Trixie's face, trying to decide whether telling her about this will ruin whatever is blooming between us. But maybe she's the help the cards meant.

Trixie looks at Jack, who's now sitting on the ledge looking in, watching the discussion. If I had to use one word to describe his facial expression, it would be unamused.

I honestly don't know how much protection he actually offers.

I take a deep breath, bracing myself to tell Trixie the truth. "If I tell you, you're going to have to promise not to freak out."

"It can't be that bad," she says.

"It really is," I say. I take a deep breath, but it catches in my chest. I glance at Silas, convinced he's watching me, but his back is to me now, more students having joined his booth. I drop my voice to just barely above a whisper, bracing myself for Trixie's disgust. "I touched Silas."

"Okay . . . I'm sure that happens from time to time."

"It does, but not like this," Felix says.

Trixie looks back at me. "What do you mean? Was it gruesome?"

"You could say that."

Trixie looks at Jack again. "That wouldn't be enough for your familiar to begin tailing you. What else?"

Sighing, my lips pull into a thin line. She's probably going to hate me for this, but I can't keep lying to her forever. I drop my voice to a murmur. "Well, I was the one who killed him."

"What?" Trixie leans forward.

"It was me. In the vision, who kills him," I say. I've had enough time to come to terms with what happened in my vision. While I may not like what I saw, I can at least say it out loud without vomiting.

"You what?"

"Don't make me say it again," I groan.

Trixie visibly grays. "Why?"

I want to recoil from the way she's looking at me, but I force myself to hold steady. "I don't know. It doesn't work that way."

She shakes her head, her expression clearing. Shifting, she looks over her shoulder at Silas before her eyes return to me. "Have you looked into it?"

I heave a sigh of relief. I think part of me was afraid she'd think less of me for this murder I haven't actually committed. Yet.

"Yes," I say at the same time Felix says, "No." I glare at him. "It's why I've been so focused on my magic."

Trixie's eyes narrow as she pieces it together. "You think it may have been a false vision?" I nod. "Have you had one before?"

"No," I admit.

Trixie's lips pull into a frown. I can't help but notice that Felix is waiting for her answer just as intensely as I am. "It's not impossible," she says finally.

Felix lets out a visible sigh of relief. I told him the same thing, but coming from Trixie, he'll believe it.

"How will you test it?" she asks.

I was hoping she wouldn't ask this question. "I guess I'll have to see if the vision happens again, after ascension." A shudder courses through me.

Trixie gives a little nod, the wheels in her mind still turning. "Well, we get your magic under control as much as we can, and go from there."

"You can't tell anyone," I say, a little louder than I intended. I get my voice under control before continuing. "Seriously, the coven hates me enough already."

Trixie nods. "Of course."

I don't voice my other fear, the one that's been clawing at the back of my mind since I started this wild plan. If it doesn't work, and I still see myself killing Silas, I might need the trust of the coven to get me through whatever comes next.

"So," I say, choosing my next words carefully. "You hear I might be a murderer, and you want to help me?"

Trixie's brows knit together. "Absolutely. It's like the best thing that's happened in a while." She holds up her hands in surrender when I go to speak. "That came out wrong. Obviously, I wish it never happened, but now I get to help a friend and learn a bit more about your gift in the process." She does a little bobbing dance in her seat. "I love mysteries."

"This is not how I thought you would react," I say.

"How did you think I'd react?"

"Horrified," I say at the same time Felix says, "Freaked."

Trixie considers us for a second before she speaks.

"Maybe someone who didn't know you. Nothing's happened yet, and if it's going to, I'm sure there's a reason. You're a good person. Anyone who talks to you would see that. Let's figure out what you need to know, and we can make a study plan, okay?"

I nod, not trusting myself to speak. It's such a relief now that she knows and that she doesn't think I'd murder someone in cold blood.

I just hope she's right.

CHAPTER

11

TRUE TO HER WORD, TRIXIE spent most of the weekend helping me take steps in gaining control over my magic. She only left for the dance Saturday night—she went with a group, not a date; I asked— but was back Sunday afternoon to meet me at the library while I was on shift. The library may not be busy, but it was still almost always open. Another strange Windrop quirk. I think she would have followed me home if I hadn't convinced her that doing so would tip Gran off that something was up.

Besides, it's not like I wanted to have to leave her even when it was time to go. Not once has she looked at me like a monster or some anomaly that needs to be fixed. She looks at me as a friend, the same one she knew before I told her about Silas.

I think sometimes she might look at me like more than a friend. I don't know what to do with that information, but it makes my insides turn to Jell-O.

She was waiting for me before school and immediately began quizzing me on types of mushrooms. She doesn't miss a beat as we enter the AP History classroom. Steve has his back to us when we enter, smiling at Krista over the several open seats. He stops abruptly as I sit at my desk, quickly turning back around. Sighing, I start pulling my books out of my bag when I notice Trixie watching me.

"Why do you look so angry?" she asks.

"This is just my face," I say, gesturing at myself.

She shakes her head. "No, that's you're *I'm scary* face."

"I didn't know I had an *I'm scary* face."

"You don't put it on for me, but you certainly did just now. You look like an ax murderer half the time. A hot ax murderer, but an ax murderer all the same. It's probably why you think people don't like you."

My stomach does a somersault at her words. Trixie sees the look on my face and backtracks.

"Oh Goddess, I'm sorry. I didn't mean it like that."

"It's fine," I say, waving her off. "Jen said something similar."

At the sound of her dead best friend's name, Krista looks up at me. I quickly duck and face the front, where Mr. Whitaker's scribbling some notes on the board about a group project. I can't help my groan.

Trixie follows my gaze. She smiles. "Don't worry. I'll be in your group."

My stomach does another bout of acrobatics.

Why teachers think group projects are okay is beyond me. No one likes them, and I always end up doing the work for the entire group. Though I don't see Trixie doing that to me.

"I thought we were safe from group projects in this class."

Trixie adjusts the bun of dark curls on top of her head. "They probably had a meeting about interactive assignments and were 'encouraged' to do some."

"They should be encouraged to *not* do them."

"True. I'm surprised we made it this long without having to interact at all. He's not like our other teachers. Just reads and assigns questions."

"No, he's not." I peer at Mr. Whitaker, who's still scribbling. My eyes fall to Silas's empty desk.

Trixie lowers her voice. "Is it weird being in the classroom with him since, you know?" I nod. "Oh no, the art class!" Trixie exclaims.

"It's okay," I say hurriedly. "It was worth it." I don't explain why it was worth it, but Trixie's cheeks darken anyway.

The warning bell for class rings and the room is already buzzing as students enter and take in Mr. Whitaker's growing directions on the board. Groups are already forming, even though it doesn't say if we get to pick our own.

I've always hated when teachers set up picking our own partners. For obvious reasons, no one ever wanted me in their group, and Felix has always been torn between going rogue with me or joining his other friends. But with Trixie, for once it's okay.

My heart stutters as Silas steps into the room. He slides into his desk, offering no more than a brief smile before sinking into his seat. He barely acts like he recognizes me most of the time.

Trixie and I exchange a look, and she shrugs.

I nearly jump out of my skin when he spins around in his chair.

"Hey!" He beams, looking over between Trixie and me.

"Greetings," I say, waving my hand in front of him in a mix between a beauty queen wave and an alien wave.

Okay. It's official. I've lost my mind.

"You seem excited," Silas says, smiling.

"Yup," I say, nodding like a loon. My heart is thudding so loud in my chest that I swear the whole class can sense it. "Gotta love a group project." If my behavior hasn't tipped him off that something's up with me, that response should.

"How have you been feeling? You seemed okay at the art class, but I haven't talked to you since then." Silas's voice is gentle, like he's trying not to startle me again.

"Fine," I say automatically. The silence stretches on awkwardly and Trixie cuts in.

"Hey Silas," she says with a smile. "Want to join our group?"

The air leaves the room. I want to ask her what in the hell she thinks she's doing, but I just sit awkwardly frozen to the spot.

"Actually, I was just turning around to see if I could work with you two. I'd love to, if you don't mind," he says, looking at me.

"Nope, nope, don't mind at all." If I didn't have the reputation I do, I might worry that he senses something off in my words. But, thanks to my signature weird-girl persona, I'm just playing to my stereotype.

"Awesome. That's a relief. I've always hated trying to find partners for group projects. Especially being the new guy."

"I can understand that. I hate it too. I'm sure George does as well, don't you, George?"

"Yeppers, sure do."

Yeppers?

"Well, let's find out the assignment and get to work," he says, spinning around.

Glancing at Trixie, I see her shoulders visibly slump.

"What are you doing?" I mouth to her.

"Reconnaissance," she whispers.

I try to glare at her, but I can't muster any heat behind it.

Fifteen minutes later, we have our desks pushed together as we go over the assignment from Mr. Whitaker.

The project seems simple enough. We have to create an X account for a historical figure from World War II and interact with the other groups' accounts like the war is going on. I have a feeling he just copied an assignment idea that was forcibly suggested to him, but all in all, it's not terrible. We've definitely had stranger assignments. Mr. Whitaker is walking through the groups, distributing sheets with the personas and specifications.

"As far as group projects go, at least this one isn't that much work." Trixie sits back in her desk. "So . . . Silas, tell us about yourself."

"What do you want to know?" he asks, quirking his head to the side.

"What do you like to do? How are you handling moving back after so long? Et cetera."

"Ah," he says. He drums the desk, his manicured nails dancing in rhythm. "Moving wasn't too bad; I've always liked it here. And I like to paint, which you probably already guessed." His smile is borderline shy.

His paintings are beginning to pop up around the school and some places in town. One is now in this classroom right behind Mr. Whitaker's desk. It's a little elaborate for my taste, but still it's obviously done by a skilled artist.

There's something about them. They're beautiful to look at, but I always feel off if I look at them too long.

"Well, how do you find inspiration for what to paint?" Trixie asks. "When I saw your work at the class, it didn't seem like there was a particular theme."

Silas's lips lift in a hint of a smile. "I let the paints speak to me. It's almost like they have a life of their own." His smile widens a bit.

"Neat . . ." I say, unsure how to respond to that.

Trixie coaxes out a few more answers from Silas about his favorite food—fish—and what shows he likes—he prefers painting. I just watch him as he interacts, trying to decipher if anything sinister lies behind his answers.

He's certainly too handsome for his own good and has a confidence that screams he knows it, but he's not a typical hot-boy asshole. He's a bit of a loner, but can I really fault him for that? People suck. Other than that, he just seems kind of normal.

Which is not what I was hoping. I would have liked to get the vibe that he has a basement full of bodies, anything that would make him a bad person who deserves what I do to him.

For all intents and purposes, he seems innocent. And I don't want to think about what it says about me if I murder an innocent.

"What do you do with your free time, George?" Silas asks. I tear my gaze away from Trixie to find him watching me. I didn't realize I was staring at her.

"Um, work at the library, study." Have secret meetings in our basement with other witches.

"She writes, too," Trixie says with a wink. It feels so carefree. She should be an actress. I try to give Trixie a look that says *no one else knows that*, but I don't think she catches it.

"You write?" Silas asks.

"A little," I say, a chill creeping down my spine. I don't want to tell him anything more about myself than I absolutely have to. It feels too personal, like creating a connection will solidify what I saw.

"What do you write?" He's so relaxed too. At least I can say with certainty that he doesn't know I kill him. Or he's a really good actor too.

"Mostly fantasy. Maybe a bit of fan fiction." Silas nods. "It's nerdy, I know," I add quickly.

"It's not," Silas says. "I think it's cool. I wish I had the talent."

"I wouldn't say I'm talented," I say, rubbing the back of my neck.

"I'm sure you are," Trixie says, tapping my desk.

I'm torn between smiling at the compliment and sinking under my desk. I doubt anyone but me has ever sat between their friend and their future victim. If I'm wrong and this has happened to someone else before, I pity them.

"Felix is the only one who's read my stuff," I say finally.

An emotion I can't place skitters across Silas's face before he speaks. "Felix. I've seen you with him . . . a lot. Are you two like . . ."

"A thing?" I finish. I'm used to this question. It's probably the second most common question I get, right after "Why the gloves?"

Trixie laughs before I respond. I cut her a glare, but she just waves me off. "They're like the weirdest brother/sister pair I've ever met."

"Thanks? I don't know if I should be offended or not."

"Definitely not," Trixie says, regaining her composure.

Sighing, I turn back to Silas even though I'd rather look anywhere but his face. "She's right though. Completely platonic." The thought strikes me he may be asking because he's interested in Felix. "He's single, though, you know. I can put in a good word?"

"What?" Silas asks, a look of surprise on his face. "Oh, no. I'm not interested in him like that."

"Really? I don't think most people can say that. Felix would be heartbroken to hear his charms don't work on everyone. I can't wait to tell him." I laugh at my own joke, but it's a little too choked to be natural.

"He certainly is charming, but I just am not interested in him . . . like that."

"You mentioned that," Trixie says, glancing at me. "I'm definitely telling him. Until a few weeks ago, he thought the only person immune to his charm was George, but now there are three of us." Trixie leans forward, propping her chin on her fist. "Are you seeing anyone?"

It isn't until that moment that a new thought crosses my mind: maybe he isn't interested in Felix, but he might have been asking because he's interested in me. The thought is too absurd to dwell on.

Silas shakes his head, a few wisps of dark hair skimming his temples. "No." His eyes find mine again. "I'm on my own currently."

"Bummer." Trixie is single-handedly carrying this conversation. Thank the Goddess for that too, because I can't find anything to say when he's looking at me like that.

I open my mouth to speak again, but Mr. Whitaker speaks from behind me.

"Hello ladies and Silas," he says as he lays his hand on my shoulder.

Every muscle in my body tenses. My focus narrows into the heat radiating from his hand, to how little protection my thin charcoal T-shirt provides. My breaths come in shallow spurts as I try to remain still. Teachers don't touch students, but I think Mr. Whitaker is too old to remember that rule.

Trixie notices my discomfort as concern weaves across her face.

The ringing in my ears drowns out everything he says.

I almost cry tears of relief when he releases my shoulder and moves to the next group.

"Are you okay?" Trixie whispers.

I nod even as I feel Silas's gaze. I roll my shoulders, trying to play off the discomfort.

"Did I miss something?" He cocks his head to the side, like a dog who has just found something interesting.

"No, George just doesn't like it when people touch her."

"I got that, you know, from the gloves," he says, dipping his head toward my hands, which are sporting purple leather gloves with a black lace frill today. A smile plays at his lips, but he doesn't press further.

I pull them under the desk reflexively.

He rolls his shoulders before changing the subject. "So what else do you two do for fun?"

I'm still reeling from the unwanted touch. Thankfully, Trixie carries on the conversation. "Oh, you know, read, go to Matt's, the usual. There's not a lot to do here."

"Oh, I don't know. Small little town like this? According to mystery shows, they're always hiding secrets."

I chuckle nervously.

Every once in a while, someone will pick up on the magic surrounding a coven. Attention can be a dangerous thing for a wielder, even in this day and age.

"No secrets here," Trixie says. She tightens the bun on her head, one of her curls slipping free. A nonchalant gesture to most, but I can see it for the nervous tick it is.

"Bummer. I'm disappointed by the art scene here. No one truly appreciates my work."

The snort that comes out of me is completely involuntary. His work is good, but I didn't take him to be that conceited. Though I don't know a single teenage boy who looks even a little handsome who doesn't think he's a gift to the world.

-◄◄◆►►--◄◄◆►►--◄◄◆►►-

TRIXIE AND I are standing in front of the bathroom mirrors pretending to adjust our makeup when the bell for the next class rings.

We ran straight here after class, but we have yet to be alone. The tardy bell ushers the last senior out of the room and on to class.

My breath comes out in a whoosh as I turn to Trixie.

"That was weird. And miserable. Why'd you invite him to be in our group?"

"What's that old saying? Keep your friends close and your enemies closer?"

"We don't know he's an enemy," I say, raising my brows. I don't add that I hope to every Goddess that he is.

"What? You think you kill him because he's too handsome for his own good?"

"Keep your voice down," I hiss.

Trixie rolls her eyes. "Calm down. I can't feel anyone; we're safe."

Part of me had forgotten that tidbit about Trixie. It's one of the gifts that spans across both blood and death witches: the ability to sense a person. For a blood witch, it has more to do with their heartbeat, but for a death witch, it's the life she can sense.

"So, you think he's handsome?" The lance of jealousy speared through me catches me off guard.

Trixie smirks. "That tripped you up?"

"Who's handsome?"

My hand flies to my chest and I spin around to find myself nose to nose with Jen.

My heart is a wild thing in my chest, and I swear that Jen looks pleased with herself for startling me.

"I'll banish you if you keep sneaking up on me."

"No you won't," she says. She hops up to sit on the sink, legs swinging. "Who's hot?"

"Who are you talking to?" Trixie asks.

I cringe. In being startled, I forgot she was here. I turn around slowly.

"Jen Monroe?"

"Why are you saying my name like a question?" Jen asks. I wave her off.

"Yeah, I also see dead people from time to time. Normally they leave me alone, but Jen won't take the hint."

I wait for Trixie's response, but she peers around me looking for Jen. "Really? I don't sense her."

"Yeah, that's normal. It's not like when a spirit makes themselves known. You won't sense it because their connection is too weak to make ripples."

Trixie's eyes widen. "So you're basically an antenna, picking them up?"

"I guess so . . ." It's not something I have considered, but it doesn't sound like a bad way to describe it.

"Earth to George!" Jen says from behind me. "I repeat, who is hot?"

My expression must change because Trixie asks, "What's she saying?"

"She wants to know who we were talking about."

"Oh," Trixie says to the middle of the bathroom. "Silas."

"She's on the sink," I say.

It's hard to tell, but I think Trixie blushes as she turns her body that direction.

Jen makes a fake barfing noise behind me, and I turn to her.

"What? Don't agree?"

"No way. He is not what I would call attractive. Plus, he gives the others the creeps too."

Trixie raises her brows, but I give her a small shake of the head.

My heartbeat picks up. Jen has been reluctant to talk about the others. And anytime I've brought them up, she immediately changes the subject. "I thought you didn't really interact with them."

Jen sighs, leaning back against the mirror. I wonder how much work it's taking her to look like she's in such a relaxed position. "I mean, I don't, but death is so boring. And there's so many of them, I was hoping at least one would be cool enough to pass the time with. Obviously not, since I'm back talking to you—"

"Wait, what?" I ask, cutting her off.

"I'm talking to you—"

"No, the other part."

Jen looks at me like I'm dense. "There's so many of them."

Trixie is watching me, but she doesn't interrupt.

The wheels start turning in my head.

"How many are there, Jen?"

"I don't know? A lot." Jen frowns. "Why don't *you* know?"

"I try not to interact," I remind her.

She scoffs. "Too good for us?"

"Jen, focus."

"Ugh, there's just a lot. A lot of people die here." She shrugs.

My brain tries to process what she just said. Jen died a few weeks into the school year. There was a death over the summer, someone's grandfather I think. And at least two others the year before . . .

I can't tell if that's a lot of deaths. It seems normal to me, so maybe there are just a lot of ghosts because they're tethered to me instead of moving on. Which would suck for them and would totally be a reason to seek justice . . . on me.

"George?" Trixie asks.

"Huh?" I look up to find they're both staring at me.

"We should probably get to class," Trixie says.

"Right. Jen, I gotta go."

"Fine," she says, disappearing from the sink.

"She's gone."

Trixie claps her hands together. "I didn't know you could see them."

"What did you think I meant?"

"That you could commune with them. Most witches have to work to call on a spirit. They don't just randomly appear." She claps her hands again and goes so far as to bounce on her toes. "George, this is so good!"

"Why? It's actually pretty inconvenient, dead people popping up at random times."

Trixie's excitement abates a little as she looks at me. "Not only do you have two gifts, but they're extremely strong gifts."

"And . . . ?"

"And that makes you a powerful witch. And it's perfectly logical that your magic would act up more than usual approaching ascension, which would explain you-know-what."

"You mean when I—"

"Shh!" Trixie hushes me. "Not here."

"Why?"

"I don't want anyone," Trixie widens her eyes, glancing around the room, "to hear."

"It's not as if Jen can tell anyone."

"You never know."

I roll my eyes. I'm actually pretty sure I do know, but I don't want to bring Trixie down when she looks so excited. "Fine. Let's get out of here."

CHAPTER

12

OVER THE YEARS, I'VE GROWN used to the gloves, as much as I loathe to admit it. They've become just as much a comfort to me as a burden. Even in the heat of summer, when their oppressive weight threatens to strangle the life from my fingers, their protection is a balm to my soul.

Except for tonight.

As I sit in the basement library of my house, I'm fixated on peeling them from my hands.

The council members sit in the front of the room, faces obscured by their hoods. But I know who they are. I've had a Quarterly exam every three months since my lessons began on the Friday following my tenth birthday.

If I didn't know them from those encounters, the weekly Friday evening lessons have burned the mannerisms of each of the council members into my head.

They don't acknowledge me, but I can feel their disdain anyway. They think I'll fail. I can't though. This is the last Quarterly before my ascension next week. I need to pass this to prove to myself I'm gaining control over my magic. And to show my coven that I have a chance of passing my ascension trials.

Gran is among them, resplendent in robes of forest green. She hides behind no hood. Her role as Supreme is fated, divined by the Goddess, while the members of the council are voted in, meant to be the faceless voices of the rest of the coven.

Dedicants file in, dipping their heads as they pass Gran, mummering greetings of "Supreme Esme" until all eight of us are in seats. Even though I can't see her, I can feel Mistress Rowina sneering at me.

The clock chimes midnight and Gran stands from her seat. I glance to my right to find Trixie two tables over. She offers me an encouraging smile. My stomach does a nervous flip, but there's no telling whether the cause is nerves or her.

"Dedicants, your fall Quarterly will take place tonight. You will undergo three trials to mirror the three trials you will need to pass for your ascension. Successful completion of all three is needed to receive passing marks. The trials have been constructed to meet you at your current level." Gran pauses here to glance at the lone ten-year-old boy in the group. He's the youngest one by two years and this is his first Quarterly. Poor boy looks like I feel.

Like he's about to hurl.

"You will have thirty minutes for each trial," Gran continues. "No more, no less. Use your time wisely. The council will instruct you on the first of your tasks."

I've done this what feels like a million times, but this is the first time I've ever been nervous. But, if truth be told, it's also the first time I had anything to lose. If controlling my magic will help me change my vision, this is the first—and last—real test of that control before my ascension. I worked for it. And somehow, I started to care about it.

It isn't until the other dedicants move that I realize I missed something.

"I'm sorry, can you repeat that?" I shake my head, trying to clear the ringing in my ears.

An audible sigh. Must have been Mistress Rowina speaking then. She starts from beneath her hood. "Your first trial is to curate a collection of geodes based on your given ailment."

I blink. That's it? It seems too easy.

Pushing back from my table, I follow the other dedicants to the front, where the cards are labeled with our names. Trixie hangs back.

"You got this," she whispers to me before snatching her card and heading back to her seat.

The card almost slips from my fingers as I pluck it from the table.

Anxiety. Seven geodes.

I look up at the assembled council. It's such a basic ailment.

"Is there a problem, Dedicant Georgiana?" Gran asks from behind the table. Formal, always following protocol.

"I think I have the wrong card."

"You do not. Return to your seat."

I blink at Gran. She dips her head the tiniest bit. This is my task. I return to my seat, catching Trixie's eye.

Even Trixie looks a little worried by what her card says.

A slew of geodes appears on my desk as I sink into the chair. In fact, all of the tables are covered in geodes.

"Dedicants," Gran says as she stands. "Please use the geodes on your table to curate your collection. Your card also indicates how many geodes you should be choosing. Line your selected geodes in front of you, and when you have completed your task, the others will disappear and someone will be by to check your work. You have thirty minutes. Begin."

Trixie immediately hunches over her geodes. I watch her for a moment before turning to mine. I've been wearing crystals for some form of anxiety for most of my life. I mean, the constant presence of ghosts alone is enough to drive anyone to anxiety. My eyes scan the table for the first ones that pop into my head. The peridot at my neck may do very little to shield me from emotions, but that's still its role. I don't see it on the table though.

I spot rough cuts of amethyst and amazonite first and drag them to the empty space in front of me. The amazonite is right next to the turquoise. I wonder if that's purposeful. A less trained eye wouldn't be able to tell the difference. A cut of smoky quartz next along with black tourmaline, the dark colors of the stones calling to me. The pink of the rhodonite is next. I scan the table again, just to get a feel of what's available. I snatch the white howlite as my eyes pass over it. Glancing down, I see I have six arranged. Scanning the other stones, some would work, but they're not what I'm looking for.

"Aha!" My fingers wrap around the moonstone as I realize everyone is looking at me. "Sorry," I mouth, laying the last stone in front of me. I arrange them all into a straight line, double checking my choices. The moment I settle back into my seat, the rest of the geodes vanish.

Mistress Rowina stands from the front and strolls toward my table. Her eyes run over my collection before she grunts.

"Does that mean I passed?" Hope floods my chest.

"Yes." It sounds almost as if she's grinding the word from between her teeth. She doesn't spare me a second glance before returning to her seat, but I could swear I see Gran smile.

The rest of the half hour drags by, Trixie just barely finishing her arrangement before the time is up. I assume it's because she's more of a perfectionist than anyone else I know. All other students finish in time as well, all seeming to pass. I'm surprised by the feeling of pride that flows through me, both for myself and for them. The next trial is much the same, this time a reading of tea leaves. If I didn't know any better, I'd say these trials are rigged for me.

It's all I can do not to go to Trixie's side. She excels in all things scholarly, but with readings, as with geodes, it's more of an art than a skill. Thankfully, she passes.

I let out a sigh of relief. One more trial.

"Dedicants," Gran begins. "For your last trial, you will brew a draft." Gran's eyes flick to mine as my stomach sinks.

I feel Trixie's eyes on me too. If there's anything I struggle with most, it's drafts and tinctures.

"You'll once again have thirty minutes. The directions for your specific draft will appear on your desk momentarily. Good luck."

Time slows as I wait for the paper to appear. *Please be an easy draft. Please be an easy draft.*

Finally, the sheet appears on my desk along with a small burner, pot, and the ingredients. The words on the paper are mocking me.

Sleeping draft.

Out of all the drafts I could have gotten, I don't know many that would be worse. Sleeping drafts are inherently tricky. One wrong move and the draft could send someone into a coma, or worse, kill them. I glance at Trixie, but she's already working.

Okay, I can do this. Trixie's been working with me every waking moment for two weeks. We've worked on drafts. Trixie's words flash through my mind.

Follow the directions exactly and you'll make a passable draft. Exactly. The timing is the most important.

Just follow the instructions. I can do this.

Squaring my shoulders, I get to work.

It doesn't take me long to realize that following the directions is simpler than it sounds. It's slow going at first before I finally get a liquid brewing in the cauldron. The directions are so specific, right down to how many times the brew should be stirred at each step. This one needs forty-seven stirs, but I stumbled somewhere around twenty-eight. Is this stir forty-six? Or forty-seven? I hesitate for a moment before I give it one more stir just in case.

Tensing, I watch the cauldron as I pull out the stirrer. Nothing happens, and I let out a sigh of relief. Only two steps left and I'll have created a passable sleeping draft. It's when I reach for the last ingredient that things start to happen.

While I believe my draft should be a milky white color and consistency, it is quickly thickening and becoming this dark, gray mass in my pot.

"No, no, no, no," I repeat under my breath. Picking up the direction card, I skim the directions again. I did everything right. It should be fine.

Except that last stir. Maybe it was one too many. I peer back into the cauldron. One extra stir surely couldn't ruin it. Right? My bangs are plastered to my forehead with sweat as the mixture continues darkening.

I can fix this. Just keep going. Calm down and I'll find the solution. Magic is intention, so maybe the draft is reacting to my intention. Sweat slips down my spine as I read over the directions again.

Tossing the last ingredient in, I give it ten stirs as directed. Instead of the opaque white draft Gran makes, this one now looks like a rotting mushroom.

"Time!" Mistress Rowina calls from the front. My stomach sinks. The hope from earlier drains as I deflate. I look up from my pot to find her smirking like a cat.

I can bet she was enjoying watching me struggle.

She moves from student to student, glancing into their pot to assess their brews and offering praises for everyone in the room.

She comes to me last.

"Dedicant Georgiana," she sneers. "I believe you had a sleeping draft?"

I clench my hands into fists at my side. "That's correct, Mistress Rowina."

"And what do you call this?" She gestures at the now black mass in my pot.

"I'm not sure where I went wrong—" This is my last chance to prove I could do it, both to myself and the coven, before my ascension. The feeling of blood coats my skin.

"Fail," Mistress Rowina announces to the room.

The weight of the stares from the other dedicants is stifling. I can almost feel Trixie's pity radiating from her.

It's that one word that sums up why I haven't tried. Even when I do, I disappoint.

All of that work. For nothing. I still couldn't pass, even when I tried.

CHAPTER

13

THE OTHER DEDICANTS SLOWLY TRICKLE out, receiving congratulations from the council members as they leave. They barely
spare me a glance. Most are used to my failing.

They don't know this is the first time that I'm surprised by it.
It's not that I thought I would excel, but I just knew I would at least
pass. All Trixie and Gran have been saying for weeks is how powerful I am and how much potential I have, yet even after practicing,
I couldn't pass my Quarterly. Shame heats my cheeks as each dedicant passes me.

Trixie lingers by the front, probably waiting to see if I'll stand
up. But I won't. She speaks with Gran quietly before Gran ushers the
council members up the stairs and out of the basement.

Trixie's steps are quiet as she heads to me, stopping just off the
side of my desk.

"George?" Her voice is quiet, almost a whisper.

Tears pool as I stare at my gloved hands, but I refuse to cry. I don't trust myself to speak without them spilling over, so I just shake my head.

"George, you did wonderfully."

I can't stop them. The first tear spills over my lashes. I failed at keeping them from falling, too. I'm still staring at my gloves as the silent tears fall when I speak. "I still failed."

Trixie steps away, and soon the sound of a dragging chair fills the library. She settles into it before speaking again. "But you passed two trials. Have you ever passed two trials before?"

"No," I say reluctantly. I think one time I might have passed a trial completely by accident when I was about eleven. Since then, I have boycotted any participation.

"See, that's an accomplishment. Two out of three. You can't have expected perfection overnight."

"We've been working for weeks."

"And you should have been working for years."

I drag my eyes from my gloves to glare at her.

"Don't look at me like that. It wasn't a barb, just the truth. You know I'm right."

"Well, when you put it that way."

"I'm serious. With our ascensions so soon, most of us have been practicing our craft consistently since we were ten. And the trials are meant to challenge us, to test us in preparation for the ascension and the full weight of our magic. They aren't meant to be easy."

"The first two trials were easy."

"Because, whether or not you realize it, you are a talented witch. Naturally. Some things are going to be easier than others. What draft did you get?"

"A sleeping draft."

"See, sleeping drafts are notoriously difficult. It is understandable that you failed. You have about a first year's experience brewing drafts and most don't accomplish a sleeping draft until the year they ascend."

"So, I'm as dumb as an eleven-year-old." It's not just the ascension that's upsetting me. I'm embarrassed. Not just because the coven saw me fail, but Trixie did too.

It's Trixie's turn to glare. "That is not what I said, and you know it. You have as much practice as an eleven-year-old, and when it comes to magic, practice makes a great wielder, not whether they received a strong blessing of magic. George, you are behind. And you have made leaps and bounds since you started applying yourself, but you will need to continue to work to catch up. It's that simple. You have another couple weeks until your ascension, and you can make significant improvements by then if you continue to apply yourself, but in the end, your improvement is up to you." When I remain silent, she continues. "Nothing to say?"

Her words sting, but she's right. If I wasn't the granddaughter of the current Supreme, the coven would never even let me attempt the ascension trials. Guilt claws at me again; it's just another way Gran has had to carry a burden due to me. She's been so lax with my learning.

Even though her role of Supreme dictates she do what's best for the coven, I'm still her granddaughter. And I think the combination of the death of my parents and the weight of my gifts always makes her hesitate from pushing me. Even when I deserve it. "I don't have any witty retorts."

"Because you know I'm right?"

"Because I know you're right," I admit reluctantly.

Trixie smiles triumphantly, causing the ghost of a smile to lift my lips.

Sighing, I wipe the tear streaks from my cheeks. "So, what now?"

"Well, your birthday is on October twentieth, right?" Trixie asks. I sniffle and nod. "So we keep practicing and studying until you're ready to pass your ascension trials. I'm assuming you don't want to retest next year?"

"Definitely not." I can't.

If haywire magic is causing me to see myself as a murderer, I wouldn't survive another year of waiting.

"Keep putting in the work and I think you'll catch up. You were chosen as Rising Supreme for a reason."

"It follows the familial line," I say. Trixie gives me a look. "Most of the time," I add.

"Right. Most of the time. If you weren't worthy, the Goddess would have chosen someone else as Rising Supreme. You're gifted. Imagine where you'd be if you'd been applying yourself the whole time."

"I'd be on your level."

Trixie snorts again. "I study. And practice. I'm not particularly talented at anything. I just put in the work to be where I am. If you put in even half of my effort, you'd far surpass me."

"Now you're just exaggerating."

Trixie's expression turns solemn. "No, I'm not. Look, I'm not saying I envy your role as Rising Supreme. It's a lot of weight for one person to carry. Especially because you weren't supposed be next in line after your gran. But you need to be aware of the power the Goddess has gifted you with. Honestly, I'm interested to see what rune you receive during your ascension."

"I've tried to avoid thinking about that."

"You can't avoid everything." Trixie glances at the stairs, then back at me. Her words sting, but luckily she doesn't see my flinch. "Are you getting up?"

"I guess so." I push back from the table and stand, stretching my limbs. "When will your mom be here?"

"She's not coming. I'm staying here." She darts a glance at me as she says it.

Despite the pit of despair currently occupying my chest, a smile tugs at my lips. "Just inviting yourself for a sleepover now?"

"Sure am. Plus, your gran said there were going to be cheese sticks coming out of the oven shortly. I never pass up a cheese stick."

"I knew I liked you for a reason." Despite the weight of my failure, a smile lifts my lips. "Let's go then."

Trixie turns and heads up the stairs. My eyes scan the room for Jack. I know he's in here, but I haven't seen him since the beginning of the trials. I find him perched on a bookshelf a few rows down, tucked between the books.

"You coming?" I ask, raising a brow.

He hops down from his spot on the shelf, landing on silent paws and coming to weave between my legs. His purr is almost deafening.

"Come on, you big softie." Jack rubs his head against my ankle one more time before following Trixie up the stairs.

Sighing, I look around the library again before following them.

When I reach the top of the stairs, an acrid stench stings my nose. "Is something burning?" My words drift off as I see Gran and Trixie standing in the doorway, looking out into the front yard.

"Georgiana, come here," Gran says softly.

I move to her side, both anxious and dreading what I might see when I make it there.

In the front yard, just beyond what I assume is the barrier line Gran has drawn, stands Jen. She is unmoving in her vigil.

My mouth goes dry. "Can you see her?"

"We can," Gran says. Trixie's eyes are wide, but she says nothing. "How?"

"They can make themselves known to others if they deem it necessary. I think she's waiting for you."

Indeed, when Jen notices me in the doorway behind Trixie, her shoulders sag in relief.

"She's gone," Trixie says.

"No, she's still here." I clear my throat and Gran at least realizes I need her to move so I can go out to Jen. "I'll be right back."

Trixie stays rooted to the spot as I pass her. "Does anyone else feel that?"

"Yes," Gran and I say at the same time. The answer leaves my lips before I have time to swallow what she's asking, but I do feel it. There's an oily dread pooling in my stomach and the hairs on the back of my neck rise.

Someone's watching me. But that's impossible. There's no one outside other than Jen, and certainly no one made it past Gran's defenses. Still, I can't shake the feeling.

Rolling my shoulders, I head out to Jen, Jack on my heels. When I stop in front of her, he sits on my feet, placing himself between her and me.

"Hey." I look her over, the strain in her features clear even in the low light of the night. "Did you miss me?"

The joke falls flat.

"Where have you been?" Jen's tone is harsh, unlike her normal snipes and jokes.

"Inside. We had coven stuff tonight. What's wrong?"

"I've been waiting for you. Something's happened."

"What's happened?" That oily dread uncoils, stretching out and slinking up my spine.

"I don't know, but something did." Jen sucks her lip between her teeth and bites hard. If she were alive, I'm sure it would draw blood.

"That's not a lot to go on."

"I know. But there's something . . . wrong. Something's changed. It's noticed."

"What noticed? Noticed what?"

Jen opens her mouth to speak, but it's almost as if the words are choked from her. "Help us." Her voice comes out in a rasp.

Before I can ask her what she means, Jen's gone.

-◄◄◄◆►►►- -◄◄◄◆►►►- -◄◄◄◆►►►-

ICY FOG WRAPS itself around me, but I barely notice the chill. My eyes are fixed on the space Jen just occupied, now empty except for the night air. I'm vaguely aware of time passing, but I don't know how long I've been standing there when I hear Gran's voice behind me.

"Georgiana, go inside."

There is no arguing with her. It's the voice of the Supreme and instinctively I yield to the command in her tone. She stays where I just left as I head inside. Jack trots in front of me, eyes scanning and tail wide.

"What was that?" Trixie asks as I walk past her into the house.

"I'm not even sure." I turn back to see Gran, arms raised in the yard.

"She's strengthening the wards," Trixie says when she sees what I'm looking at.

Gran raises her arms again. I can't hear what she's saying, but I don't need to. "I figured, but why? They still stopped Jen."

Trixie's watching her too as she says, "I don't think it's Jen she's worried about."

The feeling of being watched intensifies as we wait in the doorway, making every hair on my neck stand on end. It takes everything in me not to turn and look behind me: nothing could be back there. Even so, the feeling remains.

Finally, Gran's shoulders sag as she brings her arms down. Her steps are heavy as she approaches.

"Girls, go into the kitchen."

We obey silently. The smell of burnt cheese sticks still lingers in the air, but there's no sign of the ruined food. Trixie slides into a chair at the kitchen table, her features pinched with worry, but I stay standing as Gran comes in behind us.

"What did she say?"

"Nothing really."

"What did she say, Georgiana?" Gran's words are clipped.

"Just that something was wrong. And that it knows, whatever that means."

"What knows?"

"I don't know. She disappeared before she could say more, but . . ."

"But?" Gran presses. She doesn't even know about Silas, yet she's still so on edge. For the first time, I start to wonder what's really going on in the coven.

"She looked like she wanted to say more but couldn't."

Gran's lips pull into a thin line. "I don't like this."

"What does it mean?" Trixie's not looking at Gran when she speaks. Her eyes are still fixed on the table.

"Nothing good. We had a large concentration of magic here tonight, as is true with any Quarterly." Gran's eyes flick to me before she paces to the sink, gaze fixed to the yard beyond the window. "But George's magic has never been a part of that collection."

"You think her warning was because I used my magic?"

Gran shakes off the look of unease that's been on her face since Jen appeared. Once again, she's stoic, controlled. She's the Supreme of a powerful coven of death witches. "Trixie, your mother is here. I called her to come get you. George, to bed."

Trixie gives me a look, torn between arguing with Gran and obeying the Supreme, before heading out the door. My heart sinks, the prospect of more time with Trixie swept away by Jen's cryptic warning.

A part of me wants to ask more questions and to tell Gran everything that's been happening. That part wants to crawl into her lap like I did when I was a child and cry, letting her brush my hair while she sings.

But that hasn't happened since my touch started, and it can't happen now. I've only just started to earn my place within the coven. After tonight's failure, I don't know if I'm any better off in their eyes than I was when I started. Either way, I won't bring Gran into this, not until I have to.

CHAPTER

14

SINCE THE INCIDENT WITH JEN, I've been tense. My standing with the coven, while slightly improved from a few weeks ago, wasn't helped by failing the Quarterly.

The thought of it still stings.

Gran hasn't said a word about Jen appearing in the yard other than a brush-off comment that it must be my magic acting up ahead of ascension. I hope she's right.

The alternative is much, much worse.

The town library is empty except for Felix and me. Similar to the school, the library is also in a state of disrepair. The building is small, with fading carpet and dim yellow lighting filling the damp and musty space.

It has a few rows of bookshelves, but many of the books are older than I am. In fact, I don't know the last time the library got a new book that Felix or I hadn't donated.

Felix sits at the table nearest the front desk, one of the three collections of tables and chairs that pass for furniture in our one-thousand-square-foot building. They were actually old dining sets donated to the library, chairs replaced with mismatched ones when one breaks. His books and the remnants of takeout from Matt's are spread out in front of him as he furiously scribbles. He's lost in his words again, oblivious to my discomfort.

I lean over my chemistry book, which is perched on the front desk, trying to figure out why anyone would want to learn chemical equations when potions are so much more effective. Though, I've never really wanted to know either until recently. I startle when someone clears their throat in front of me.

I look up, ready to tell whoever it is not to get their panties in a bunch, only to find Trixie standing on the other side of the desk.

The breath whooshes out of me at the sight of her. Her curls are free around her face, and there's a sparkle to her eyes.

She's smiling so bright it's like the sun has turned its attention to me.

I've been spending a lot of time with her recently, but I don't think I'll ever get over how beautiful she is. My brain can't move past the realization.

Her smile falters a bit and I realize I might have been staring. "Hey," I say, dragging out the word. I see Felix's head lift from the table out of the corner of my eye.

Her smile returns. "Hey! I only have a second, but my Kindle bit the dust, and I'm in desperate need of a book. I'm thinking of a little spa night with a bubble bath, a book, and some candles, but I have nothing to read."

Every inch of my skin feels too sensitive at the mention of her in the bath, and it once again takes me far too long to respond to her.

"Why don't you just read one of your own books?" The words rush out before my mind comprehends that I sound like a complete ass. What is wrong with me? This is my friend, Trixie. I should not be acting like someone with a crush.

But I am.

Luckily, Trixie seems to equate my awkward banter as normal because she says, "Our apartment is really small, and I had to get rid of most of my books when we moved, so I've been relying on my Kindle, but like I said, it bit the dust."

A car horn honks, and she turns around to wave at the glass doors.

"Sorry, my mom is waiting in the car."

A choking noise escapes my throat. Trixie furrows her brow.

"Are you okay?"

"She's just confused," Felix says as he leans against the counter next to Trixie. "It's been so long since anyone has actually come into the library to get a book that I think she's in a state of shock."

He's smiling as he says it, but I don't like the way he's raising his brows to me.

"Umm, there's not a lot here. I mean most of the books that are here are donations from Felix and me because our bookshelves at home are to the point of bursting, so none of our favorites are here." I'm rambling.

"That's okay," Trixie says, still oblivious. "I just need something new. Point me in the right direction."

Felix gently grabs her shoulders and spins her in the direction of the books we've donated. "That way."

It's such a casual gesture, and neither of them thinks anything of it. I want nothing more than to reach out and touch her, to feel the warmth of her skin against mine.

But I can't. I won't. I wouldn't survive living her death. I tuck my hands into my pockets.

She's my friend, I remind myself. But that still doesn't explain the butterflies taking up residence in my stomach. Or the shy glances. Or the way her smile makes my entire day. She steps away and disappears down one of the three rows of shelves.

Felix turns to me, eyes wide.

"Shut up," I hiss at him.

"What was that?" he says, a smirk on his lips.

"Not another word," I say, cheeks flaming.

Trixie pops out from a stack only to disappear behind another.

"You like her," Felix croons.

"Shut up. Shut up. Shut up."

Trixie pops back out, book clutched in her hand. "I guess I'll take this one," she says, laying down a smutty fantasy book on the counter.

"Nice choice," I say, pulling the card from the front. The stone age the library lives in means we don't have a computer system for checking out books. Not that anyone ever checks out books anyway. "Just write your name here and I'll file it. It'll be due back in seventeen days."

"Seriously?" Trixie asks, raising a dark brow.

"Seriously," I say. "That's Windrop for you. We like to skirt the edges of normal."

"Tell me about it," she says, that radiant smile returning to her face. I feel heat climb up my neck as Felix looks between us with a shit-eating grin.

The silence stretches on like she's waiting for me to say something, but I can't move. "I'll see you tomorrow at school?" she finally says as the car honks, scooping the book from the counter. There's a hopeful edge to her words. Has that always been here? Or am I just imagining it now?

"But I mean, go Owls, right? Hoot hoot." Trixie just laughs as she runs out the door.

Thankfully, Felix waits until the door shuts behind her to croon.

"What was that?" he says, another smile on his face.

"I can kill you, you know."

"But you won't. You know that."

"Fine, but I can do worse things."

Sort of true. I should ask Trixie to help me learn how to turn him into some kind of rodent.

Trixie. Just the thought of her name makes my skin tingle. What is happening to me? I mean, I've seen her plenty of times. Sure, I might have felt a twinge of something here or there, but I thought that was just nerves of making a new friend. It's never felt like . . . this.

Then again, I've never taken the time to really *look* at her. And when she looks like she did tonight . . .

"Maybe, but you won't." Felix's words break me out of my thoughts. He glances back at the now closed door. "You like her."

"No, I don't." Heat rushes up my neck as Felix raises a brow. There's no tricking him. "Fine, maybe."

"Why didn't you tell me before?"

"I didn't know. She's my friend."

"It's not impossible for you to have a crush on a friend."

"I wouldn't know. It's not like I've really ever had either before."

"Hey now," he says in a mock offended tone.

"You know what I mean."

"I know what you mean," he agrees. It's a minute before he speaks again. "Are you going to tell her?"

I don't voice the obvious argument that she might not be into girls that way, let alone me, so I stick with the one that trumps all others. "It doesn't matter. Nothing can come of it."

Felix frowns. "You don't know that."

I can't think of a retort. Felix is wrong though; I do know that. A relationship with no contact isn't the kind of relationship I want.

Thankfully, Felix changes directions. "You've never had a crush before."

"How would you know?" I ask. He lifts a brow again. "Stop doing that. No, I've never had a crush before. It's never seemed like a worthwhile pursuit."

"I just, I mean you never told me, that you . . ."

"Huh?"

"That you like girls," he mutters.

"What? Oh, I mean, I never thought about it. I don't know that I have a preference either way. Is that an issue?"

"No!" he half shouts. Clearing his throat, he begins again. "No, I just want you to know that I'm, like, cool with it."

"While I appreciate the sentiment, I would be surprised if you found an issue with whom I have a crush on after accepting that—I don't know—I'm a witch and ghosts are real."

"Fair point. But the world is crazy, and people are assholes," he says as he scoops up the takeout wrappings from the table.

"Ain't that the truth." I drop my eyes to my textbook before looking back up. "Felix?"

He looks at me. "Hmm?"

"Thanks. You're a good friend, you know, for being a guy and all." I give him my best smirk.

"Yeah, yeah, yeah," he says, but there's still a smile on his lips. "I've got to head home. My parents are in town for dinner tonight."

I gesture to the wrappers he's now putting in the trash can. "You literally just ate."

"Because you know what they'll serve there. Some mess of greens with nothing good on it."

"Probably true."

"Don't you spend too much time pining after Trixie. You have homework to do."

"Hilarious. Get out of here." After crumpling up a piece of paper, I toss it at his head as he leaves.

It falls short.

WHEN JEN'S FORM appears sitting on the counter next to my chemistry textbook, I don't even jump.

"I thought he'd never leave."

"Who? Felix? He left like thirty minutes ago."

Jen's brow furrows. "Really? I could have sworn the door just closed behind him." She turns to look at the door before turning back to me.

"Why did you want him to leave?" I close my textbook. As long as she's here, there's no sense in even attempting to study. "He knows you exist."

"Yeah, but you'll ignore me if anyone's around. Even Felix."

"Can I ignore you even if no one is around? Will you go away?"

"You think you're so funny." Jen tosses her blond hair over her shoulder. "But I know you miss me when I'm not around."

"You caught me." Bracing my hands on the counter, I hoist myself to sit next to her. "Any more unrest in the land of the dead?"

She wrinkles her nose. "Ew. Don't call it that."

"Don't get hung up on semantics."

Jen sighs. "Just the same old same. Being dead is kinda boring."

I frown. "Yeah, I guess it would be." Looking down at my dangling boots, I try to decide what I should say. "Jen, do you think they act normal, for ghosts?"

"How would I know? This is the first time I've been dead."

A laugh almost chokes me.

"I guess you're right. You're funny, you know? I didn't know that."

"You don't know a lot about me."

My lips pull into a thin line. "I'm finding that a common theme." I take a deep breath, wondering how to approach this subject. "Do you remember showing up at my house the other night?" Jen shakes her head, so I explain further. "You showed yourself to Gran and Trixie."

"What? I don't even know how to do that."

"I think you have to desperately want yourself to be seen. It doesn't happen often."

"Are you sure it was me?"

It takes everything in me not to roll my eyes at the ridiculous question. "Positive. It was like you were trying to give me a warning. You said 'it knows' and then disappeared."

"What knows?"

"I don't know. You disappeared, and this is the first time I've seen you since then."

Jen's brow furrows as she tries to think back. "I don't remember . . . any of that."

My lips pull into a thin line. I'm the one to shiver now. "I wonder why."

Silence settles between us while I try to figure out how Jen could show up and not remember before she speaks again. "Do you mind if I just kinda hang out?"

"What do you mean?" Her question startles me from my thoughts.

"Like sit in a chair. Maybe look at a magazine? You don't have to talk to me, just maybe turn the page for me occasionally."

"Uh, sure." Strange, maybe a little heartbreaking, request. "Magazines are over there. Just let me know which one you want, and I'll get you started."

Jen goes over to look at the magazines while I carry my textbook to the table Felix vacated earlier. I watch Jen as her eyes scan the magazines. It doesn't take her long to find one she wants.

"This one." She points.

After walking over, I pluck the magazine from the shelf. "*National Geographic*?"

She follows me back to the table. "I always wanted to travel."

There's no way to tell if the wave of sadness that sweeps over me is Jen's or my own. I've spent so much time avoiding their emotions, I never realized that their grief isn't just reserved for the big things in life. It's the little moments, like enjoying a magazine, that are gone too.

CHAPTER

15

JEN'S HOVERING. EVER SINCE THE night in the library, she's decided that she needs to spend every moment observing my life. I pick up a book and turn it over to read the cover. Jen sighs over my shoulder. Turns out we do not have the same taste in books.

I ignore her, adding the book to my pile. She still hasn't told me what happened at the edge of Gran's wards, but I'm trying not to push her.

October is my favorite month in Windrop. Even with my ascension looming over my head, I still can't help but love it. Downtown Windrop, if I can even call it that, is decorated like the cheesy Halloween store threw up all their decorations on the storefronts.

It started out as a joke, a bit of an inside thing among the magical community of Windrop. It was a way to celebrate being a witch without calling too much attention. But the regular folks of Windrop took to it as well, and now everyone goes all out.

If there's one thing Windrop residents like more than Halloween decorations and knitting—A Yarn and A Leg, the yarn store, is also packed today—it's buying books. Which is probably why no one comes to the library.

"What about a romance?" Jen asks. This time, I glare at her.

"Are you going to read over my shoulder too?"

The middle schooler next to me gives me a strange look then shuffles away, right through Jen. Jen throws up her arms, but no one notices.

"Go lurk on Felix. He's in horror three shelves over," I say.

Jen deadpans. "Kissing, not killing."

That earns a snort as I dip my head, telling Jen to follow. I carry my stack over to him, which he eyes, mentally counting the number of books.

"I'm still deciding," I say. I'm weighed down with one too many fantasy novels, even though Felix is only paying for three. It's tradition: on our birthday, the other buys us three books. No more, no less. And since I will be occupied on my actual birthday, Felix has chosen today to celebrate.

"You better be," Felix says, tucking a book under his arm. "I don't even know when you have the time to read all those between school and your extracurricular activities."

"A bookworm never tells her secrets," I say, hoping he doesn't press it more. I'm still not sleeping after the incident with Silas, even if things have calmed down. My ascension will be the true tell if my magic was just acting up or if the vision was real.

Only five more days until I find out. The thought makes me nauseous.

We turn around another shelf and I come face-to-face with Mistress Rowina. She looks so different outside of ascension lessons, her usual robes replaced with black slacks and a cream sweater. Her cane is still clutched in her hand. And she's . . . smiling.

That smile falters when she sees me.

"She definitely doesn't look happy to see you," Jen says behind me.

If I could elbow a ghost in the ribs, I would.

"Georgiana," she says, eyeing my stack of books. "What a surprise." An older Black woman with short-cropped hair and warm eyes comes around to Mistress Rowina's side. It's Mistress Rowina's partner, a mortal. It's not unheard of for a witch to marry a mortal, but for Mistress Rowina, a pillar of rules, I've always been surprised by it. I've never seen her up close though. My go-to move when I see other coven members in public is to turn and run. "Have you met my wife?" Mistress Rowina asks.

"Nellie," the woman says, holding out her hand. I stare down at it, taking a step back. Nellie's smile falters.

"It's not you," I say quickly. I hold up a gloved hand. "Just don't do handshakes." I smile and Nellie relaxes. "I'm George."

"My nephew tells me it's an old lady habit anyway," Nellie says with a laugh. "George . . . your birthday is soon, right?" Nellie muses. "I think Rowina was just talking about you. All good things," she says when she sees my face.

Mistress Rowina sucks in a deep breath, obviously irritated to admit she said anything nice about me. "I simply said that a previously disinterested student has been putting in an effort." Nellie bumps Rowina, nudging her on. "And that the coven has noticed."

Pride blooms within me. The coven is paying attention. More than that, I didn't realize I wanted Mistress Rowina's approval so much. Now that I have it, even begrudgingly, I feel like I'm seeing the sun for the first time after a long winter.

"Thank you," I say. Mistress Rowina dips her head in response.

"We should get going," she says to Nellie.

"It was nice to meet you," Nellie says, and it's easy to see she means it.

"Georgiana," Mistress Rowina says as I'm turning back to Felix. "I will see you at your trials. Perhaps you will pass." She purses her lips. "Happy early birthday."

I'm too shocked to say anything as she turns and walks away. Felix, who heard the whole exchange, comes up next to me.

"Isn't that—"

"The mean old crone? Yes." I wonder if I can still call her that after what can only be considered a friendly exchange from her.

"Was she just—"

"Nice to me? Good, I'm glad I'm not the only one who heard that."

"I heard it too," Jen says.

Felix carries on, oblivious to Jen. "Quite the turnaround, don't you think?"

"That's one way to put it," I muse, watching Mistress Rowina and Nellie leave the store.

⟪◆⟫ ⟪◆⟫ ⟪◆⟫

IN THE END, Felix conceded to buying me four books, stating that since it was a big year for me as a witch, I deserve an extra present.

Jen and I lean against the brick wall of Caffeine & Cones—the coffee slash ice cream shop—waiting for Felix to come out with hot chocolate. Jen's eyes are trained on the river just beyond the shop.

"What is it?" I ask, trying to figure out what she's looking at.

"It's just strange, being so close to . . . to where I died," she says.

Chewing my lip, I glance at Jen. I can't help the bloom of pity that fills my chest. "I guess so."

Jen turns to me with narrowed eyes. "I can feel that."

"Feel what?" I spot a couple walking across the bridge, hands intertwined. My throat tightens. If the ascension doesn't go well, will I ever be able to do that with Trixie, or anyone?

"The pity. You feel sorry for me."

My attention jerks back to Jen. "Wait, you can feel what I'm feeling?"

"Sometimes. Maybe it's only when the emotion is strong. But that was a pretty powerful wave of pity."

I don't know how I feel about that. It's bad enough that I experience their emotions. The brush of grief or the press of longing is one of the many reasons I've stayed away from the ghosts. I don't want them knowing mine as well. "I didn't know that."

"You don't know much about us. Maybe that's why I follow you. To educate you." She smirks again.

"I don't know why you want to. You never liked me much when you were alive."

"True. But I don't think you liked me much either."

"Also true." I turn back to her. "But things change."

Jen's smile lights up her face. Felix comes out of the shop then, one hot chocolate in each hand and gives me one. We pull our jackets tighter around ourselves as we walk down to the bridge over the river, Jen just ahead of us.

Windrop has several bridges over the river throughout town, almost like the people who built the town were trying to see how many times they could make the roads cross it.

It's late afternoon, and the river is beautiful. It's all sparkling golds and reds, reflecting the turning leaves and sunlight. It looks just like Trixie's painting. A few couples along the river sit on blankets or play frisbee, trying to get in their time outside before the first snow falls in a few weeks.

I lean against the railing, cupping my hot chocolate between my hands for warmth.

"Are you going to be able to carry all of those books back to the car by yourself?" Felix inclines his head to the books dangling from the bag on my arm.

"You'd be surprised at the strength I can muster to carry books. Besides, you're one to talk. You bought twice as many books as I did."

Felix beats his chest with a closed fist, the other tugging on the strap for the backpack slung over his shoulder. "Big strong man, remember?" he asks in what I can only describe as his caveman voice.

"Yeah right, cinnamon roll," I say, rolling my eyes.

"I'm extremely well-rounded."

I snort. "You should add conceited to your list of attributes."

"That's why we're friends: we have so much in common."

"Ass," I say with a laugh.

Felix chuckles and leans on the railing.

Out of the corner of my eye, I see Jen stopped down the street, right where her bike fell the night she died. Her face is scrunched up, like she's trying to puzzle out how she ended up there. It's a dangerous corner. Felix's brother died about ten feet away, and this is the bridge that took my parents. So much death for something so beautiful.

"Huh," Felix says. For a second, I think he sees Jen too, but then I follow his line of sight.

Silas is set up by the river, a half-painted canvas perched on an easel. He has a variety of water cups in front of him, each a different hue.

"That kid really loves painting," he says, watching Silas. Silas's concentration is fixed on the river in front of him, his brush slowly moving over the canvas.

"It's basically all he talks about," I say, trying not to stare as well. I can't help it though. This is the first time I've been able to look at him without him noticing. He's fully absorbed in his art, in whatever story is unraveling on his canvas. It's hard to tell from here, but it kind of looks like a bubblegum-pink hot-air balloon over a field of green.

Then, he pauses his brush midstroke, and turns slowly to look at the bridge. His eyes meet mine and I freeze. So much for watching him without notice. A smile spreads across his face and he gives us a wave. Instinctively, Felix and I wave back.

Then he's back to his painting, like the interruption never happened.

"What are you going to do if the vision happens again?" Felix says softly. He hasn't brought up the incident in a week, trusting Trixie to guide me through the ascension. The questions are still there, written on his face anytime he sees Silas. He's concerned, and I love him for it, but I'm also grateful he's let me try this without pushing too much.

"It has to work." Hopefully Felix doesn't notice the tremor in my voice.

"But if it doesn't?" he asks.

I sigh, watching Silas again. I don't want to tell Felix all the thoughts that have gone through my mind while I lie awake at night. That maybe I'm not a good person, and a murderer is what I've always been. That all of Trixie's help and Felix's faith is for nothing because I'll still end up covered in blood, body and soul.

"I don't want to be a murderer," I say quietly.

For a moment, I think he wants to give me a hug. My stomach clenches as I realize I want that too. Just one carefree hug. Just one. But he just turns toward me.

"You're one of the best people I know. The crankiest, sure, but also the best."

I laugh, but it's thick with tears I can't stop from clawing up my throat. "Don't exaggerate," I say.

"I'm serious. I love you. I'm pretty sure Jack might love you, though it's hard to really tell."

We both turn to look at my familiar, his lanky form arranged in a seated position in the middle of the sidewalk. His face is schooled into its signature unamused expression. I can't help but let out something between a laugh and a sob.

"Maybe."

"You are not a bad person. If your ascension doesn't change things, we'll think of something new. Promise me."

"I promise," I say, but I don't feel any conviction in it.

Felix wants to ask more questions, to press me further. But he doesn't. Instead, he looks me over, then wraps his arm around my shoulder. He pulls me in tighter, making sure no skin is touching. My composure cracks and tears sting my eyes. He stands with me in silence watching the river until Silas finally packs up his paints and I'm shaking from more than just the cold.

CHAPTER

16

"TRIXIE!" GRAN'S VOICE ECHOES DOWN the staircase. "It's time to go."

"I don't know why she's being such a stickler," Trixie grumbles as she gathers her things. "You get to stay for my trials."

"I don't know if 'get to stay' is the right description. More like I will be forced to stay because as Rising Supreme I need to be involved in all coven affairs."

"You make it sound like torture. I think it might be fun."

"It's not so bad in years when we have only one ascension or the blessed years we have none. But we have four of us this year. And we're all in the same season. It's a lot."

"I guess so," Trixie admits. "At least we're in the first batch?" she says, lifting her shoulder as she makes her way to the stairs. I follow but we stop at the base of them. "You'll do fine. Really."

"Only because of you," I say.

I cross my arms over my chest, but that feels so closed off, so I grasp them behind my back. Nope, too formal. Finally, I settle on sliding them into my pockets. Ever since I realized I do, in fact, have a crush on Trixie, I'm reading into everything she says, every look she makes. And apparently I don't know what to do with my hands.

"Nonsense, you're a better witch than you know." Trixie hesitates, shifting on her feet. "I want to hug you right now."

"I feel the same," I admit. That zing from the library hasn't faded, but my anxiety currently occupies every inch of my brain.

Trixie's smile is sad. It's like a punch to the gut. "Good luck. Text me after."

"Duh," I say as she ascends the stairs out of the basement.

I turn back to examine the space. Candles float around the edges of the room, casting a warm glow throughout. The table Trixie and I were studying at will remain. One chair for me and one for the Inquisitor.

I return to my seat, smoothing the skirt of my black satin dress. The dress has short sleeves, but in combination with my opera-length gloves, I look like I stepped out of the wrong century after attending a particularly boring funeral.

But Gran insisted it be this dress. It was the same dress my mother wore to her trials, and Gran wore before her. I take a breath to steady myself, but it's shaky. I try again. By the fourth breath, the trembling has ebbed.

I've sat through at least two dozen trials. Only one of those trials ended in a failure. It's not like they'll kick me out, I tell myself. I'll just have to stay in courses for a year and test again, like Mildreth did three summers ago. That was the original plan, anyway.

And live with the fear that my vision is real.

No pressure, right?

I think I would feel better if I knew what was coming. But that's the thing about the trials. They are never the same. They are meant to test the strengths and weaknesses of every witch or wielder, and just like the person, the tests are unique. I could be asked to call upon dark magic or make a soup. The test reveals itself to the Inquisitor.

The door at the top of the stairs from the house opens and footsteps sound. Mistress Rowina, followed by Gran, descend. Mistress Rowina carries something covered by a cloth. As they reach the bottom, Mistress Rowina situates the object in front of me so that I have to look around it to see her and Gran. Gran's mouth is pulled into a thin line, but other than that, her face reveals nothing.

"Where's the rest of the coven?" I ask, peering around them. Something's not right. The entire coven doesn't always attend, but usually at least a dozen members are present. I thought for mine there would be more.

Gran's face tightens further, but it's Mistress Rowina who answers. "It seems the coven chose to await the outcome of your trial."

Sweat slicks my palms under my gloves. I open my mouth to say something else, but I have no words. They didn't even bother to show up. If they won't show up for this, they certainly won't help me if my vision is true.

"Georgiana Colburn, the night of your trials has arrived," Gran says, but it's the voice of Esme, the Supreme of the Death Witch Coven of the Northeast, that rings out. I square my shoulders, sitting up straighter. They didn't show, fine. The only thing to do is move forward. "Should you pass, you will proceed to your ascension tomorrow night. Are you prepared?"

I've always thought it was strange when they asked *Are you prepared?* when the dedicants have no idea what they're to be prepared for.

"Yes," I say. I don't think a smart aleck remark would be appreciated by Gran. I glance at her, but her eyes are void of emotion. Ever the impartial Supreme.

"Very well," Mistress Rowina says, steepling her fingers. "You only have one test tonight." Her expression looks softer tonight, but that could just be in my head. She gestures at the item on the table. I reach for the cloth. "Ah, ah, ah," she tsks. I lower my hand. "Not so fast. You don't even know what it is."

"Don't play with her, Rowina," Gran scolds.

Gooseflesh pricks my skin. Gran never intercedes in coven matters on my behalf, at least in public. That would show favoritism. If anything, she gives me less help than she gives anyone. If she's stepping in now, this must be bad.

Mistress Rowina shifts in her seat to glance up at Gran but doesn't say anything.

I look at the object. "What's under the cloth?"

There's something like pity on Mistress Rowina's face before she speaks. "Veritas."

My stomach feels as if I ate a meal of rocks as it plummets. Just further confirmation that while I thought the coven was beginning to trust me, I was wrong. With a trial like this though, they must hate me more than I knew.

"I thought that was a myth," I choke out through too-dry lips.

The origin story is never the same, changing from coven to coven so each can claim their own heritage to the item, but its power is always the same.

Veritas is the mirror of the true self. Only the strongest wielders can look into it without going mad. And even the ones who survive the process are changed forever.

I don't know what's worse: facing Veritas or becoming a murderer.

"Many believe that, but it is all too real." Mistress Rowina hesitates before speaking again more gently. "If you can look into Veritas without shying away, you will pass."

Sweat coats my hands under my gloves. "Why do we have this?"

"It can be called upon when needed," Gran says. If I didn't know her so well, I wouldn't be able to hear the pain in her words. She didn't want this.

I swallow past the lump in my throat. "Is this allowed to be used for trials?"

"The coven thought it best, given your previous disinterest in magic, to give the Rising Supreme a test of character instead of a test of skill," Mistress Rowina says.

The coven, not the Inquisitor. It was a group decision. If that's true, it breaks a tradition that's been upheld for a century, if not longer. I search Gran's face. I should have asked what was going on in the coven; maybe I would have been more prepared.

"I've been trying," I say, but my words are shaking as badly as my hands.

"Recently," Mistress Rowina admits. It occurs to me she was part of the decision to bring in Veritas. I wonder if that was before or after the bookstore, and if it even matters. "But it did not negate the disinterest you have shown since you began ascension lessons. If you are truly to be our next Supreme, the coven has put forth this test. Pass and you will have our trust."

"Gran?"

She doesn't look at me when she speaks. "You must, child. The trial has been chosen. There is no other way." She's done so much already, made so many excuses for my behavior. Her hands are tied.

Part of me understands why they chose this, as much as I hate to admit it. My interest in the coven is recent. If I wasn't fully committed, I wouldn't risk insanity for the mirror. Still, this might make them trust me more, but it doesn't go both ways.

"I could fail," I blurt out. Even the humiliation of failure sounds better than this.

"Yes, you could. But this could very well be your test next year as well."

With those few words, the fight leaves me. I don't even need to think about it. I know she's right. This will always be my test. I'm the disinterested Rising Supreme. I've been ignoring lessons, skipping coven meetings, and mocking the coven for years. Even if I'm taking the role seriously now, the coven doesn't take *me* seriously.

And as much as I loathe to admit it, this may be the only way. I set my jaw. "Fine," I say through gritted teeth.

"Whenever you're ready," Mistress Rowina says. I may be imagining the pride in her face at my answer. She looks like she wants to pat my hand but thinks better of it. She gestures at the covered mirror instead.

Closing my eyes, I recall the main thing Trixie has been trying to get me to remember since she's been tutoring me.

Intent. Magic relies on intent.

I don't know that any kind of magic will help me face Veritas, but maybe the same applies? Couldn't hurt.

I intend to face my true self. I intend to face my true self. I intend to face my true self.

The motto repeats in my head as I open my eyes, as I pull the cloth from the mirror and face what lies within.

⫷⫸⫷⫸⫷⫸

WHEN I FINALLY sit back, I don't know how much time has passed. It could be seconds or years. Cold brushes along my cheeks and I realize they're wet. Was I crying? The room comes into focus as my eyes find Gran.

She's still standing, steady as a pillar, but relief shines in her eyes as she takes me in. Whole. Not insane. At least, I think I'm not.

"What did you see?"

I swallow past the lump in my throat. "Myself, and the role I'll play for the coven." It's all I can give them for now.

True self is a lackluster term for what was revealed in the mirror. It wasn't so much me—I can't recall seeing a reflection of myself at all. More than that, I can't remember seeing anything. It was more like combing through every inner corner of myself. I saw every flaw, every fear, every weakness. I saw good mixed in as well, but the insecurities will be what haunt me as I'm on the verge of sleep.

I'm not ready to talk about it. Part of me thinks I won't ever be.

At least I didn't see myself covered in blood. That was a relief. And I'm here, and I don't feel any more insane than I did before. I tuck away the rage. I'm angry that I had to do this in the first place, yes, both with myself and with the coven. But I'm also angry that I spent weeks practicing, anguishing over whether or not the skills I've learned will be enough to get me through the trials, and it wasn't even a factor. It gets filed away, to be dealt with later.

Mistress Rowina looks relieved. She smiles a bit, just barely enough to notice. I'll take it.

"Georgiana Colburn," she says. "You have successfully survived your trials. You have the blessing of the coven to ascend."

"Thanks for that," I say, swiping my cheeks as I stand. "I'm done right?"

"You're done," Gran says. Her way of approving my retreat.

"Awesome," I say as I bound up the stairs. Another set and I'm in the upstairs bathroom, closing the door and turning the water as hot as it will go.

I rip the dress from my frame, only half noticing the tear when the zipper gets stuck, and the rest of my clothes until I slip into the near scalding water and let it wash me away.

By the time I emerge from the shower, Gran and Jack are already perched on my bed.

I hiss as I move, my skin raw and tender from scrubbing. Snatching a pair of pajamas, I disappear back into the steam-filled bathroom.

Returning to my room, I sit on the bed next to Gran. Jack rubs against my back, curling into a ball behind me.

"I'm very proud of you," Gran says.

"I don't know how to respond to that."

"I suppose you're right. Being proud isn't a large enough consolation for what you went through."

"Yup." I'm angry with her, although I know it's not fair. "Why'd you let them pick that for me?"

I know, deep down, that Gran had no say in what trial was selected for me. But I can't help but feel betrayed. Did she know ahead of time and not warn me?

"You know I didn't let them do anything. I found out just before you did. It's a ridiculous system, really, Supremes not being allowed any say in the trial. It's what determines the viability of any wielder in our coven ascending to their full power. One would think the Supreme should have some input."

"You'd think so . . ."

"Georgiana, I'm sorry. But truly, the hard part is past you. The ascension is a beautiful experience."

"I don't want to talk about it."

Silence descends on us. "Would you like to stay home from school tomorrow?"

The question startles me from my daze. I turn to her, eyes wide.

If Gran is offering to let me stay home from school, she must truly be feeling guilty.

"Who are you, and what have you done with my gran?"

"Don't be so dramatic. You went through an ordeal. And besides, it's your birthday. I've let you stay home on your birthday before."

"Once," I say. "And it was only because I had a one-hundred-and-four-degree fever."

"But I let you stay home," Gran says, lifting a white brow.

"Technically, you did let me stay home," I concede. "But no, I don't want to. I'll just dwell on the ascension." And what it means if my vision wasn't a fluke.

"Very well," Gran says as she stands. "Never say I didn't offer."

"Ever the benevolent Supreme."

"That tongue will get you into trouble one day."

"That's what I hear."

Gran pauses in the doorway. "Tomorrow will be a new day," she says finally before pulling the door shut behind her.

CHAPTER

17

ON THE NIGHT OF MY seventeenth birthday, I'm standing in the middle of the forest. Most teenagers get to have a party or maybe even a car. I get a torrent of magic pouring into me in the middle of the night.

My breath frosts in front of me as Gran casts the warming spells on the area. I should be shivering, but I find some part of me relishes the cold. It distracts me from what's to come.

I'm glad Gran let me choose the dress tonight. Black velvet sleeves cling to my arms, ending in golden embroidered leaves at my wrists. The velvet slips down my form, pooling at my feet, golden trees stitched into the hem.

The setup is the same for every ascension: the five candles arranged in the pentagram, a dagger and stone in the center. The only difference is that I don't have any family to stand in for me. Since Gran is the Supreme, she has to fill her role as the Supreme. Trixie's helping Gran finish the setup, and I say a silent prayer of thanks to the Goddess for bringing her into my life. If nothing else, I didn't have to have one of the instructors stand in.

Gran turns, inspecting her work.

"Are you ready?"

"As ready as I'll ever be." At least the coven didn't choose to come to this as well. That, or Gran didn't let them. Either way, I'm glad I don't have to worry about one of them trying to kill me at my weakest point. Before last night, I wouldn't have thought it was an option. But Veritas could have easily killed me, so I'm not ruling anything out.

Gran ignores my remark and gestures to the pentagram. "Then enter."

Air tickles my bare fingers as I step into the circle and kneel before the knife and stone. Gooseflesh rises on the back of my neck, the feeling of someone watching weighing on me. Trixie and Gran kneel before two of the candles and place their hands on their knees, palms to the sky.

"Goddess, we present to you this dedicant. She has survived the fires of the trials and waits before you for your blessing. As the clock strikes midnight on the dawning of her seventeenth year, accept her offering and welcome your daughter into your warmth."

The familiar prick of gooseflesh doesn't come tonight. Instead, a swirling storm of nerves ravages my stomach.

Gran and Trixie begin the chant.

"Mother keep her. Sister welcome her. Goddess protect her. Mother keep her. Sister welcome her. Goddess protect her."

Bennington stares at me from Gran's shoulder.

"It is time, Georgiana," Gran says, inclining her head.

My hand shakes as I reach for the knife. I told myself I would be braver than this, but now that I'm here, every part of my body trembles. I press the knife to my palm, willing my hand to steady as

I slowly drag the blade across my skin. The crimson flows from my palm to the stone below.

"Mother keep me. Sister welcome me. Goddess protect me."

I wait for the familiar zing of magic coursing through the air, but a savage force barrels into me. My mouth opens in a silent scream as my head is wrenched back. Every nerve in my body is on fire, begging for relief.

But none comes. Power courses through me from the earth below and the sky above. I'm a conduit, lost to the swirls of power and magic until all thoughts eddy from my head. Time slips away. I'm suspended in some place between life and death, unable to move or break free before the darkness takes me.

—««◆»»‒‒««◆»»‒‒««◆»»—

"GEORGIANA!" A WOMAN yells from very far away.

Gran? I sense her, at a great distance, but I also sense something else. Another presence lurking on the edges.

"Georgiana, wake up," Gran calls again. Her voice is thick but still full of command.

I twist on the ground, the ache in my body a living thing.

The presence slinks back.

"Good girl. Get up. You must get up on your own. We cannot break the circle."

I don't understand her words. Break what circle?

Shifting to sit up, a hiss escapes through my teeth as I blink around me. The candles are still lit. Gran and Trixie sit just outside of the circle. Trixie's face is wet with tears.

"What—" I start, but my mouth is dry, so dry, and my throat feels like I've been screaming for weeks. "What happened?" I try again.

"The magic took you. Nothing out of the ordinary," Gran says. Her voice is smooth now, calm and calculated, but I hear the slight tremor. She's lying, though about what, I don't know. "Take your stone," she says, still the commanding tone of the Supreme.

I pluck the stone from the ground and stand. A groan escapes my lips, but I make it to my feet to stumble out of the pentagram before crumbling back to the ground. Out of the corner of my eye, I catch Trixie moving to catch me. But she stops herself.

Gran kneels beside me, careful not to touch me. "What is your rune?"

My rune. I thought that would be the first thing I thought to look for after my ascension, but I feel almost as if my head has been stuffed with cotton. I open my palm as the three of us peer at it.

A crescent moon is etched into the stone. My mind spins to recall the name, but Trixie finds it for me.

"Night," she whispers. She clears her throat. "Night," she says more clearly.

"I'm a night witch?" I can't recall anything about night witches.

"The technical term is nocturnal witch, but yes, essentially," Gran says, the solemn tone in her voice drawing my gaze.

"Is that bad?" It feels bad.

"Not bad, but just—" Trixie starts before Gran cuts her off.

"Nocturnal witches wield great power, and it is very rare. It is not surprising, considering you were blessed with two gifts when many witches receive none. Some of the most influential witches and wielders of all time have been nocturnal."

"I feel like there's a but in there," I say cautiously.

"But, so have some of the most dangerous," Trixie says when my gran doesn't finish.

Gran nods. "Some will be drawn to your rune and the magic you can wield because of it." A warning is laced in her words.

Darkness, I remember now. That's what it is. Nocturnal witches excel in magic that treads the line between light and dark, life and death. The ghosts, the deaths . . . they're tied to this.

"Why?" I ask. "Why couldn't just one thing be easy? Why couldn't I be a garden witch or something generic and warm? Why do I have to be the witch whose magic teeters on good and evil?"

"We do not always get to choose our paths," Gran says.

"Don't give me the philosophical shit right now. Be my grandmother, not the Supreme."

"I am being your grandmother," she says, voice raised. She takes a deep breath before continuing at normal volume. "I know you've had a rough go of things, but we didn't do this to you. It is just your path."

"I've had a rough go of things? That's what you have to say?"

"I will not suffer you acting like an insolent child," Gran says as she begins to stand.

My movement isn't even a conscious decision. It's so stupid, I just reach to grab her arm, to stop her and make her talk to me.

But my gloves aren't on.

The moment my fingers connect with her skin, I have an instant feeling of hope that my gift is gone, or at least controllable.

But then I'm the one who's gone.

⠀⠀⠀⠀⠀⠀⠀⠀⠀⠀⠀⠀-«‹◆››»- -«‹◆››»- -«‹◆››»-

THE RATTLE IN my chest is painful for even me to listen to. Her hand is wrapped firmly around mine and I run my thumb along the smooth skin. I know it's her, even though I can't see her through the darkness of my eyelids.

Ever loyal until the end.

Every breath is a raging fire in my lungs. I know part of me should be angry with her. She grows stronger as I grow weaker. But I cannot. This is the way of things.

Another breath, another rattle. Her lips brush my forehead. My sweet girl, my Georgiana.

I WRENCH BACK from her, the horror I feel cut into her features.

"Georgiana," Gran starts.

"No," I say. "No, tonight was supposed to be special, supposed to be something different than this," I say gesturing to myself. "But it's just more of the same."

"George," Trixie says from behind me.

"I'm fine. Actually, I'm not fine, but I will be. I just—I just need some time. I need to be by myself for a while."

I stomp toward the house, Jack trotting along behind me.

CHAPTER

18

THE FIRST WARNING BELL RINGS just as I get the door to my locker open. I dig around, trying to find a rogue lip balm in its depths, glad for the general lack of ghosts since my ascension

"You seem different."

I freeze, the song I was humming now a lump in my throat. I didn't even notice him until he spoke. Slowly, I remove my head from my locker to find Silas leaning against the one next to me. The smile on his face is just as warm as it's always been, but alarm bells still sound in my head.

"I'm not sure what you mean," I say, trying to swallow down the lump in my throat.

"There's just something different about you." His arms are crossed over his chest. "You had a birthday this weekend, didn't you?" The door of my locker is blocking my retreat to the back. If I want to move away from him, he has to move first, or I risk touching him as I squeeze by. My only exposed skin is my face and neck, but I still don't want to risk it.

"I did." The second warning bell rings. "Well, we better get to class."

"That must be it then." He takes a small step forward. I press back into my locker door, but he's still too close.

"Wh-what?" I almost choke on the words.

"Do you feel any different?"

"I mean it's just another birthday? Didn't even get a car or anything." I try to laugh, but the sound is choked. He's too close. I know I should test my theory about my vision, but now that he's here, invading my space, I can't bring myself to do it.

He watches me for another moment before taking a small step back. I almost slump with relief.

"You left your painting a couple weeks ago. Would you like to pick it up?"

Back to painting. Thank the Goddess. "It wasn't any good."

"Oh," he says. "You shouldn't speak that way about art. It's an expression of soul."

I chuckle again and it's a little less choked. "My artwork certainly didn't come from my soul." There would be no way to paint what I saw in Veritas, the dark and the light warring within me.

"I could teach you, if you want?"

I'm shaking my head before he even finishes. I think if I have to spend any more time in the same area as him, especially learning how to paint, that might be the thing that sends me over the edge into murder.

"I could," he continues. "You could learn the art of putting soul onto a canvas. I think you have the skills in your arsenal."

"You have a lot of faith in me." The gap between us is just wide enough now, I should be able to step away from the lockers without bumping him.

"You have no idea." He cocks his head, the movement more predatory than curious. "You have something on your face."

"No wait—" I say, trying to stop him. My head slams back into the locker. There's nowhere to go. I scan for someone to save me, but it's too late as the tips of his fingers brush my cheek.

⫸⫷⫸⫷⫸

I WAKE GASPING on the floor. A small group of people crowd around me, but Silas is gone. My stomach lurches and I choke down bile. If I don't get out of here right now, that fluffernutter is coming back for an encore. Pushing to my feet, I grab my bag and shove my books in before closing my locker. The vision was exactly the same as before. My chest aches from the impact of the knife as I try to blink the tears from my eyes. The crowd tightens around me. I think I hear someone ask if I'm okay. I'm trapped. Without shoving through, I have no way to get out. Another death experience is not what I need right now. My stomach lurches again, and I gag. The crowd steps back, the fear of vomit too much for their curiosity. A small gap opens, and I rush it, hoping for the best. By the time I emerge from the gaggle of onlookers, Felix is already hustling down the hall. I guess that's a perk of a small school: word travels fast.

"Who was it?" he asks, turning and matching my stride as I head toward the door at the end of the hall.

As soon as I'm free from the confines of the hallway, I turn and hurl into the bushes off the steps. There's a chorus of "gross" from students lingering, but I don't care. I keep retching until there's nothing left. I spit and stand up, wiping my mouth on my sleeve.

"Silas. It was the same as last time." Felix's face pales. "It's time. I need to tell Gran."

⫸⫷⫸⫷⫸

THE SMELL OF lavender lingers in the air as we sit at the small table in my kitchen. Gran must have been making a tincture when we came in, probably a salve for the arthritis in her hands.

Now the ingredients for whatever it was lay scattered across the kitchen, long forgotten. Her white hair is pulled into a bun at the base of her neck. She's wearing dark slacks and a cream sweater, a canvas apron tied over her clothes. My brain is still a fog. It felt like trudging through mud to tell Gran what happened, and as we sit in silence now, a heavy exhaustion seeps through me. Even staying upright to sit in the chair feels like too much.

"Tell me again what happened," Gran says. Her face is hidden behind her steepled fingers, as if it will help her figure this out better. Bennington sits on the perch Gran installed in the kitchen. He keeps shifting from foot to foot, mirroring the discomfort Gran obviously feels.

"I've told you three times," I say, leaning back in the creaky kitchen chair. Jack shifts on my feet. He always does this when he's upset, sitting on my feet to make sure he knows when I move. Just now, though, I wish he was in my lap.

"Again." The voice of the Supreme.

"I slipped in a puddle leaving the bathroom. I hadn't put my gloves back on because I had literally just washed my hands, and no one is ever in the halls during class. He caught me as I fell, and I was pulled into his death. I thought it was a fluke because of the blood drive, or maybe a lack of control over my magic, but it just happened again."

"That's what led to your sudden interest in learning your magic," she says, putting the pieces together.

I nod guiltily. I see all of her questions buzzing through her green eyes. She's trying to work out a solution. But this isn't a spell we need a counter charm for. I may have had to tell her the story three times, but thankfully, she's only made me repeat what I felt once.

"Was the vision the same each time?" she asks. I nod. "Georgiana, I need you to be sure it was exactly the same."

"I'm pretty sure every detail is burned into my brain. Hard to forget seeing yourself murder someone, you know." The words are harsher than I meant for them to be, but I can't help it. Because every time I close my eyes, I can see myself, slicked with blood and lifting the blade again.

My stomach turns again, even though there's nothing left.

"Felix." Gran turns her attention to my friend. He straightens in his chair at her gaze. He's always been a little afraid of my gran, but right now, he doesn't balk. "Did you meet this boy? Anything off about him?"

"I've met him. We knew him as kids, but his parents moved out of town years ago." Felix doesn't mention the part about calling him Snotty Silas, which I'm sort of grateful for. Something about teasing the boy I'm supposed to kill doesn't seem right. "He just seems like a normal guy. A little old school, from what George says. Maybe a little too good-looking for his own good, but other than that, normal."

"Old school?"

I shrug. "He just has that vibe? Like he's taking midcentury modern a little bit too much to heart." I shift on my seat, not looking forward to this next part. "Except for today."

Gran and Felix both whip their heads to me. "Explain," Gran demands.

"Today, he was still perfectly friendly, but something felt . . . off. He was asking about my birthday." At that, Gran's frown deepens. "And when he touched my face, it felt purposeful, like he knew what was going to happen."

"Is it possible he does? Like, could he be a witch from another coven?" Felix asks.

Gran purses her lips. I know her answer before she says it. "It's highly unlikely." Nothing we've said seems to have quieted the questions in her eyes. If anything, she probably has more now. She inhales deeply and slowly releases her breath before addressing me again. "Tell no one."

"Like that even needs to be said," I scoff.

"Don't sass me, young lady. This is serious."

"I know it's serious. I'm the one who just felt myself killing someone for the second time." It comes out with less bite than I intended, with me stumbling over the last words. That's what I saw, but it doesn't make saying it any easier.

Gran's lips pull into a thin line. "I know, child." She sighs, sitting back. "No one. Even Beatrix. She seems like a nice girl, but we can't risk the coven hearing of this. Not until we know what it means."

Felix and I share a look. Gran clocks it.

"She already knows, doesn't she?"

I grimace. "I told her a few weeks ago."

"You should have told me," Gran scolds. Her eyes flick to Jack, the cat curled at my feet. "Have Jack come with you when you leave the house from now on."

"He's already been following me," I say, looking down at him.

Gran's frown deepens further.

"Will you involve the coven?" I ask. I don't know why, but the thought of bringing them into this terrifies me.

"Not yet. I fear this may be too closely intertwined with your gifts, and I do not want to cause a stir when there is no need for one." I hear what she means: that my place in the coven is still on shaky ground and something like this may destroy any progress I've made with them. They may be *slightly* impressed I survived Veritas, but like Mistress Rowina says, it's not going to change things overnight.

"Should I be worried?" I ask quietly.

Gran's face falls, finally making her look her age. "Yes, I think you should. I think we all should."

CHAPTER

19

"MY ASCENSION DIDN'T CHANGE ANYTHING." It's not entirely true—I've been able to ignore the ghosts more easily and my magic feels calmer, even in its strengthened state—but it didn't change my vision.

Trixie is sitting across from me at one of the tables in my basement. She was the first call I made after Felix went home.

I think I was dreading this conversation more than telling Gran. But it needs to happen. When I first told Trixie, she barely batted an eye, but now that my hope of my magic just being haywire is gone, she might change her mind.

"And you know this how?" she asks. Analytical as always. I launch into the same story I told Gran, about how he touched my face in the hallway, ending with telling Gran.

My heart is in my throat when Trixie nods. "So that's why she gave me that look when I got here."

"Probably," I say. "She wasn't really pleased I told you."

"Is she informing the rest of the coven?" she asks. I shake my head. "That's not surprising. I'm assuming she was worried about your place as Rising Supreme. Coven members have been known to kill a Rising Supreme to roll the dice again."

"You think someone in our coven would kill me?" The thought of my own coven murdering me seemed unlikely until recently. Thinking I was worthless, sure. But I didn't think they would resort to something so drastic.

Unlike death, the future isn't set in stone. Veritas made that clear, and yet there were at least a half dozen paths it showed me that might make some wielders plot my assassination. A chill rakes down my spine.

I dismiss the thought as soon as I think it. Gran would never let that happen. Though it would explain why she has been on edge.

"No, not in our coven," Trixie says quickly. I don't entirely believe her though. "But it's not unheard of. There's a small coven in the mountains of North Carolina, and the rumor is that their last Rising Supreme fled out of fear."

"Is that the one with the magical bloodlines?"

"Yup."

"That sounds like a shit coven."

"Or a bad apple? We don't know. And besides, it's just a rumor."

Rumor or not, there's weight in what she's saying. Maybe Gran's avoidance in telling the coven wasn't just to keep their budding respect for me, but to keep me safe.

It would be just my luck to have a bunch of ghosts and a coven after me at the same time. Let alone be responsible for the murder of a classmate.

Trixie is quiet a moment. I don't say anything either, letting her process the information while silently praying to the Goddess she doesn't choose now to ditch me as a friend. And, despite my best efforts, the hope for something more seems to have taken up permanent residence in my chest.

I tug on the edge of my glove, the silence yawning before me.

"So, what's the next step?"

I blink at her. While this reaction feels perfectly aligned with Trixie as a person, it's still a bit of a shock.

"Umm, you understand I'm a murderer right?"

"And you understand I'm of the camp that there must be a reason why."

I grin, hope blooming in my chest. "I no longer have any doubts." I've thought about the next steps a lot since my worst fears were confirmed. My first instinct was to stick my head in the sand and forget any of this was happening. But my old habits don't work for me anymore. "I think it's time to figure out what that why is."

"Excellent plan," Trixie says, beaming at me.

"There's more too," I say.

"Tell me," she says, leaning forward.

"Do you remember a few weeks ago, when Jen mentioned this town has a lot of ghosts?"

"Yes?"

"Something's been bothering me since then. She showed up when I was walking home a few days before that and told me that there are others, and they're getting restless."

"Restless?" she asks.

"Complaining. About justice . . . for their deaths. And then she just disappeared without another word. I've tried to press her about it, but she won't say anything else. I let it go because I had so many other things going on. But with that and her weird warning after Quarterly . . ."

"You think the ghosts and Silas might be related," Trixie finishes for me. I nod. "I think that's a great place to start." A bubble of pride grows in my chest.

"Do you think we have an abnormal amount of death here in Windrop?" I ask.

"I would have said no," Trixie says, frowning. "But I haven't really thought about it before now."

"What if no one's really thought about it? Why would that be?" I press.

"I'm not sure," she says.

"Can something like that be shrouded? Like with magic?" My mind races, trying to remember Gran's talks about wards and shrouding when she was explaining how she hid me from the ghosts in the house, but I can't think of anything.

"Maybe? It'd have to be some kind of cloaking spell or something similar. But if it's a spell, wouldn't it have to be put in place by a wielder? Who would do that?" Trixie's frown deepens. "And if it's cloaked, why and how did Jen notice?"

That's the question that concerns me the most.

<hr />

"WHAT'D YOU FIND?" Trixie asks an hour later. She's been hunched over an old tome while I've been scouring the internet for information. She's still beautiful; the way she gets her face so close to the book, like she's trying to literally absorb it, makes it hard to look away from her.

"We are well above the national average," I say, clearing my throat. "Best I could find, the national mortality rate is somewhere around point five percent. Last year, the town's mortality rate was five percent."

"How is that sustainable?" Trixie asks, looking up. "Like, how hasn't the entire town disappeared?"

"That's the thing: deaths have been going up for the last thirteen years or so. Steady, but slow enough not to notice. I hadn't really thought about it before"—my eyes flick to Trixie—"that we have a lot of deaths in such a small town. That's weird, isn't it?"

Trixie's lips pull into a thin line. "Definitely weird."

"Maybe we're just unlucky?" I suggest, but it feels weak. An abnormal amount of deaths in a small town is one thing. An abnormal amount of deaths in a town that has the largest coven of death witches is another. Then it hits me. I look down at the notebook where I've been keeping track of my findings. "It started getting worse around thirteen years ago, right after my fourth birthday."

Trixie looks up, mouth dropping open as realization dawns. "Is that . . ."

"When I started seeing the ghosts?" Dropping my eyes, I stroke Jack's fur. "Sure was." And I started experiencing the death of anyone I touch soon after. I suck in a deep breath, scrubbing my hand over my face. I don't know what that connection means, but something tells me it's not good. "I just don't see how Silas could be involved in that. He just got here. And besides, he would also have been like four years old when this started." The same age as when it started for me.

Trixie bites her lip. My heart stutters before picking up its erratic beat. I take a deep breath, trying to will it to calm. No luck. I have to look away. "Anything else?" Trixie asks.

"Nothing much," I say, grateful for the change in topic. "Not one death is suspicious." Accidents or natural deaths. All of them. There was one murder-suicide when I was a toddler, but that is the only death even remotely suspicious.

But Jen was right—there have been so many.

She spins her book open in front of her to me. "Look here."

"Calling the Spirits?" I say, reading the title of the spell she's pointing to. "Why would I need to call the spirits? They're basically stalking me as it is."

"Can you see all of them at the same time?"

"Not usually," I admit. "It's too draining to focus on more than one. With Jen, it's a little different, I think because she wants to be around me instead of needing me as a vessel. Most of the time it takes enough of my energy just to ignore them."

Trixie taps the page. "See, that's what I mean. I want to call them all together at once."

I pull back from her. "What? What for?"

"I have some questions." She looks so excited I don't think I could refuse anything she asked of me.

"Are the questions like 'what's it like being dead' or 'why does George kill our classmate?'"

"Definitely the latter," she says firmly.

It's not a terrible idea.

Rather, it's actually a pretty good idea. Still, the thought of all those spirits at once, pressing in on me with their desires and emotions and fears . . . it's too much.

"I don't want to." Trixie doesn't say anything, just waits for me to admit defeat. "But I will," I say finally.

"Great, so let's go get Gran—"

"Wait. Now?"

"Yes, now. When did you think I meant?"

"I don't know, in a few days?"

"No, now."

"Don't you have to go home sometime?" Even I hate myself a little for asking the question. All of me never wants her to leave.

"Nope. My mom has decided the education of the Rising Supreme outweighs her desire to see her daughter." When I eye her, she clarifies. "Basically, I'm allowed to stay here as much as I can to help you. At first, it really was to help you with your magic, but it's the perfect excuse for me to keep researching." Trixie pauses, chewing on her bottom lip again. "Why? Sick of me already?"

"Only when you start suggesting we talk to dead people."

For a moment, Trixie looks worried, until she sees my smile. "Stop being a Negative Nancy. It could be fun. Jen's not that bad."

"That's putting it nicely." I wrinkle my nose, but my heart isn't in it. I've started to get used to Jen being around. A part of me even misses her when she's gone.

"She's not and you know it. But there are others. And I want to talk to them. I think you do too."

Sighing, I take a sip of my tea before responding. The peppermint emboldens me. "Fine. Just once. And if it doesn't work, I never have to try this again."

Being in a room with as many spirits as I can hold definitely feels like it should be a onetime thing.

"Deal." Trixie gathers the book in her arm and starts for the stairs. "Now we just have to get Gran and start putting together the séance."

"How do you know she has everything?" I ask.

Trixie turns around to glare at me, then notices the look on my face. "That was a joke, wasn't it?"

"It was," I say with a laugh. Gran's got enough supplies to keep the whole town in witchy business.

"If we get started now, we'll probably be ready by midnight." Trixie's at the top of the stairs, opening the door into the foyer.

"Why does everything magical have to happen in the middle of the night?"

Trixie deadpans. "It's not called the witching hour for nothing." It takes me until a smile forms on her lips for me to realize she's joking.

"Oh, you think you're the funny one now," I say, smiling.

"Couldn't resist. Magic works better in the dark. Something about our connection to the lunar cycles. It's one thing I don't fully understand. I'll go tell Gran now. I think it'll sound better coming from me."

She's already heading into the kitchen to find Gran when I call after her. "You sure now is the right time?"

Trixie turns and shoots me her mischievous smile. "No, but you know what they say: no time like the present." I wonder if there will ever be a time when that smile doesn't make me do whatever Trixie's asking.

CHAPTER

20

SWEAT COATS MY PALMS AS I sit with my back to the fire in the living room. I could barely focus as we set up the room.

Meanwhile, Gran and Trixie carried on like they were almost excited about the prospect of inviting a bunch of ghosts into my living room.

"I think we should reschedule," I say. Since my ascension, it's been so much easier to keep the spirits away, also as easy as breathing. It seems counterintuitive to call them to me when I've spent my whole life wishing they'd leave me alone.

"Absolutely not," Gran says from her reading chair to my left. "Tonight is an excellent night for a séance." Bennington caws in affirmation.

"Shut it, Benny."

"Don't take your contempt out on him," Gran scolds.

"Done!" Trixie declares as she stands up.

Two dozen or so black candles are spread out before me, flickering in the glow of the fire. Their flames are orange, ready to receive.

"Why do we need so many?"

"I don't know how many will come." Trixie shrugs. "I want to have room for as many as possible."

"You say it like you're waiting to see who comes to a party," I grumble. Jack senses my irritation, shifting in my lap.

"It is kind of like a party. A ghost party." Trixie wiggles her eyebrows at me.

"Gotta make it creepy."

"No way. This is fun. Oh, don't look like that. It's not like they'll hurt you."

I shift uncomfortably. "You don't know that."

"They haven't before," Gran says from her seat. "Besides, I am ready should you need assistance. This is your gift, Georgiana. It's time you embraced at least a part of it."

"I've been studying the tarot! I've even gotten quite good at the pendulum." I look at Trixie for confirmation. "I've embraced my magic!"

Gran remains unimpressed. "And that is wonderful, but those are such small parts of your magic. It's time you test it, especially after realizing your full power at ascension."

A shiver rakes its nails down my spine.

"Jack, leave us," Gran commands. Jack hisses his disdain but obeys. She is the only person besides me who can give him commands. He hops from my lap and trots to sit next to Bennington's perch. His hackles are still raised, but he's quiet.

"Are you ready?" Trixie asks. She sits cross-legged on the other side of the candles.

"No, but I don't think I'll ever be."

Trixie nods but doesn't offer that we stop. She wants to do this even more than Gran does.

While I do think it's necessary, part of me was hoping Gran would shut this whole thing down. But apparently when Trixie asked her, she turned right around and started pulling every black candle we had from the cupboard.

I filled her in on all my suspicions as we worked. Gran has all the same questions we do about what has the spirits riled up and what role Silas plays in all of this. She hasn't said it outright, but I can see it in the way she watches me, in the tension in her shoulders.

The other question we're all skirting around, the one I'm not even sure I really want the answer to is: *why am I at the center of it all?*

"Remember: intent." Trixie gives me an encouraging nod.

"I'm going to have that inscribed on your headstone when you die." Closing my eyes, I lay the backs of my hands on my crossed legs, palms toward the sky.

No gloves today, no barriers between myself and my magic.

Gran pulled down the wards on the house for tonight. She wanted it to be easy for them to come in.

I take a steadying breath. Let it out. Another, trying to focus my intent on the spirits.

"Spirits of Windrop, make yourselves known. We want to . . . chat."

"Not quite formal, but I suppose that will work," Gran mumbles from her chair.

I force my eyes to remain shut and focus on the feeling of the room. My inner self is searching, calling. If nothing else, looking into Veritas has made it much easier to connect to that part of myself.

For a long while, nothing happens. I begin to think I did it wrong. Or maybe Gran missed a ward.

I hear Trixie's sharp intake of breath as the first emotions crash into me.

Despair, confusion, anger, longing.

One right after the other, they consume me. The emotions swirl around inside me. I clench my jaw against a wave of nausea at their volume.

It's a fight to leave my palms open, receiving.

"George," Trixie whispers. "George, open your eyes."

I peek open my eyes.

Every flame has turned to black. Spirits litter the room, some familiar but many I've never seen before.

"What the shit," I breathe.

"Language, young lady!" my third-grade teacher says with a glare. "Always were a little troublemaker."

"Can you guys see them?" I ask. By the looks on their faces, I already know the answer, but I can't help but ask.

"I wasn't expecting so many," Gran says quietly.

I feel all of them. Not only their emotions, but their pull on my magic. It's straining within me, and a sweat breaks out across my skin.

"Oh, there's more," Jen says from beside me. Though the others are all on the other side of the candles from us, Jen apparently took a different stance.

"Hey Jen." Part of me is relieved to see her. "More?"

"Loads, but they can't move as freely."

"Why?" Trixie asks.

Jen looks puzzled, as if the question never occurred to her. "You know, I'm not really sure."

"Some are held with a tighter grip," an old woman croaks from the sofa.

I peer around Jen's ghost to look at her, but I don't recognize her. She must have died a long time ago. The spirits seem to acknowledge her as their speaker, all of them turning their focus to her.

Except Jen, who remains next to me.

"Renee?" Gran breathes.

"Esme." The old woman smiles with closed lips to my gran, but there's something sad in the gesture.

"It's been, what?"

"Almost thirteen years," Renee says.

"She was—is—a dear, dear friend." Gran is still looking at Renee, but she's speaking to me. A faint line of silver appears on Gran's lashes. I don't think I've ever seen her cry. "And a trusted member of the coven. Georgiana, direct your questions to her."

"I will answer the best I am able." The ghost of Renee adjusts on the couch to sit up straighter.

"Okay," I start. I know there're things I'm supposed to ask, but my mind can't grasp any of them. "Um . . . how many of you are there?"

"That number is too hard to pin down. This is the largest gathering I've been a part of," Renee says. "I think the better question is when."

"When what?"

Renee's lips pull into a thin line as she shakes her head. "I can only help you so much. There are . . . limitations."

A bead of sweat slips down my temple. I don't know how much longer I can hold them. I rack my brain, dragging up the only question I can think of: "When did you start gathering?"

"There you go, child. I was one of the first in the group, a few others arriving within weeks."

"Write that down." Gran whispers to Trixie, our designated note-taker for the night.

My mind is spinning too fast, weighted down by the emotions in the room, and I know I'll need some record of this conversation.

"Already on it." Trixie's pen scratches on the page.

"Okay," I continue. "Jen mentioned that some of the spirits were agitated, talking about justice. Why?"

Renee's eyes flick to Jen, who shrinks under her gaze, before returning to mine. "They feel they linger unjustly."

"Why do you linger? Why not just move on?"

Renee shakes her head again. "I cannot answer that either. Be specific."

I chew my lower lip. "Do you linger because of my gift?"

"Yes and no."

That answer doesn't make me feel any better. If it's my fault they're still here, they would probably want justice for that. "Can you explain?"

"Ask a specific question." She's only been here a couple of minutes and already she sounds like a broken record.

"Are my gifts the result of the spirits that linger?"

"Some yes. Some no."

I don't like this game. "Um, is there another force keeping you here?"

"Yes."

Now we're getting somewhere. My limbs are trembling from the weight of the magic. My entire back is now slicked in sweat. "A bad force?"

"Yes."

"Who?"

"Specific."

"Silas?"

She cringes at the mention of the name. "He has his role to play."

"How? He just got in town and you just said you've been lingering thirteen years."

"Specific."

"Ugh." This is frustrating. I shift a bit, trying to relieve the numbness in my butt. It doesn't work.

"She's great, isn't she?" Jen says from beside me. I can feel her sarcasm.

Renee glares at Jen. "Continue."

I try a new tactic. "Who lingers?"

"All."

"So every person who's died in this town since I got my first gift still lingers here?"

"They started gathering a little after that, but yes."

My parents died three weeks after I saw my first ghost. There were still balloons in my bedroom from my birthday party. Hope soars in my chest. Renee must see what I'm about to ask before the words leave my mouth. Her pity turns palpable. "My parents?"

"Are with us," she says begrudgingly.

"Where are they? Can I see them?"

"They are allowed very little freedom," Renee says.

"What does that mean? Who allows them? Why aren't they here?"

"Too much," Gran says as Renee begins to fade.

"Wait!" I call, but she still fades. Her candle turns from black to orange.

"Well, I guess she didn't want—" I'm cut short as I turn to look at Gran. Fresh tears line her eyes as she looks to the place where Renee just was.

Renee's candle is once again black.

Pride swirls around me.

"Monica?" Gran whispers.

Time stalls and I'm moving in slow motion as I turn my head to see my mother perched on the couch.

She looks exactly as I remember, chestnut hair flowing down her back and emerald eyes sparkling. The only difference is her missing brooch, the same as Gran's. Well, that and there's now panic etched into her beautiful face.

"Georgiana." Every bit of anxiety written on her face is present in her voice. "You must release them. Now. This has been noticed."

"Mom, what? Who's watching? Where's Dad?"

"I don't have the time. Release us. Let this go." I want to stand. I need to go to her, to be closer to her, but that would require breaking position, and it's hard enough to hold them as it is. She holds up her hand to stop me as if she senses my thoughts. "Let this go. It isn't safe."

"Mom, what isn't safe? What are you talking about?"

Candles flicker and go out around the room as spirits disappear. Even Jen is sucked from the room. Emotions are now ripping from me. I push out with my magic, trying to hold on to them, to pull them back. But I don't have enough strength left in me.

"I'm out of time. George, I love you. Let this go. It's not—"

She's cut off as she's ripped from the room.

CHAPTER

21

WE SIT IN THE DIM light from the smoldering fire. I fix my eyes on a candle, smoke from the wick rising in a haphazard line. I've decided that was the candle my mother grasped on to, though I really have no way to tell. But for whatever reason, I can't stop staring at it like it's the only piece of her left.

Finally, the silence is broken.

"Was that . . . ?" Trixie starts, trailing off.

"My mother?" My words are choked, pain lancing through my chest. "Yup."

"She was very beautiful," Trixie says softly.

Was. The word clangs through me. Though she's been gone almost thirteen years, the reminder is just as painful. Standing, I start heading out of the room. "I guess."

"Wait, George, where are you going?" Trixie asks as she starts to follow me.

I hear Gran say, "Let her go," as I turn the corner and head for the stairs. Their muted voices follow me, probably talking about their theories, or how I should have held them longer.

I don't care.

Though he makes no sound, I can feel Jack's presence behind me as I enter my room, and I pause to allow him to follow before shutting the door behind him. I drag off my boots before crawling into bed and waiting for the tears to come. The sheets are cool as I sink into them. Soon, Jack's weight lands on the bed and his warmth sinks through the sheets as he settles in behind my knees.

I figured I could at least make it here. If I made it to my room, then I could let myself fall apart. But as I lie between the ice-cold sheets, staring at the wall, I feel . . .

Nothing.

It's like the emotional tidal wave from the spirits has left me dry, leaving not even an ounce of feeling to mourn the loss of my mother, even though seeing her again makes it feel like a fresh wound.

My eyes are fixed on a blank space on my wall as a knock sounds on the door. I don't respond, but the door opens anyway. Gran comes in, setting down her tray on my nightstand before sitting on the bed. I don't look at her, continuing my vigil of the wall.

Gran gestures to the tray. "I've brought you some hot tea."

"Tea doesn't fix everything."

"No," she says solemnly. "No, I don't suppose it does. But it will fix this."

I break my stare-down of the wall to eye her.

"There's a draft in it. Should lift your spirits and fill your cup, so to speak. I imagine you're drained."

Pushing myself up, I pick up a cup from the tray and sniff it. Orange and licorice with a hint of honey and basil.

"Strange combination," I say before taking a sip.

"Whole thing, dear," Gran says as I begin to lower the cup.

I lift it again, downing the lukewarm tea before setting the cup back on the tray. Gran refills the cup and gestures at it. I repeat the process two more times before she seems satisfied.

"Give it a moment and tell me how you feel."

At first, I just feel like I have a full belly of mediocre tea, but then it's just as she said. My feelings return as if they're being poured back into me, the heartache settling like a weight.

"Worse," I say, lying back into the bed.

"You might think so, but even pain is better than nothing."

"How did you know I didn't feel anything?"

"It's part of the process. I've known many less gifted mediums than you, and they always felt drained after hosting just one spirit. You had over two dozen at once. Both an impressive feat and one that I believe must have been very draining."

"Hmm."

"Ask your questions."

"I don't know where to start." There are too many for me to figure out what I want to know first.

"Start with the first one that comes out of your mouth."

Taking a deep breath, I try to push aside the pain and focus on what we learned.

"So they're here still?"

"It appears that way, yes."

"Why didn't Dad come?"

"I don't know that I have an answer to that, but I'm going to guess it has something to do with what your mother and Renee were saying. They don't have the freedom." Gran pauses. "It seemed to be a heavy strain for your mother to come here tonight."

Her brooch catches the light from the open door. I vaguely remember my mother's, the same as Gran's. The rune was also the same, almost unheard of in covens.

I wonder why I didn't get it too.

As she says the words, I know what she means. It seems silly that I even needed to ask the questions, but some part of me needed to speak them out loud, to have the fear that my dad didn't love me enough to come explained away.

The question is out of my mouth before I have time to think about it. "Why?"

"That is as good a question as any," Gran says. "I was beginning to think we would never understand your vision and why so many spirits are lingering. While I don't know any answers to those questions, I do think we at least have somewhere to start."

The weight of this suddenly feels like too much. "What if I don't want to start?"

"I don't know that is an option any longer."

"I'm tired of this." I don't say what this is, but it seems the right word for everything.

I'm tired of my gifts. Of not being able to touch anyone for fear I may feel their deaths. Of magic. Of being different. Of being an orphan. Of the weight of responsibility that no high schooler should feel. And on that note, high school.

"I know. For now, you can rest, recover after the strain of this evening. We will refocus after that."

Gran scans my leg. She seems to deem the fabric sufficient coverage, so she pats my knee twice before standing. We've never been the type of family to wallow together. Grieving in solitude has always been our way.

"Gran?" She stops, turning in the doorway. Her emerald eyes find me. I've grown so used to seeing them in her face, I forgot she gave them to my mother, who then gave them to me. Until I saw them in my mother's face tonight.

The knife in my heart twists again.

"I have one more question."

"I thought you might."

"Do you . . . I mean, do you think my parents' death wasn't accidental?"

Gran heaves a sigh. "Your mother was young, but she was powerful. You're a lot like her in that way: raw, untapped power. She might have become even stronger than I was in my prime, if she had lived long enough to hone her craft." Anguish skitters across Gran's face. "I would have been suspicious if there was a reason. Jealousy is not uncommon in covens." My mind skips back to Trixie's earlier words about covens killing a Rising Supreme to get a new pick. "But the ice was thick that night. And the bridge has claimed more than a few lives over the years . . ." Gran's eyes glaze over, as if she is lost in thought, before she continues. "But no, I didn't think it was anything other than a terrible accident. I thought the fact that they didn't try to speak to you confirmed that." Gran reaches up to pinch the bridge of her nose. Her age once again settles on her. "Now I think there may have been other forces."

"Like what?"

Gran sighs, releasing her nose. "Right now, I need to think. I will sleep on it." Gran begins shutting my door but pauses again. "Georgiana?"

"Yes?"

"I love you."

Tears burn my eyes. "I love you too, Gran."

-《《◆》》--《《◆》》--《《◆》》-

SLEEP WON'T COME. Every time I close my eyes, I'm met with the vision of my panic-stricken mother or my blood-slicked face. Neither are conducive to sleep.

Jen left with the others, but I can feel her, just outside the wards. Gran put the protections back up following the séance, but I think I'm strong enough since my ascension to work around them.

Maybe I should have asked her how they work, just to be sure.

I'm struck by the thought that Gran may sense what I'm doing, and she'd know I was puncturing her wards, but I push it aside. I need answers, and there's no time like the present, right? Trixie would be so proud.

Crossing my legs, I place my hands palms open to the sky and close my eyes.

Intent.

I feel her hovering right on the edges. Calling to her, tugging on the bond between us, I pull her in until she's sitting in front of me.

Jen looks around my room, eyes wide. "Is this your bedroom?"

"Hey, Jen," I say. "Yeah it is. Look, I have something I need to ask you."

"I've never seen your room before," she says, still looking around. "Actually, I've only ever seen your living room, and that was tonight. Why is that?"

I don't have time for this. "Gran puts up wards to keep you out."

"That's not very nice."

"It's not for you in particular," I sigh. "Just your kind."

"My kind." She draws out the word in disgust. "Well, that's not very nice either."

I don't have time to argue the nuances of judging all ghosts the same with her tonight. "Jen, focus," I say, snapping my fingers in her face.

"Geez, touchy today."

"Why'd you leave me during the séance?"

"Huh?" Her eyes glaze over as she tries to remember. "Oh, didn't you send me away?"

My brow furrows. "No, I definitely didn't."

"You must have."

"I'm positive I didn't. Try to remember."

Jen bites her bottom lip as she thinks. "I don't—I don't know."

"My mother was talking to me, then she was gone. You all were. It felt like the spirits were being ripped from me." Running my hands through my hair, I try another way. "Jen, do you know if Silas is what's keeping you here?"

Jen shudders as fear courses from her. "No."

"Why'd you just tremble?" Is Jen lying to me? It isn't something I've considered before, but it could be possible, though I'm not sure why she would be. I try to scan her emotions to see if there's anything telling. I don't feel any deception from her, but come to think of it, I've never tried to figure out if one of them was lying to me. I'm not even sure it's possible.

"I did?"

"You did."

She looks down at my bed, eyes searching the comforter like it holds all the answers she needs.

"Think," I encourage.

Jen's face scrunches. "It's fuzzy . . ."

"What's fuzzy?"

"My head. I'm trying to think, but it's just fuzzy."

She looks up at me again, and if her emotions weren't coursing through me, they'd be easy enough to see: they're painted across her beautiful face.

She's terrified and has no idea why, which scares her more.

"Curious," I muse.

Jen's eyes narrow. "You're looking at me like I'm a roadside freak show."

I blink. "That's not my intention. This is just a weird situation."

"What does it mean?"

"I don't know," I admit.

"I don't like it," Jen says.

"I don't either."

"Things were easier when I was alive."

I look at her again. I can't be sure if the ache in my chest is my response, or hers. "That makes sense."

"I hate to say this, because it sort of sounds like I'm glad to be dead, but I'm glad I got to know you, even though it took me dying to do it." She drops her eyes from mine, almost like she's embarrassed by the admission. "I wish it hadn't taken death for me to be nice to you."

I want to give her a snarky comeback, but something tells me it's not the right time. If, even three weeks ago, someone had told me Jen Monroe would be the person to soften me up, I would have laughed in their face.

But here we are, building a friendship between a witch and a ghost. I would say stranger things have happened, but I honestly don't think that's true.

"I'm glad I got to know you, too. You're not as terrible as I thought you would be."

The tension in the room melts a bit as she sticks her tongue out at me. "And you're not as prickly as you pretend to be."

"Always calling me names," I say with an exaggerated roll of my eyes.

"If it fits, it sticks," she says.

"I'm pretty sure that's not how that goes."

We both laugh for a minute, the humor too exaggerated for the joke, but it still feels good.

"Do you want to, I don't know, stay for a bit?" I ask.

Jen tilts her head. "With you?"

"Yeah, for a while. We could listen to music?"

"Sure. I think I might like that."

Jen and I settle on the bed, her form not touching mine as I pull up my Spotify playlist.

"What are we listening to?" Jen asks.

"It's called Angsty Teen. I made it myself."

"You're a strange one," she says, resting her hands on her stomach. "In a good way."

We lie there, listening as the songs click through my playlist, for a long time.

Finally, Jen speaks again. "Are you going to try?"

"Try what?"

"To figure out what's happening in town?" she asks quietly. There's hope and longing in her words, and something else I can't quite place.

"Yeah, I think I am."

"Good," Jen says.

We lie there until my eyelids droop and the world becomes hazy. I feel Jen fading as I slip away, my magic no longer able to hold on to her in sleep.

CHAPTER

22

GRAN MAY HAVE FORGONE THE large ceremony for my ascension, but that doesn't mean I don't have to be at every single one of the others.

At least it's Trixie's tonight.

As Rising Supreme, I've seen dozens of ascension ceremonies since I started my ascension lessons, but I've never lost my wonder at it. Even after mine, I'll always secretly like watching them.

Trixie's trembling. I can see it from here. The night is cold, bordering on frigid, but the warming spells my gran and Trixie's mom put in place keep the circle warm.

Her hair is down, freed from the tight buns and braids she normally wears it in at school. The red lace dress she's wearing flows onto the forest floor and pools at her feet. The bell sleeves sway as she rubs her arms. She looks like a goddess, an ethereal light in the dark.

I shuffle over to her as Gran and Trixie's mom prepare for the ceremony.

"You look really pretty," I whisper to her.

She offers me a nervous smile. "Thanks. I couldn't wait to wear it but now it seems like a silly choice." She glances down at her dress.

"It's perfect. Really!" I add when Trixie lifts a dark brow. "You should see some of the things the others have worn. One guy showed up in a tank top and slides." Once again, my nerves make nonsense tumble from my mouth.

"No," Trixie gasps.

"Yup. Gran grumbled about disrespecting tradition for a full week."

Trixie chuckles. "I feel a bit better then." She runs her hands down the front of her dress.

"You look great. And that color is amazing on you." That's an understatement.

"Thanks. I always thought red looked great with my skin." She takes a steadying breath. "So what happens next?"

"There aren't any surprises," I say, turning to where Gran is chanting the opening spells. I didn't tell her about my ascension, about the power that ripped through me. Gran said it was uncommon for it to be that strong, so I figured it was best not to worry her. I hope I'm right. "It's just like what we've always heard. You'll present your offering to the Goddess just as the clock strikes midnight and ascend. And you'll end your first day being seventeen."

"Oh yeah, and there's that," Trixie laughs nervously. I want to reach for her, to pull her into a hug and assure her she'll be okay. To take her fingers in mine and squeeze them, offering her the comfort I so desperately needed before my ascension.

Instead, I have to settle for the hollowness of words. "Relax. You passed your trials with flying colors."

The tension in her shoulders releases a bit. "I did."

"We're ready," Gran interrupts before I can finish. Unsaid words hang between us as Gran gestures to the candles arranged on the ground among the leaves.

The five-pointed star.

I remember when I was little, I always thought the candles were arranged in a circle. Gran would get so mad at me for failing to understand they represented the five points of the pentagram and that calling it a circle was basically sacrilege within the coven.

None of the ghosts were present at my ascension, not even Jen. I didn't think anything of it at the time, since maybe my realization of power was keeping them away. But they've been at every other ascension, always testing to see how close they can get. Actually, they're everywhere except the house, thanks to Gran's wards.

I glance around for confirmation, but there's not a single one here. And the last time I even felt Jen was when we fell asleep a few nights ago.

Trixie looks to me, pulling me from my thoughts.

It takes me a moment to realize she's looking at me for reassurance. I give her a small nod after which she squares her chin and marches forward.

No one has ever looked to me for reassurance.

In the center of the pentagram rests a knife and a smooth stone no bigger than a quarter. Trixie kneels in front of the two objects. Gran, Trixie's mother, and I kneel at three of the five candles. I present my palms to the sky with the others.

"Gloves," Gran hisses. There's a flash of something across Trixie's face but it's gone too soon to nail down. I think she was almost as hopeful as me that my ascension would change my gift. And just as let down when it didn't.

I tug the gloves off and resume position.

"Goddess, we present to you this dedicant. She has survived the fires of the trials and waits before you for your blessing. As the clock strikes midnight on the dawning of her seventeenth year, accept her offering and welcome your daughter into your warmth."

No matter how many times I hear her say it, gooseflesh still spreads along my skin. As Gran finishes speaking, Trixie's mother and I begin the chant.

"Mother keep her. Sister welcome her. Goddess protect her. Mother keep her. Sister welcome her. Goddess protect her."

Bennington caws from Gran's shoulder.

"It is time, my child," Gran says, inclining her head.

Despite her earlier nerves, Trixie doesn't hesitate to lift the knife and drag it across her palm. Red blooms in an instant, dripping over her hand onto the stone and leaves.

"Mother keep me. Sister welcome me. Goddess protect me."

The knife slips from her fingers to the ground.

The forest goes still as magic settles in. Trixie's head is thrown back in some mix of ecstasy and pain as the Mother's magic flows through her. I feel it coursing along my skin, zinging and tingling as it coalesces in her.

It's almost as if time is standing still as Trixie lifts from the ground, hovering within the pentagon.

Our chant becomes a frenzy, the power that feeds Trixie's ascension.

Finally, Trixie lowers to the ground, eyes closed as we continue to chant.

This is the part I've never liked, waiting for them to wake. The unworthy never do, and part of me suddenly fears Trixie will be one of this unlucky few.

I barely have time to think the thought before her eyes are fluttering open and she's pushing up.

"Very good, Sister Trixie," Gran says. High praise from her.

Trixie shakes the daze from her head before moving to look at the small stone.

"What is it?" I blurt. Gran gives me a look but says nothing.

"Vines," Trixie says softly.

We stand and crowd around her to look at the stone perched in her hand. Indeed, the rune is plain as day. I told Trixie it looked like a shrugging man just the other day, so I recall its meaning immediately.

"Growth. You've been blessed as a lifebringer!" I say, looking up to beam at my friend.

She bites her lip and nods, tears forming in her lashes.

The blessings of the Goddess are fickle, with many witches and warlocks finding themselves blessed with the more common water or sun runes. Rarely are there lifebringer witches. They are coveted almost as much as a draconian gift. Still a death witch, Trixie can pull her power to heal and grow, using her connection to death to come full circle in life. It makes sense since she's able to sense someone's life force.

"Oh my girl," Trixie's mom says, scooping her into a hug.

My heart aches as I watch their embrace. Gran rests a hand gently on my covered shoulder. "I am so proud of you, Georgiana."

I know what she's trying to say, that her pride in me stems both from my recent ascension and from my growing involvement in the coven, even making a friend. But just as I try to smile, my eye catches on the bloody knife on the ground. Memories of the knife in my hands come back. The smile falls from my lips.

⫸⫷ ⫸⫷ ⫸⫷

TRIXIE GETS BALLOONS. The living room is filled with them. They're mismatched, too, which means her mom wasn't the only one who brought them. I'm surprised how much that stings. They're the first thing I notice when we walk into my house. Gran doesn't usually lend out our home for post-ascension celebrations, but since it was Trixie, she made an exception. Trixie and her mom immediately make the rounds, saying hello to all the guests gathered around Gran's sofa.

There are only about a dozen people, but it's still a dozen more than who showed up after mine.

"Had I thought you would enjoy something like this, I would have thrown you one too," Gran says. We stand in the archway between the foyer and the living room, watching Trixie receive her, rightfully earned, congratulations.

"I wouldn't have," I lie. Somehow, between the equinox and now, I've shifted from coven pariah to active participant. And I kind of like it.

Gran gives me a knowing look before something catches her attention. "I think someone is calling my name."

"I don't hear anything," I say as she moves away. Then I notice Mistress Rowina heading straight for me.

"Georgiana," she says with a dip of her head. She's standing a little straighter than usual, a glass of red wine gripped in her free hand. I knew she was just putting the crone thing on for show. "It is good to see you." She notices my frown and sighs. "I mean, it is good to see you participating."

"I think it's becoming a trend," I say. I wish I had a glass. Not necessarily of wine, but just of anything. I need something to stop my fidgeting hands.

"A good one, I think." Mistress Rowina takes a sip of her wine. "I hear Beatrix is a lifebringer? Curious, to have two such opposing runes so close together." My body tenses, and Mistress Rowina tracks it. Something in her face softens and somehow she looks younger. "That is not an attack, just an observation." She takes another sip of her wine, like she needs time to collect herself. "I am impressed by your recent commitment to your magic. It makes me . . . hopeful for the future of the coven."

"Thank you," I say, surprised by the tightening of my throat.

She dips her head, turning to leave, but pauses. "While the Veritas would not have been my choice, I do think it was the right one. No other single action could have helped you make up so much ground with the coven."

She leaves me standing in the archway to mull over her words. She's right, but just the mention of the mirror makes me break out in a cold sweat. I take a steadying breath, then a second, before heading to the food. There are cupcakes, and cupcakes make everything better.

Trixie finds me almost as soon as I finish my cupcake. She's beaming, practically bouncing on her toes as she pops over to me.

"I don't think I'll ever be able to sleep," she says, picking up a cupcake. It's chocolate with blue frosting and a smattering of rainbow sprinkles. Fun and chaotic, just like Trixie.

It's just after two in the morning, and I can feel the weight of all the sleepless nights bearing down on me. I smile anyway. "Me either." Trixie nods, taking a bite of the cupcake. "How are you, other than excited?"

She chews before speaking. "Honestly, overwhelmed. Before, I could sense people if I was actively trying, but now they're just . . . there. All the time. I can feel everyone here. Even you." The look she gives me is searing. She can probably feel the way my heartbeat kicks up from it.

"I can imagine," I say, looking away quickly. Watching her too long might make me do something stupid, like declare my feelings as if I were in a cheesy, yet highly underrated historical romance. Or ask her out, which is just as ludicrous.

"Is this what it feels like for you, with the ghosts?" she asks. The question catches me off guard.

"Probably," I say, though I'm not sure. "It gets easier though," I add when the adorable line between her brows appears. "You'll find your own way to tune it out and it will be like background noise unless you're looking for it."

She relaxes a little at that, a bit of the giddiness returning to her face. Hank, a witch one year older than us, waves Trixie over. I watch her go, the words of Mistress Rowina playing through my head. Trixie's gift is so similar to mine, only in its opposite, as in her rune. I don't know what that means, but I'm beginning to think there are no coincidences.

CHAPTER

23

HISTORY CLASS IS EVEN MORE painful than usual. Every time Silas shifts in his seat, I'm convinced he knows something. Every time he turns his attention my way, I hold my breath, certain he's going to call me out.

Seeking me out the other day felt purposeful, like he knew what would happen if he touched me. But since then, he's gone back to normal. Still, I watch the back of his head, waiting for him to make a move.

But he just does his work like nothing is amiss.

My eyes refuse to focus on my textbook, deciding they need to flick to the back of Silas's head every thirty seconds against my will. I can't make sense of it: there doesn't seem to be anything evil lurking beneath his skin.

There isn't even a hint of something that would be causing deaths in town, let alone connected to whatever is trapping the souls here. Even after the creeps he gave me the other day, he seems so harmless, more cocky than terrifying.

Maybe desire to find some tangible reason that I kill him is driving me to see things that aren't really there.

No, that isn't it. The look in his eyes right before he touched my face is burned into my memory. And then I think about Jen and how she flees whenever he's around—her warning the other night on the lawn. There are too many coincidences. If he's not the reason for the deaths, he's connected in some way.

The hand on the clock ticks ever closer to the end of class, and I brace myself.

The sound of the bell ringing clatters through me. Despite the gloves, I know my hands are white-knuckle gripped on the desk. But Silas just packs up his things and leaves from the room, waving to someone in the hallway as he disappears.

I don't relax until he's gone.

Trixie lets out a whoosh of breath as she begins packing up. "I thought for sure he was going to know what we think about him."

"Me too," I say, finally starting to move. It's then that something takes over. My life could be over any day now, either figuratively or literally. All of Felix's and Jen's prodding about Trixie finally settles in.

I would say it's a possession, but I know far too much about spirits to even pretend that's the truth.

I almost chicken out. Almost.

"Would you want to go for coffee one day?" The words are out of my mouth before my mind has had a chance to register them. I'm horrified by myself, but it's too late now.

Trixie blinks her wide eyes at me, probably more put off by the shocked expression on my face than my question. I try to school my features into a smile, but I'm pretty sure it's a grimace.

"Like after school?" she asks.

My way out is so clear then. I could just play it off like I was just asking as a friend, like I wasn't just overcome by the sudden and all-consuming urge to ask her on a date.

But I don't back down. Maybe it's because I've grown bolder over the past few weeks. Maybe it's because it feels like something's coming, and there's no time like the present.

Or maybe, just maybe, Jen's right and it's me who's been holding myself back.

But I will never, ever admit that I think she's right. I'll never live it down.

"No," I say. "Like at night, by ourselves." My heart is thundering in my chest, and I shove my hands in the pockets of my leather jacket to keep them from trembling.

She blinks once. Twice. "Like a date?"

Again. A way out. I don't take it. "Yes, like a date." When she doesn't immediately respond, I charge forward. "You can totally say no and forget about it if you want. I know you've been helping me with my studies, and you're basically like one of my only friends, so I really don't want to mess this up but—"

Thank the Goddess that Trixie cuts me off because I have no idea what I was going to say next. Her smile is wide when she speaks. "Definitely. I would like that."

◄◄◆►►· ◄◄◆►►· ◄◄◆►►

THE BLEACHERS ARE icy today. Though, after this morning, every part of my body is warm.

Trixie whispers a few words, a warming hex spreading around us.

Who knows, maybe I'll cast it next time. My hand goes to the crystal hanging from my neck. I hope my parents would be proud of how far I've come.

"Bold move," I say around a mouthful of sandwich.

"I'm not trying to freeze out here. And no one will bother us anyway."

"Can I ask you something?"

"Sure." Trixie's gaze meets mine and there's that look again. It's like my limbs have turned to Jell-O. My heart tells me it's hope, but my mind won't tolerate that thought.

I press on. I haven't voiced this feeling yet. I suck in a deep breath. "Just that I think there's something sinister going on, and if I'm connected like I think I am, it would be dangerous to get too close to me." My eyes meet Trixie's. "It's probably dangerous for you—and Felix too."

Trixie's shoulders sag. "That wasn't a question. Did you change your mind already?"

I'm shaking my head before she even finishes. "Absolutely not. I'm more trying to give you an out, if you want one."

Trixie relaxes. "Well, it's too late for us."

"Trixie, I'm serious."

"So am I," she says, leveling a look. "I can speak for Felix when I say we're in this with you. So stop worrying about us and start worrying about Silas. Which brings me to what I've been thinking: I think Silas is the reason people are dying."

I've been thinking the same thing, although part of me hasn't wanted to say it out loud, probably because I wasn't sure if it was just wishful thinking. But if Trixie thinks that, there has to be something there.

Then there's the other part of me that knows I have to face the fact that *something* is going on with Silas. But by admitting that, I'd be acknowledging that I actually kill him, something I can't think about without being struck by a wave of nausea. There's been so much death already, I don't want to add to it.

"But how?" I ask, mouth full of sandwich again. I chew quickly and swallow. "He just got here." That's the first thing I can't figure out. It's like a one-thousand-piece puzzle where I don't know the image and half the pieces are missing.

"That's what we have to figure out."

"And he's what? Seventeen?" I barely hear her. Those pieces are bouncing about in my mind, begging me to put them together. "He would have been a child when my parents died. And if this has been happening since before then, he would have only been a toddler. How would he kill anyone?" I take another bite and chew slowly while I think. "How would we even start looking into this?"

"I've been thinking about this." Trixie perks up. "I don't have a clue what would keep spirits here or cause deaths, let alone do both, but if there's anywhere with information that could answer those questions, I think it's your gran's library."

"Okay," I say with another mouthful. "What happens if we figure out he's the cause?"

Trixie frowns like she's been anticipating this question. "We should tell the coven, if nothing else than to have their help in preparing you to . . ." She trails off, unable or unwilling to say *kill him.* "But ultimately, the choice is yours."

Despite the absolutely terrible topic, my heart warms at that. She trusts me enough to make my own decisions, despite what she knows happens.

"You drive a hard bargain."

"You agree?" Trixie says, perking up.

"I agree, but if we don't find anything, you and Felix are out of it," I say. Trixie opens her mouth to argue, but I cut her off before she can. "If we can't figure out what's going on or how Silas is involved, I don't want you involved further. Can't have you an accomplice to cold-blooded murder."

The last words land how I intended them. Trixie's argument dries in her throat, but I know I haven't heard the end of it.

"Deal," she says finally.

My eyes scan the field, then return to Trixie. "You know what's weird?"

"I think we can establish that there are lots of weird things going on."

"You're a real smart-ass, you know."

"Look who's talking."

Trixie levels a look my way. A smile lifts the corner of my lips even though I try to fight it.

"Fine, but for real. I haven't seen any ghosts in days."

Trixie stops midchew. "Really?"

I haven't said it out loud, partly because it feels like jinxing it and partly because it feels like admitting a failure on my part. I've wanted them gone for most of my life, but now that they are, the world feels empty without them. "Really. Not since before your ascension."

"Not even Jen?"

I grimace. I feel Jen's absence the most. And for some reason, I don't want Trixie to know that I called on Jen after the séance. "No, none of them. They've just ... disappeared."

"Have you tried calling them? It should be harder to get rid of them with your full magic."

"I know," I say. They should be pushing to get in at all times. There's usually a relearning period for wielders when they have to navigate the full strength of our magic. I was expecting that, not ... silence. "I called gently for Jen this morning. She didn't come. And I'm not that desperate to start trying the others yet." Instinctively, I scan the field again. Nothing. "Actually, it's not that. I've wanted them to go away for most of my life, but now that they're gone, I might miss them?"

"You say that like you don't know."

"I guess I don't. I mean, Jen was terrible when she was alive, but I actually like having her around."

Trixie considers. "I don't think there's anything wrong with that." She looks out over the empty football field. "It's connected, isn't it?"

I nod. "I think it is." The missing ghosts. Their call for justice. The unnatural deaths. Their restriction at the séance. Silas. Me. I'm filled with this sense of dread that we're all connected. The only question is how.

Trixie's gaze catches mine before she looks back over the field. "We'll figure it out. Then we can focus on something better."

She's still staring ahead when she says it, but I can't help but hope that something better, is us.

CHAPTER

24

THE CHEER OF THE CARNIVAL chafes against my mood. I'm not usually one for large social gatherings anyway, but today I find it especially unbearable. I'm already anxious and excited about today, and the large crowd of people bumping around isn't helping.

While I suggested coffee, I shouldn't have been surprised that Trixie picked the Halloween carnival as our first date. Towns like Windrop don't have much to do, so when there's an event—a school play, a festival, a football game—everyone goes. I try to avoid it, but Trixie wasn't having any of that.

"Give me a donut," Trixie demands, reaching for the bag I'm holding.

I pull out another apple cider donut from the bag, still warm from the fryer, and hand it to her. She takes a bite, sighing in contentment. I have to forcibly stop myself from brushing the sugar from her lips.

Jen smirks like she can read my thoughts. She's hovering about ten feet away, the compromise we came to when she all but begged to let her stay at the carnival. She could have asked for anything though. I was so relieved to see her, I probably would have agreed to letting her tail me forever.

The smirk feels like interfering, which she promised not to do. Jen raises her hands like she'll back off.

"I had something a little quieter in mind," I say with a mouthful of donut, then shut my mouth quickly. Talking while chewing probably isn't date appropriate. Transitioning from friend to being on a date is a lot harder than I realized.

Trixie smirks. "I know you did. But the donuts help, right?"

"The donuts help," I admit after I swallow. It's safe to say my cheeks are going to hurt from smiling by the end of the night.

"It's hard for me too," she admits. "Not this," she clarifies, gesturing between us. "But being around such a large group when I'm already nervous. I can feel everyone, their lives and heartbeats." Her eyes dart to mine before looking away. "And I can't tell if I'm this nervous or if your nerves are influencing me."

"I didn't know you could feel that." A flush spreads up my neck. First Jen, now Trixie. I feel like soon enough my emotions will be on display for everyone.

"It's getting easier," she says in an obvious attempt to make me feel better. "I can block people out most of the time. And the healing piece is nice. I got a paper cut yesterday while researching, and it was gone before a drop of blood welled."

"Okay, that's bad-ass."

It's Trixie's turn to flush. Our first research session didn't deliver anything substantial, just a list of creatures that eat souls, and a very short list of curses that could be causing the high death rate in town. Neither held any clues for how Silas could be involved. Even though I should probably still be at home researching, I'm grateful for the break from death. Trixie's been cautious since we arrived, close enough that I can almost touch her, but not so close that she'll accidentally bump me. I don't know what to do with my hands. They want to reach for her, so I end up just shoving them in my pockets when I'm not actively eating.

"So, rides or games?" Trixie asks.

"Games," I say quickly. Trixie eyes me. "What? I'm surprisingly good at rigged games."

"This I have to see," she says, as we change direction toward the games. "You can win me a teddy bear." My stomach does that flipping thing at the thought. That seems like a date thing, for sure.

"Easy. But don't even think about trying to pay for it. It's not a gift that way."

Trixie narrows her eyes but the smile on her lips negates any of her glare's heat. Something catches her gaze behind me and her smile falls. "Incoming," Trixie says under her breath. She nods behind me.

Turning, I see Silas strolling through the carnival. Heads turn as he passes, everyone seemingly unable to keep their eyes off him. Despite the dorky nature of his childhood nickname, he isn't lacking admirers.

But he doesn't seem interested in anyone else.

A chill creeps down my spine as I watch him. Even though I've seen him outside of school before, it's more unsettling after the incident at my locker. He walks with the kind of confidence that says he knows everyone is watching him, and he enjoys it.

I scan for Jen, but she's gone. Whether it's a coincidence or something to do with Silas is the question.

"I don't think I realized just how cocky he is," Trixie says, taking another bite of donut.

He turns his head then, like he could hear Trixie's words, and his eyes find mine. I'm frozen as he looks at me. A ghost of a smile lifts his lips, then he winks before turning his attention back to the school building.

"Did he just . . . ?" Trixie asks.

"Sure did," I say. Every hair on my neck is standing at attention. "He turned right as you were talking about him."

Trixie chews her bottom lip before speaking. "Maybe it's another clue," she says, but the bravado feels forced.

⫸⫷ ⫸⫷ ⫸⫷

WITHIN AN HOUR, Trixie's arm is tucked around a stuffed whale. She did not fight me when I paid for the game but was adamant about buying the corndogs. She now has two obnoxiously long corndogs clutched in her hands as she walks back to me. I'll never be able to eat that with any kind of grace.

"Thanks," I say, taking the corndog as she hands it to me, careful not to let her fingers brush mine. "I still think you should have let me pay. I asked you on the date."

Trixie pulls a slew of napkins from her jacket pocket. "That's just because I didn't get a chance to ask you first."

My stomach does a flip like I'm still on one of the rides.

"Wait!" Trixie says as I go to take a bite. She pulls a small plastic container out of her pocket and hands it to me. Ranch. It's such a small gesture, but my heartbeat kicks up all the same.

The earlier weirdness of seeing Silas has worn off, along with the tension of the first date, and we managed to ride almost every ride here, which actually isn't that many. We walk along, watching townspeople stand in line for rides or sip their beers. She takes another bite out of her corn dog before turning to me. Trixie watches me, her eyes falling to my mouth. A tingle dances along my skin.

I'm suddenly very aware of my hands and how awkwardly they're hanging beside me. What I wouldn't do to be able to touch

✳ 193 ✳

her. If she keeps looking at me like that, I might forget all about self-preservation.

"Fun house?" I ask, basically just so I don't do something stupid.

Trixie blinks a little, eyes clearing. "Absolutely."

Fun house is a gracious name for it. In reality, it's a room of mirrors and glass. And it's empty except for us.

One of the mirrors make you bigger, body parts larger than normal. Another makes Trixie look like she only comes up to my knees, which sends her into a giggling fit that takes her a full minute to recover from.

Near the back of the fun house, there's a wall of glass. The glass is opaque, but it distorts what's on the other side. It's not much, but it makes me feel like I'm looking through water.

Trixie walks around the wall, peering at me through the glass. She looks ethereal through it, like something plucked from a fairy tale. I lift my gloved hand, pressing it to the glass. Trixie looks at it before lifting her own, pressing hers to match mine. I would have been content to stay there all night.

A trio of middle schoolers comes in, arguing about a video game, and the spell is broken.

Back on the row of rides, a quiet has settled between us. It's not uncomfortable, but the easy conversation from earlier is stilted now. We stop and grab a bag of cotton candy, eating it while we survey the rides we haven't been on yet.

"Ferris wheel?" she asks, pointing at the very last ride on the list.

My throat tightens. "Or we could skip it?" I say.

"George, are you afraid of heights?" Trixie asks in mock astonishment.

I look up at the Ferris wheel again. "It is one of my many fears," I admit.

"That's strangely endearing," she says, eyes dropping as the color in her cheeks deepens. There's another split-second hesitation as my mind wars over making Trixie happy and not tragically falling to my death.

"I will make an exception for you."

If there was one power I wish I had, it would be reading minds, if only to find out if that's really longing in Trixie's eyes. I want to kiss her so much it physically hurts. She bites her bottom lip, smiling, and leads me to the Ferris wheel.

The mostly empty cotton candy bag is death gripped in my hands. Nervously, I reach in, pull off a chunk, and shove it in my mouth, savoring the rush of sweet as it melts over my tongue. It steadies me, a little. I don't know why this is so different. I've sat across from Trixie at Matt's or in my basement a dozen times or more now. Yet here, in the chill of the October night with screaming children and the clattering of rides, this feels like the first time.

The line moves at a glacial pace until we're finally being ushered into one of the seats. It's just wide enough for us to sit side-by-side with a small space in between. I want the space to be greater and smaller at the same time.

We start moving, rising higher in the sky, the cotton candy bag now squished between my hand and the rail as I hold on for dear life. Trixie is smiling so wide, it makes this almost worth it.

"How are you doing?" she asks.

"I'm okay," I say as we start the descent. My grip loosens. "It's not so bad." And I mean it. Logically, riding a Ferris wheel is exponentially better than seeing yourself kill someone.

We start rising again, and the Ferris wheel stops at the top.

I groan. "I forgot they did this." Still, I look out at the town, lights speckling the dark. "It is pretty though."

"I wish I could hold your hand," Trixie says quietly.

Her hand is next to mine on the bar, just inches away. If I decided to, I could reach out and grab it, the fabric of my glove protecting me.

"I wish I could kiss you," I say, my mouth once again working faster than my mind. Trixie blinks at me in surprise, then she starts calculating.

"Can I have some cotton candy?" Trixie asks. Shocked, I hand over the bag, one measly chunk of sugar the only thing left in the bag. She straightens it out. "Do you trust me?"

Now, I'm the one surprised. "With my life."

"Then turn toward me and close your eyes."

When I don't move fast enough, Trixie uses her hand to motion hurry up. I close my eyes, turning my face toward her. I only have to sit in confusion for another second before the plastic of the bag reaches my lips. I almost pull back, until I feel the warmth of Trixie's lips against mine. I lean into it, wishing that time would stop, leaving me in a perfect first kiss at the top of the world.

CHAPTER

25

"CRAB RANGOON IS SUPERIOR. It's not even a question."

"Says who?" Felix points the dumpling he's holding in his chopsticks at me. "Shumai. Always."

"I, for one, am a fan of all of it," Trixie says, ever the diplomat. She convinced her mom to bring home Chinese takeout from the place in the next town over when she was on her way home from her shift at the hospital. The food covers one of the tables in my basement—not the ones with the tomes we were using for research—that would be irresponsible, according to Trixie.

"If you weren't already one of my favorite people, this would have cemented your spot." I fish out another piece of honey chicken. It's certainly not authentic—maybe one day I'll travel and eat food from all over the world—but for now, it's a nice change from Matt's.

Trixie pulls her lips between her teeth like she's trying to bite down her smile. "Maybe my intention was bribing you."

Even though my stomach is full, the butterflies still pick up their fluttering.

"The way you two are looking at each other is making it really weird for me to be here," Felix says around a mouth full of food.

I snort and reluctantly break eye contact with Trixie. "Says the man I've always been the third wheel for."

"Fair point," he concedes. When I glance at Trixie again, she's still smirking.

"Back to work," Trixie says as she closes up her containers. She grabs a wet wipe and wipes the food from her hands before heading back to the table with the tomes. Sighing, I follow suit.

"Your gran's here." Trixie doesn't look up from her laptop screen as she speaks.

Felix cocks his head, pointing his ear toward the ceiling, as he walks over. "How can you tell? I didn't hear anything."

"I sensed her arrival," Trixie says, opening a book.

Felix puts down his notebook. "You what now?"

Trixie finally looks up. "Oh, um, I can sense a life force. It's a witchy thing."

"So, I can't sneak up on you?" Felix asks, coming over to join us at the table.

Trixie laughs. "No, but that's nothing new. You just didn't know about it."

"Can you track me?"

Trixie cocks her head, considering. I find I want to know the answer too.

"I think so, but that's only because I'm so familiar with you. It doesn't work over long distances, but I can find my mom if we get separated in the grocery store."

"She can heal minor wounds too," I say. Trixie's cheeks darken. "She'll be able to heal larger wounds as she learns to harness, maybe even bring someone back from the brink of death."

"Damn," Felix says, a little shell-shocked. "Can you do that too?" he asks me.

I purse my lips, my earlier pride in Trixie fizzling out. "No," I say. "It's something Trixie discovered in her ascension." I debate describing runes in full but decide against it, opting for a summary. "Mine is different."

"I didn't know that. I just thought you could do magic; I didn't know there were variations of it. How is yours different?"

As much as Felix has been involved in my life, I've kept him separate from the magic. I haven't really used mine, so it never felt necessary. Now, I realize I've been keeping a part of myself hidden from him in the process.

"Trixie's magic is almost the opposite of mine," I start, trying to right some wrongs by at least explaining this. "Both our magic works along the lines of life and death, but hers is more life and mine is more death. Though I haven't been able to really test what that means for me yet."

I haven't wanted to is a better description. Eventually, I know I'll have to, but it's just felt like another thing to worry about. Trixie's magic became more intense, which is usual for most witches. Mine just got . . . easier.

Calling on the ghosts is almost effortless, and I changed Jack into a fox with ease when he was being pissy the other day, but I don't know what that means for the actual death components of my magic.

Plus, now that I know my rune, some of what I saw in Veritas is making more sense. The darkness I felt while looking into the mirror is lurking in me, yes, but it's my magic too, woven into its very core.

Eventually, I'll have to do something with that information.

"Actually," I say, "that might be something to look into."

"What is?" Trixie asks.

"My magic. At my ascension, Gran mentioned some creatures would be attracted to my magic. Could something else, something other than a wielder, be attracted to it too?"

A line forms between Trixie's brows. "Theoretically." She nods. "It at least gives us something to look for next."

Flipping back through the pages of my notebook, I try to see if there are any connections I might have missed before. Maybe I'm smarter now that I'm fed. We've been trying to make a list of all the deaths that have occurred in Windrop. I'm working backward from the most recent, Trixie from five years ago, Felix from ten. The point was to try to find any connections or similarities between how they died. So far, I haven't seen anything.

It took three brutal hours to put my list together—name, age, wielder or mortal, and date and location of death—and I've got nothing.

"I think I've got everyone," Trixie says, leaning back from her laptop.

"Same," Felix says, pushing his list toward her. I do the same, if only so I don't have to look at it anymore.

Trixie scans the lists, frown deepening. "I was hoping something would jump out at me."

"We could put pins on a map?" Felix says. Both Trixie and I turn to him, eyes wide. "What?" he asks, looking between us. "Is that a bad idea?"

Trixie pats the top of his head as she stands from the table. "No. It is an excellent idea. I'm just sad I didn't think of it first." Trixie disappears into one of the rows and comes out a minute later with a giant map of town.

"Where did you get that?" I ask as she spreads it out on an open table.

"There's a whole map section. It's fascinating, actually, since they aren't just present maps but historical too. I can show you?"

My heart kicks up at the inflection in her tone. "Yes, please."

Felix snaps his fingers. "Focus, ladies. Flirt later."

Trixie rolls her eyes but nods anyway. "I don't have pins so we're just going to have to draw on it." She frowns like she just said she was going to commit a crime. "We'll each take our lists and mark the spot on the map." She walks back to her backpack and digs around until she pulls out three red pens. I don't ask her why she has so many red pens in her backpack. It seems like an entirely Trixie thing to have.

The process of marking up the map takes another hour, mostly because I wait until Felix and Trixie are done before I start marking so I don't accidentally touch them. Better safe than sorry.

I thought looking at the list of names was hard, but the amount of Xs on the map turns my stomach.

"That's a lot," Felix says. Trixie nods, hand at her throat.

I scan the map, trying to ignore the thought that every X is a life. I don't discern a pattern to them. They're not in the same place or even clustered together. Some are closer to each other than others, like in the spot where Jen died, but it's a small town; there isn't much space to die within town limits to begin with. Then I see it.

Jen. I remember her standing by the river, looking at the spot where she died. Where my parents died. Where Felix's brother died.

"They're all by the river," I say. As soon as I say it, it's like it comes into focus. The Xs snake along the river. They're not always right next to the river, but close enough that I could see the river if I were standing in each spot.

"They are," Trixie says. Her hand's still at her throat, but she doesn't look as ashen. "They're not drownings though."

"No," I say.

"It's something, right?" Felix asks.

Trixie looks up at me, a sad smile on her lips. "It's something."

CHAPTER

26

IT IS NO SURPRISE THAT Halloween is the favorite holiday in the wielding community, especially in a coven full of death witches. While many do celebrate, I've never been keen to take part. Much of the holiday focuses on ceremony, gifts to the Goddess, and honoring the spirits, but since I have never been interested in magic, I haven't participated.

Tonight is different. Even though I told Felix I would pick him up from Garrett's party, I offered to help Gran set up for the ceremony.

"Be sure the candles are spaced appropriately," Gran directs from across the basement. Even though, as Supreme, she could recruit other wielders to do the setup, Gran has always done it. She says her connection to the Goddess is stronger if she does tasks of service herself. That might be true, but I think part of it is that Gran is just a control freak.

"Yes, Gran," I call back, nudging a candle over slightly. Candles are arranged throughout the room, all spaced apart in perfect five-point stars. Wielders will gather around the candles tonight to offer up bits of their magic as a sacrifice to the Goddess, a way to say thank you for the gifts she has bestowed on them. Some will meditate alone, others in groups, and reflect on the year prior and what the next will bring. It's a solemn time and will go on most of the night.

It's just past eleven now. Members of the coven should be arriving any minute. Trixie included. My heart flutters at the thought.

"Done," I say, standing up to inspect the room. None of the candles are lit. Gran looks over the room too, snapping her fingers and lighting the candles in an instant.

"Thank you for your help, Georgiana. The room looks great."

"Was that a compliment?" I joke as I head toward her.

She glares at me before heading up the stairs. "Maybe you'd get more if you didn't always give me lip."

"Lies. You hoard compliments like a mandrake, never giving them out."

"I simply have high standards," she says, lifting her nose.

"Well, that's at least true." I follow her up the stairs and head into the living room. Following the ceremony, the wielders will come up here to let off a little steam. This is where they also poke fun at the mortal holiday. The room is covered in cheesy decorations: paper skeletons hang from the ceiling, witch confetti is sprinkled on the orange-lined table, various snacks made to look like blood and brains and other gore are laid out, and a lime-green punch that fizzes is releasing smoke in the corner. No one can say death witches don't have a sense of humor.

"This looks more fun than I thought it would," I say.

"If you ever came downstairs on All Hallows, you would know."

"You never said it would be fun."

"I did. You never believed me."

I roll my eyes and pull out my phone. No text yet.

"When are you going to get him?" Gran asks, watching me stuff my phone back into the pocket of my black jeans.

"He usually doesn't stay out too late when I'm driving him, so soon."

Gran sits in her armchair by the fireplace. "You know I don't approve of underage drinking."

"I do. That's why I don't drink."

"I do not believe that's why you don't drink, but I wish Felix wouldn't either."

"Tell him that."

"He is not my child to parent."

"No, but since his have lost interest, you should probably take up the role."

Gran's lips pull into a thin line. "They're still absent from his life?"

I rub my gloved hand across the back of my neck, awkwardly standing in the middle of the room. "Yeah. Worse since Max."

Gran doesn't speak for a long while, turning her attention to the fire. Finally, she says, "I may inform him of my opinion on drinking then."

"If you tell him not to drink, he never will. He's still scared of you."

A smile lifts Gran's lips. "Smart boy." She loves Felix; I've always known that, but part of Gran revels in being feared. "Are you planning to return?"

I gesture down at the shirt half hidden beneath my leather jacket. "That's the plan."

Gran frowns at my costume. "I don't get it."

It only takes one second for me to dismiss the idea of explaining dressing as Thing 1 and Thing 2 to her, especially since my Thing 2 isn't here yet. It might make sense when Trixie arrives wearing the matching red T-shirt and her hair spelled, temporarily, blue. I'm not sure Trixie understands how big of a deal matching costumes are for me—or how much Felix will mock me.

"I shouldn't miss too much, just part of the offerings to the Goddess." In truth, I'll be rushing to get back to Trixie.

Gran nods. "Yes. But I'm happy you'll be here tonight either way." She turns to look at me then.

There's a hint of pride shining in her eyes. I look away when my heart clenches. "Don't make a big deal out of it."

"I make no promises." After a knock on the door, Gran rises from her chair. "Will you help me greet the guests?"

"I'd like that." And I mean it.

Gran and I stop at the front door, and her hand hovers over the knob. "The coven appreciates your effort."

They've noticed that I have been applying myself. Even Mistress Rowina has continued to acknowledge my presence when I see her in public. But until I figure out what's going on with Silas, I don't want to give them any more reason to doubt my intentions.

"Good."

Gran doesn't say another word as she turns the knob and opens the door.

-«««•»»»--«««•»»»--«««•»»»-

FELIX'S JEEP IS easy to find as I pull up to Garrett's house on my bike. I come to a stop and hop off before hoisting it into the open back of the vehicle. It's unlocked. Everything is always unlocked here. Windrop is relatively safe—except for the myriad of suspicious deaths, I guess. A gust of wind ruffles my hair, sending a shiver through my body. I pull my leather jacket tighter around me, grateful for the fur-lined gloves warming my fingers.

Loud music blasts from Garrett's house as I approach it. Felix parked a little way down from the house, either because the parking out front was full or to make escape easier for me, I'm not sure. He was right in thinking the quarterback would be throwing a party again.

It might even be larger than last year. The bass from the music rattles the house. It's beyond me how he manages to have a party without every cop in town being here. Perk of being famous in a small town, I guess.

I pull my phone out of the small purse slung across my body to shoot a text.

Our earlier conversation is the first thing I see.

FELIX: bestie. can you come now plese? sleepy.

GEORGE: cutting it close. it'll take me at least ten minutes to bike if I hoof it.

He still hasn't responded. I text him again.

GEORGE: the speed demon has arrived. where are you?

I wait for the text bubbles to pop up. But nothing comes.

"Why are you at a party?" Jen asks from over my shoulder.

My heart stutters in my chest. "Shit!" I whirl to her, momentarily forgetting I probably look like a psycho in the street. "I told you to stop doing that."

"This conversation is getting tedious."

I want to remind her that there are other ways to get my attention than speaking directly over my shoulder, but I haven't seen her since after the carnival. "Where have you been?"

Jen's nose crinkles. "What do you mean?"

"Well, you keep disappearing. You did it again. You were with me at the carnival, but I haven't seen you since. I called for you."

"No, you didn't." Jen looks around, probably trying to gauge where we are.

"Yes, I did. Where did you go?"

Jen's face scrunches up. "I have no idea what you're talking about. I just saw you on your date." She draws out the word *date* to get a rise out of me, but I'm not in the mood.

"Jen, that was two days ago. It's Halloween."

"Really?" She glances toward the house, where the party is still in full swing, as if trying to puzzle out the dates for herself. The slew of our classmates in costumes should at least give her a clear indication of what day it is. She looks at me, obviously trying to gauge if I'm in costume. I open my jacket, flashing the red shirt. Jen shivers, and I know it has nothing to do with the temperature. "That's really weird."

It is weird, and another thing to add to my list of clues. My eyes flick toward the house. "I'm just waiting for Felix, if you want to wait with me?" I tug my phone out and glance at the screen. Still no response.

"Sure."

Standing in front of the house, I debate going inside to look for Felix, but the risk is too high. There's not even someone I can ask to go find him. No one is in the front yard, but I can see girls in barely there costumes and football players wearing their letterman jackets in the ever-creative *I'm a football player* costume from the street.

I rub my arms to try to create heat before looking at my phone again.

Nothing.

"Are you cold?"

"A little," I admit.

"Not polite of Felix to make you wait out here in the cold."

"Tell me about it." My fingers fly across my screen.

GEORGE: *i'm not coming in there after you. let's go.*

I watch the door, but no one emerges.

GEORGE: *it's freezing out here.*

GEORGE: *i'll never come get you again if you don't come out right now.*

My threats don't work because the door stays shut.

It's not like him to make me wait. I glare at the door again, but I'm so not going in there to look for him. I turn away from the house.

Digging in my pocket, I pull out a sour cherry lollipop. Though not my preferred choice of candy, lollipops are the easiest to transport, and everyone needs their vice. After unwrapping it, I pop it in my mouth, my face scrunching at the first wash of sour over my tongue.

"Too sour?" a voice asks from behind me.

I jump, turning to find Garrett walking up to me. Usually, I don't pay much attention to the football players, but up close, he is handsome. Broad shoulders, a strong jawline, and full lips that always look like he's a little amused by something. His hands are deep in the pockets of his letterman jacket as he stops beside me.

"Just a little. What are you doing out here?"

"Do you know him?" Jen asks from beside me. I glance sideways at her with a look that she hopefully understands as *I can't answer you right now without looking like I'm crazy.*

He stares out into the empty street as the party rages inside. "I don't like parties."

"This is literally your party," I say, turning and using the lollipop to gesture at the house behind me.

"Eh, it's expected," he says. It's almost not noticeable, but if I listen closely, I can hear a slight slur in his words.

I wonder if he's drunk.

"Ah. Heavy are the burdens you bear."

He chuckles. "I guess you could say that. You know those things will rot your teeth, right?" he says, nodding at my lollipop.

"I'm pretty sure there are more important things to worry about," I say as I crunch down on the candy. I would know.

"Smart-ass," Jen murmurs as Garrett speaks.

"Has anyone ever told you you're pretty witty?"

"Once or twice," I say, though they usually say other things first.

"Waiting for Felix?" he asks, his breath frosting in front of him. It takes seeing that to realize how cold I am. My cheeks are numb.

"Yup."

"I saw him talking to Reagan. I think she may forgive him."

"Great," I say, wrapping the now empty stick in the plastic and sticking it back in my pocket. Not like she has anything to forgive him about, but I don't want to get into it.

"So, you two aren't like a thing?"

Jen snorts, and it takes everything in me not to turn and glare at her.

Maybe one day this question won't be annoying. "Nope. Hasn't he told you that?"

"He has. Just don't get it. You two are always together. And you're smoking hot, no pun intended." He turns toward me and frowns. "You've got something on your face. I think it's glitter."

"Yeah, I was setting up for a Halloween party," I say, glancing at Jen again.

Jen's disbelief slams into me before she speaks. "Oh shit."

When I look back at Garrett, his hand is moving toward my face. I don't have time to react as his fingertips graze my cheek, the cloying scent of smoke the last thing I remember before I slip away.

⋘◆⋙ ⋘◆⋙ ⋘◆⋙

WHAT? I HISS as I touch my cheek. Pulling my hand away, my fingers are slick with blood. I feel it then; the ice creeping up my waist.

Water is pouring in. I look outside my windows and see only black.

Panic consumes me: my car is completely submerged.

It comes back then. The bridge, the man, the fall.

Wrestling with my seat belt, I finally get it to release as the water reaches my neck. I jam down the window button. The windows don't move. Pushing myself back, I lift my foot to kick into the glass. Once, twice. But it doesn't budge. I can't get enough momentum through the water.

I'm almost out of time. Sucking in one final breath, the rest of the car fills.

Then, through the haze of panic, I remember the window-shatter tool in my glove box. I fling it open, sending up a prayer. The tool is always in the same spot.

I slam it against the window, and the little metal rod pops, splintering the glass. I shove on it, pushing the window out of the way. Whole chunks of glass slice into my hand before I get it free.

My lungs are screaming, the last of my air ticking away.

Almost there. The car sinks deeper.

Squeezing into the hole, I try to push through, but something is stuck.

A piece of glass snags my letterman jacket. I try to shrug it off as my lungs scream. Black dots swim in my vision as I get one arm out . . .

CHAPTER

27

I COME TO, GASPING FOR breath like a drowning man. Drowning, like Garrett.

I'm crumpled on the sidewalk where I fell. Felix is kneeling down next to me, a crowd of partygoers around me. Rolling over, I vomit on the sidewalk to murmurs of disgust.

I don't care.

"Where is he?" I say as I wipe my mouth.

"Where's who?" Felix asks, helping me sit up.

"Garrett. I felt it. Where is he?" Panic claws my throat. My eyes scan the crowd around us for his broad shoulders, but I don't see him.

He's gone. And so is Jen.

Felix's eyes go wide as he realizes what I'm saying. "Um, he was just here. I came out as he was lowering you to the ground." Felix scans the crowd. "Where'd Garrett go? He was just here." His words slur together.

"He said the freak made him thirsty, and he was heading to go get more beer." Someone, Tommy is his name, points at taillights as they disappear from down the street.

Felix puffs up, about to lose his temper over an idiot's rude words. "He's been drinking, you idiot," Felix growls. "You just let him go?"

"Felix, stop," I say, grabbing his arm. "Help me up." Felix stands, yanking me up with him. My heart is racing so fast I feel like it's going to explode. "I think it's tonight." My words are barely a whisper.

"Are you sure?"

"Yes? No. I don't know." The crowd around us is dispersing, the entertainment from the situation gone. I squeeze my eyes shut, trying to remember. "He was wearing his letterman jacket. He's wearing it tonight too."

"He always wears it. What else?"

"The water was dark, like it was nighttime."

"Good. Anything else?"

"It happens on the bridge, and there's a man," I say, opening my eyes. The river. It's always the river. The thought doesn't make me feel better. I scan the lawn for Garrett again, but he's gone.

"What do we do?"

I should say "nothing." My hands are fists at my sides. He knows the rules of what I see: there is no changing it. But I also never experience a death that I can pinpoint when it's going to happen. There's nothing I can do, there never has been.

Something inside me shifts. Not tonight. There's nothing about my vision that tells me tonight is the night that Garrett dies, but deep down, I know. I make a decision.

Why would I have these visions if I can't do anything about it? Magic is the blessing of the Goddess, and she wouldn't bless me with this gift for nothing.

"We save him," I say with absolute finality.

"But—" Felix starts, his mind still too slow from the alcohol.

"Keys," I cut in before he can finish. If it's really tonight, I don't have time for this. Garrett doesn't have time for this.

Felix stares at my outstretched hand.

"Keys. Felix, give me your keys!"

Felix digs around in his pocket. "I think they're inside. George, what's wrong?"

"Get them!" I scream at him. I can save Garrett, I know it. For once, my gift has purpose. "Now!"

"George, you can't—?"

"Tonight. It happens tonight. Right now. I can't stand around and do nothing. Go!"

The moment Felix takes to comprehend what I'm saying feels like a year before he's turning and sprinting inside. I run to his Jeep parked down the street. The icy air ravages my throat.

Felix is back as I reach the door, tossing me the keys before he hops in the passenger seat. The color has drained from his face, turning him a sickly shade of gray.

The keys slip through my fingers. Seconds, precious seconds are wasted as I scramble to pick them up from the ground and shove myself into the driver's seat. It takes too long; my hands are shaking so badly. I finally line up the key with the ignition, shove it in, and turn.

The engine turns over but doesn't start.

"Come on, come on, come on," I mutter as tears flow down my face. I turn the key again and again to no success.

I reach within myself, searching for my link to Gran. Maybe she can beat us there. But my brain is too thick with panic. Calling on her should be second nature, but I still have to think about it too much.

"We should call the police," Felix says.

"They won't get there in time. Why won't your car start?"

"I don't know, it's a brand-new battery. I'm calling anyway." He lifts the phone to his ear. "What do we do now?"

My old response almost bubbles through my lips.

Nothing.

"Save him," I say again as the engine finally roars to life. I throw it into drive and head toward Round Street Bridge. He only has minutes on us. We can still catch him. We will have time.

You can't change death.

The mantra floats through my mind as houses blur past us. All of my life it's been what I've lived by, a comfort to offset experiencing all the deaths I never thought I could fix. But not tonight. Tonight, I won't believe it.

I can do this.

I take a turn, wheels squealing as I straighten out and speed down the street.

If we catch him before the bridge, he'll be all right, at least for the night. I can't let my brain think about what happens every other night if we prevent it now. One thing at a time.

We turn another corner, tail end spinning out behind us on the icy street. But this street is empty too.

We're so close now. One more turn and we'll be at the bridge. It's okay. Maybe tonight isn't the night. Or if it is, we'll get there in time to pull him out. Hope bubbles up in me. We're going to do it. My gift will be used for something good, for once.

My heart sinks as we come around the corner. The bridge is empty, the wooden railing ripped through.

"No, no, no, no, no, no, no," I mutter as I slam on the brakes and fling the door open. I practically fall out of the truck trying to get to the edge.

The river's current is swift, but the taillights are still visible below the surface. They flicker and go out.

There's still time.

I shrug off my jacket and start trying to yank my boots off as Felix comes behind me and looks down. Blue and red lights flash in the distance as a siren peals through the night.

"George," Felix says gently.

I give up on my second boot and stand. Sucking in a deep breath, I launch myself forward, running to the edge of the bridge.

I'm ripped back as Felix's hand wraps around my arm. Stumbling, I slam into his chest.

"What are you doing?" I try to yank my arm from his grasp, but his fingers dig in deeper. "Let go."

"What are *you* doing?" he spits my question back at me.

"I can save him," I say, yanking again. Felix pulls me back against him and wraps his arms around me.

"It's too dangerous."

"He'll die!"

"And so would you." Felix's voice is thick with tears. "It's been minutes, and that water is freezing. It's too late."

"You have to let me try!" I scream, trying to wrench from his grip as the cop cars stop on the bridge. Officers begin running down to the water's edge.

"George, I won't lose you."

I struggle harder as Felix pulls me against him.

"Stop. The police will help."

"Let. Me. Go!" I yell through gritted teeth. I buck and writhe against him, tears tracking down my cheeks as rage burns through me, trying to burn out the pain ripping through my chest.

Instinctively, magic begins to build beneath my skin, ready to strike. Nothing happens though. No matter how much I want free, my intention would never be to hurt Felix.

But his arms are irons wrapped around me. He lets me scream until my voice is hoarse, but he doesn't relent. I kick and scream and writhe as the ambulance shows up. As officers begin coming up from the river's edge. As one walks over, flashlight trained on us. He never lets go. Not until there's nothing left and I'm quiet, defeated.

His grip finally loosens as I sag, boneless, in his arms. The ambulance is there, cops watching the water for signs of life. It's been too long and the current's too strong. No one will go in.

And no one is coming out.

Felix calls Gran as an officer questions me about why we're there. The words are simple: we were trying to stop him from driving after drinking. The reasons behind them aren't.

My red-rimmed eyes burn from the tears and cold as Felix settles me into the Jeep. He still can't drive after drinking, though he seems pretty sober now. I take a deep breath, my need to be home overriding everything else.

I roll down the window and let the night air numb me.

I feel them, hovering, watching, just outside my reach. He's there now too, with them. Our anguish mingles until I can't tell what pain is his and what pain is my own.

-«‹◆›»--«‹◆›»--«‹◆›»-

WHEN WE PULL up to the front of my house, I don't even have the strength to get out of the car. Felix opens my door, scooping me into his arms and carrying me up the steps of the front porch.

The layers of jackets between us provide a barrier from his skin, but I don't care anyway. I find myself longing for the peace of his death instead of this feeling.

The coven is gone, and Gran's on the front porch with Jack beside her. She must have ended the party early. As he passes with me, Felix mutters something I'm too weary to hear. They both follow him up the stairs.

He carries me all the way to my room, laying me on the bed before pulling off my lone boot as Gran watches from the doorway. She doesn't speak as Felix pulls the blanket from the foot of the bed over me, tucking it in before sitting on the edge next to me. She watches us silently for a moment longer before heading downstairs.

I roll onto my side, away from Felix, unable to look at him any longer. I want him to go, but I don't think I can stand for him to leave.

"Do you remember when you first felt my death?"

I'm unsure where he's going with this, but I don't respond.

"We were on the playground in elementary school. You always played by yourself, but I decided that was the day I was going to talk to you. No one should be alone. I marched right up to you, but you didn't see me coming. You were staring down at your book, oblivious to the world. I tapped you on the shoulder, but my hand grazed your cheek as I pulled back, and you slipped into my death."

He's telling the story like I wasn't there, but I remember every moment: the feeling of his death for the first time, the look on his face as I came out of it, and the utter acceptance as I tried to explain what happened. I think about that day often. Not many children would reach out to a loner, and certainly fewer would accept the explanation I gave him. I don't even know why I told him, but something in his eyes told me I could trust him. I've never stopped being grateful that I did.

"Do you remember the night you felt Max die?" His words are barely above a whisper.

Of course I remember. I loved Max like a brother. He was family, blood or not. I can't bring myself to respond though.

Felix continues as if I did. "You didn't know when it would be. You weren't even sure how. Just that he was out for a run and tripped. You told me he must have hit his head just right because he was gone instantly."

Silent tears slip from my eyes.

Max's death was quick, but it nearly broke me. He died eight months after my vision, and it was just like Felix said. He tripped while running and his head hit a rock off the trail. One-in-a-million odds, but it happened to him.

Felix sucks in a breath, as if steeling himself. "We spent weeks trying to figure out how to stop it, what we could do to make sure Max didn't die."

I nod. I don't even know if Felix is looking at me.

"And after weeks of discussing, we decided not to tell him. You didn't know when it would happen. You didn't know if he was young or old, only that he was still in Windrop running his favorite route. There was no way to let him know what you saw without revealing everything about who you are, and even then it would have cast a shadow over his life because you and I both knew one thing for certain: you can't change death."

"But I knew, tonight I knew it was the night." I choke on the words. "And we had time. I could have saved him if I was faster."

"No, you couldn't. There were other forces at work, not just time. I left my keys inside the house. Why were my keys even out of my pocket? I never do that."

"But—"

"And the car wouldn't start. That's a brand-new battery, and I have *never* had an issue with starting the Jeep before."

"I know, but—"

"But nothing." The weight of his hand settles on my hip. I look over my shoulder at him. "George, we've known you can't change death since we were children. How many times have you tried to tell someone how they die to prevent it and they do it anyway?" He doesn't wait for my response. "Dozens. And sometimes people change, but then they get lazy and return to their lives. I have to believe even if somehow you shift how someone dies, their life would end another way. Why tonight?"

I don't know that I have a solid answer for that. I've seen so many deaths over the years that part of me has just become numb. But I think another part of me is raging at the unfairness of the situation. Still, I can't deny the real reason I went after him.

"I was hoping I could change it this time, that I could save him."

It takes a minute for Felix to speak again. "Tonight was terrible. Garrett was a good person and my friend. I'm not saying this because I don't care that he died, I'm saying this because it's not your fault."

"It feels like it is." Despite the fact that I've known my whole life that death can't be changed, I still tried to save him when I shouldn't have, I know that, but I couldn't help it.

"I know."

Those words break the leash I had on my emotions. Sobs rip through me, threatening to destroy me. Because, while he doesn't really know, the acknowledgment is a relief and a curse.

Because I don't say the real reason I went after him, the thing the selfish part of me was hoping was true. That if I could change Garrett's death and save him, I'd be able to change my fate too.

CHAPTER

28

THE SILENCE OF THE LIBRARY makes it almost painful to be here. I've been drumming my fingers on the desk just for some noise to fill the emptiness. Even Jack is quiet tonight.

It's the first time I've left my room since last night, but I had to get out of the house. Now that I'm here though, I'm not sure it was the right decision; I should have called out sick.

Felix has a late football practice tonight, and Trixie is obviously with her mom. I've been trying and failing not to linger too long on the events of last night, but the alone time isn't doing anything to distract me.

I glance at my closed chemistry book, waiting for me to open it and do at least some of the homework inside.

Nope. Not happening tonight. Turning back to the glass doors, I watch as the parking lot lights flicker. It gets dark so early now. I remind myself to thank Felix for still coming to get me.

Windrop has never felt dangerous, but something has shifted. Even as a witch, I wouldn't want to walk the streets at night.

Jack sits on the counter, watching the glass doors. He appears calm, except for his flicking stub tail. It's the only hint that he's on edge. I don't know if it's because he knows something or if he's just feeding off of my tension.

Another twenty minutes and Felix will be here, and we can leave.

I glance back at my chemistry textbook. Maybe I should at least crack it open.

For once, I'm not startled as Jen slowly materializes on the desk and peers down at my book. "I always hated chemistry."

"Thank the Goddess!"

"That's an excited greeting." Jen furrows her brow. "What's with you?"

A smile splits my face as Jen eyes me. "Nothing, I'm just glad to see you. And you appeared so politely." I have so many questions. I haven't seen Garrett since his death, which is a blessing in a way.

Jen eyes me suspiciously from her perch on my desk. "It's quiet in here," she says, legs swinging.

"Yup."

"Where's your posse?"

"My what?"

"Your little gaggle of friends. Where are they?"

"Felix has practice and Trixie's with her mom."

"Oh . . . I wish I could do either of those things right now."

I'm not ready for the sudden rush of grief that comes at me. I look at Jen to find her picking at the skin around her nail. Such a normal thing to do and so at odds with her current predicament.

"Do you miss cheerleading?" I ask.

She looks at me sidelong. "You've never asked me anything like that before. Do you care?"

"Yeah, actually, I think I do."

Jen smirks. "Look at you, being friendly for once."

"Don't make me regret it."

Jen's smirk turns into a smile, but it doesn't reach her eyes. "Not really. I actually hated cheerleading. But I'd take practice over what I've got now," she says, gesturing at her less than corporeal form.

Somehow, that makes it worse. "Makes sense."

"I'm glad . . ." Jen starts. "I'm glad you can see me." The words tumble from her mouth like she had to work up the courage to get them out.

"Why? Because it means you still get to hang around?"

"No. Really, I mean it," she says when she catches my look. "I actually think I'd like to move on, whatever that means. It's too sad to be here all the time, especially since I'm not particularly wanted."

"I want you here," I say, chewing my lip.

"You're just saying that."

"I'm not."

She watches me carefully before she speaks again. "Then I don't mind staying so much."

The feeling of gratitude is almost overwhelming as it washes over me. I take a deep breath to steady myself before I speak again. "So why are you glad I can see you? Just because someone can?"

"No," she says, tucking a blond strand behind her ear. "Just that it's you. I think it's part of who you are. Makes you unique."

"Unique is just a nice way to say weird."

"You know what I think? Weird isn't a bad thing either."

"Whoa, look at the personal growth from Jen Monroe."

"Oh, don't be an ass," she says, rolling her eyes. "But seriously, you have friends, real friends. I can see that now. I don't think I ever really had that."

Jen's melancholy drifts toward me. "Don't say that. Jason was torn up right after you died."

"And now he's with Stefanie Delgado." She makes a gagging face. "Like, it's barely been two months."

"If it makes you feel any better, I always thought he was kind of a dumbass."

Jen laughs, and the warmth of it washes away her melancholy. "Oh, he's so dumb. But he is gorgeous."

"Keeping your standards high, I see."

Jen swats at me, but her hand passes right through my shoulder. She purses her lips as another wave of sadness rolls through me. "I'm sorry . . . about Garrett."

My anguish mingles with Jen's. "He was your friend," I say, deflecting. "Have you seen him?" I ask, even though I don't want the answer.

"I haven't, but I'm sure you can—"

The only warning I get is a wall of terror that barrels into me before Jen disappears.

A low growl permeates from Jack's belly. It's a sound I've never heard from him before and I whip my head to him, then to where his eyes are fixed.

My heart stutters in my chest, then stops.

Silas opens the door.

I try to avoid looking directly at him. The image of my hands slicked with his blood always comes when I do. But here, in the library this late at night, alone with him, I can't help it.

His dark eyes bore into me from behind his tortoiseshell glasses as he prowls toward me. The smirk on his lips sends a chill spider-walking down my spine. He's gone from the harmless, maybe even charming, classmate to a predator.

Jack hisses as he stops in front of me. Silas's eyes drop to my familiar, then back up to me.

"Not a friendly fellow, huh?"

"Um," my voice cracks. I cough. "Not particularly."

"Strange thing, to bring a cat to the library."

I take a tiny step back from the counter, unable to bear the weight of his stare. "How do you know he's my cat? Could just live at the library."

His eyes drop to Jack again. Jack's tail is almost as large as he is.

I've never seen a familiar in action, but I've heard stories. I can guess what Jack will do if he feels I'm truly being threatened. He may not like Silas, but I don't think I'm in any real danger yet.

Nevertheless, I don't like this.

"I've seen him hanging around you. It's obvious what he"—he pauses, licking his lips like he's tasting for the right word—"means to you."

"Is there something I can help with?" I try to keep my voice steady, but the words tremble as they leave my lips.

"There is, actually. I heard this town has a strong history of witch-craft." His onyx eyes drop to my neck, to the hint of chain peeking out from the top of my shirt.

The pendant turns to ice on my skin. I've never heard of crystals reacting to a presence, but it feels like it's trying to tell me something.

A warning.

"Oh? And you thought you'd come here?" Calm, George. Stay calm. "I'm sure there are tons of resources on the internet."

"I find the best way to seek something out is in the flesh, wouldn't you say?" A smile lifts one side of his lips.

The way the word *flesh* sounds on his lips turns my stomach. My blood is ice in my veins.

"Anything we have would be on that shelf there," I say, inclining my head. I don't dare lift my finger to point. The tremble would surely give my terror away.

But I think he already suspects. And enjoys it.

"Thank you, my dear," he turns on a heel and strides to the shelf.

Pulling out my phone, I type a message across the screen as fast as my fingers will move.

GEORGE: SOS

Hitting send, I watch as the text bubbles light up.

FELIX: OMW

FELIX: 5 min

FELIX: speeding

FELIX: what happened?

FELIX: r u ok?

Silas turns to head back to me before I can reply. Sliding the phone back in my pocket, I send a prayer to the Goddess that Felix will be here faster than that.

My phone buzzes again. I don't reach for it, but I swear the ghost of a smirk lifts Silas's lips.

I still haven't mastered silent contact, but I scramble around inside myself, looking for a connection to Gran. Inside, I scream into the void.

SOS SOS SOS SOS SOS SOS

No response. No way to know if Gran can hear me.

Silas lays a book in front of me. *The History of Witchcraft along the Massachusetts Coast* by Mildred Ruth. If memory serves, she was a former resident of Windrop.

"This one will do," he says, sliding the book toward me.

I almost rip the card from the book and shove it back to him. "All set."

"You have my thanks." He inclines his head in a mock bow. "I'll get this back to you soon." He has the audacity to wink at me before looking back at Jack. "Bye for now, little mean kitty cat."

When the door shuts behind him, I almost crumble to the floor in relief.

Felix's Jeep comes peeling into the parking lot just as what I assume is Silas's Hyundai starts up. The Jeep barely comes to a stop in front of the library before Felix vaults from it, not even bothering to shut it off.

Felix bursts through the doors as Silas's taillights turn on, and he backs out of the spot.

"What happened?"

I want to answer him, but I'm frozen, watching as the taillights disappear out of the parking lot.

"George!" Felix demands.

Shaking my head, I try to put the last few minutes into words. I'm not even sure it was a few minutes. It feels like it was hours, years even.

"Silas came in."

Felix's brows pull down. "And? What happened? Did he hurt you?"

"No. He was just weird. And Jack growled at him."

"That cat never growls at anyone." Felix's eyes shift to Jack. His hair is still raised. "But why is Silas blatantly showing interest in you?"

"I don't know. I wasn't at school today. It's the first time I've seen him since . . ."

"Garrett's death," Felix says quietly. It's not a secret that I was there. The cops questioned Felix and me, but since Felix told them we were just going after him to stop him from drunk driving, the rest of their questions stopped. I haven't wanted to look too closely at Garrett's death.

Unbidden, a piece of the memory rises to the surface.

"There was someone in the road," I say quietly, the ghost of icy water choking my words. Coughing, I try again. "Before Garrett went off the bridge, there was someone in the road," I say again, louder this time. "He saw him, I remember. He swerved to miss a person in the road, that's why he went off the bridge. What if it was Silas?"

"Did you see him?" Felix asks.

I shake my head. "But Garrett thought about a man right before— He was thinking about how there was a man in the road." The way Silas was looking at me tonight, it was like he knew what I could do, knew what I saw. "I think it has to be Silas. It would make sense."

Felix and I watch the closed library doors like Silas will come back and get us, even though his car is long gone.

"We need to find out who he is and what he wants before anyone else dies," I say. *And before I kill him.*

CHAPTER

29

"GEORGE!"

I pop my head from my hands. "What?"

"You were sleeping." Trixie glares at me from across the table.

Tomes cover our table in my basement library, all relating to various curses and hexes, all of them basically gibberish to me.

I scrub my eyes, pushing my glasses out of the way and ignoring the fact that mascara is probably now smeared across my face. With my current lack of sleep between researching with Trixie and the image of my blood-soaked face chasing me from sleep when I close my eyes, I should just give up on makeup. It's futile.

"I was not sleeping. I was laying my head down in despair."

"You looked like you were sleeping," she says, still glaring.

"Trust me, if I could sleep, I would. But I can't."

After our kiss at the carnival, I was worried things would be weird between us.

Instead, it's been even better, with secret glances and groans from Felix about being a third wheel.

"You could ask your gran for something," Trixie offers gently.

I shake my head. "No. I think dreaming might be worse."

My gloves lay discarded on the table since Trixie's far enough away that there won't be any accidental brushes with death. Tapping the button on my phone, I let out a groan. "It's almost two in the morning."

I see a slew of messages from Felix, mostly grumbling about not being invited tonight.

"We haven't finished. And if you can't sleep, what better way to spend our time?"

"Trix, we're not going to figure anything out if the words are blurring together on the page."

I slam the tome in front of me shut, sending a cloud of dust into the air. Coughing, I try to bat away the dust. "Can we lie down now?" I won't sleep, but I'd at least like to lie instead of sit.

"Soon," Trixie says, eyes skimming the page in front of her.

Sighing, I pull my laptop toward me and open it. We took the very long list of reasons there could be an excess of deaths in town—creatures, curses, location, et cetera—and split it between us. The only thing I've managed to do is cross out most of the creatures on it.

"I think we can rule out curses," Trixie says. "None of them seem even close to what's happening. Besides, there's no correlation between curses and your rune."

I chew on my fingernail, nodding. "Gran was convinced it was a curse, but she hasn't been able to find anything either." Gran has been down here a lot recently, basically anytime there's not another coven member in here. She still thinks it's best not to tip off the coven until we know what's going on.

I came down here with her last night, both of us researching in our own way. It was the first time I ever worked with her on something down here. It was actually really nice and made me wonder why I avoided it for so long.

Trixie piles the papers and notebooks in front of her. "Maybe she should join our next fact-finding session."

I try to picture Gran, tucked into the basement with her nose in a book while we eat Doritos and drink Cokes. I wrinkle my nose. "I think she likes to work alone." A bit of blood wells on my cuticle from where I've chewed it raw.

This whole situation has turned into a muddied mess of confusion and conjecture. We have so many questions.

Why did I see myself killing Silas? Why are there so many deaths in this town? Why can I even see deaths at all? Was it really Silas in the road in the vision of Garrett's death?

Above all else, though, is the one question that's haunted me since Jen's warning.

Why are the ghosts scared?

It doesn't seem logical for ghosts to really be scared of anything—they're already dead—but Jen's fear was almost palpable when Silas walked into the library. She hasn't been able to remember anything, even though I keep asking her. I don't know that I would have thought too much of it, except that she couldn't remember why she was scared.

What could do that? What scares a spirit? Almost nothing can interact with them.

That's where Trixie and I have come up short in research. Even the creatures we've found that go after souls absorb them. If that was the case, I wouldn't be able to interact with Jen, or any of them, for that matter.

They would just be gone forever.

I shiver at the thought.

But the souls aren't gone. They're here, tethered to the town. So not only would something have to capture souls, but I'd be looking for something that stores them too. Trixie hasn't found a single spell that would allow a wielder to do it on a large scale. It can be done once, but it's such a large drain on power, it wouldn't explain the unnatural occurrence of deaths in the town. At least that rules out someone in the coven.

The cursor in the search bar of my laptop blinks at me, a question of its own.

The problem isn't necessarily the questions, it's the fact that an answer to one rules out one of our theories. I have only a few creatures on my list but, once again, very little that would tie any of them to my magic. There are creatures that cause death where they go, but the souls wouldn't been trapped here. There are curses that trap ghosts, but not on a large scale.

But it's not just Silas that's bothering me.

It's Jen. It's Garrett. It's my parents. It's anyone in this town who has died before their time.

And if I'm being honest, it's me. I'm connected to this, somehow. But none of the answers I've found explain that.

Sighing, I type the same word into the search for what feels like the one hundredth time. "Creature that steals souls."

I feel silly even typing the words into the search bar. If it truly is a creature stealing the souls of Windrop residents, we should have been able to find it in our books.

The creatures on the internet are myth for the most part. Their truthful counterparts linger in the pages of the books Gran collects. Tales of monsters fill the screen in front of me. Every country seems to have their own version of these monsters that haunt the nightmares of their children.

As I scroll through, the same theme comes back repeatedly. Most of these creatures eat the souls. That wouldn't explain how the ghosts still linger here. If they were being eaten, I assume they would be gone forever, the same as if they were absorbed.

After what feels like an eternity of scrolling, I lean back in my chair. My eyes are aching from the light of the screen, and I take my glasses off to rub them. Trixie has her head down, speed-reading the tome. I look around to find Jack perched on the top of a bookshelf. His tail swishes off the end, the calico stub still swaying like it was a full tail.

"What am I missing?" I ask quietly.

It's not directed at him. He's a cat, after all. His eyes watch me through the dim of the room. I stare at him, going over all the things I know thus far.

The unnatural number of deaths.

The feel of Silas's blood on my hands.

The souls that seem trapped in Windrop.

My breath catches in my chest at that last part.

Trapped. Not stolen, but captured. They cannot leave, cannot pass on, yet they are still here.

Swiveling back to the computer, I try something new.

"Imprisonment of souls."

Even as I'm typing the words, electricity is coursing through me. The screen populates links just like before, but none with anything concrete.

Sighing, I click on a Reddit link.

"Looks like I'm not the only one searching for something that imprisons souls instead of devouring them," I mutter to myself as I read through the comments.

There isn't much, but one name stands out as I search.

Vodnici.

When I enter the word into the search bar, little comes up. I can't even find anything concrete about them, just whispers of myths of a creature that captures souls in glasses of water.

"Vodnici." I whisper the name in the dark, letting my tongue taste the word. Jack hisses from his perch, but I ignore him. I don't know how I know, but as soon as it leaves my lips, this is what I've been searching for.

"I might have found something," I say.

Trixie perks up. "What?"

"I figured it out," I say, the words rushing from my lips. "Silas. The deaths. Trixie, I think I know what it is—I know what *he* is."

I wait as Trixie's tired mind races to catch up. I try to calm my racing heart. I can almost feel all the deaths I've experienced over the years all at once.

"Are you sure?"

"No, but I feel it. This is it." My hands find my phone, pulling up Felix's number.

It only takes three rings for him to pick up the phone. Part of me realizes he's probably been waiting for my call, hoping we'd find something. He's out of the house before I even hang up.

TRIXIE AND I are still in the basement by the time Felix arrives, bleary-eyed and anxious.

"You both look like you've seen better days," Felix says when he opens the door at the top of the stairs.

After shoving my glasses on top of my head, I press my gloved palms into my eyes for the umpteenth time tonight. "Always the gentleman."

I probably look like a raccoon with my smeared mascara. Or maybe a blue-haired panda, but I don't care.

"Tell me," Felix says before he's even made it down to us.

"It's just a guess. I still haven't been able to find out much about it. But I started looking for something that imprisons souls instead of stealing them. I found a creature that captures souls. I found a few variations of it throughout literature. The Grimm brothers tell a story of an old man who captures the souls of the drowned and saves them in water cups."

"'The Peasant and the Waterman,'" Felix says.

Trixie and I both turn to look at him.

"What?" he says. "I like fairy tales."

"Moving on. Then there's something called a vodyanoy in Slavic mythology that basically captures souls and has them work as slaves beneath the water. They're also supposed to look like some ugly frog man, but that's beside the point. They're called vodniks in Czech fairy tales. But they all basically do the same thing: capture souls."

They both stand there, blinking at me for a minute before Trixie speaks. "But it sounds like this creature captures souls by drowning. Not everyone who dies in Windrop drowns."

"No, they don't, but they all happen near the river. Think about it."

Even in the last few months, all the deaths in the area have concentrated around the river. Jen was riding her bike on the road along the river. The former principal had a heart attack while running by the river a month after Jen died.

"Is she right?" Felix asks Trixie.

Trixie's brows are knit together as she thinks. "She might be."

"Might?"

"I can't confirm until I've done the research. But yes, I think this might be the closest we've been."

"We saw him by the river, painting in the same spot Jen died."

Trixie turns wide eyes to me. "Why didn't you mention that earlier?"

I shrug. "It didn't seem that weird at the time. It's not like it's a surprise that he likes painting."

"But now it's suspect," Felix adds.

"Understatement of the year," Trixie grumbles.

Felix glares at her. "Would your magic work on another creature?"

I suck in a breath. "It doesn't work on familiars, but that's as far as I know." Even with an answer, there are still more questions.

Trixie nods. "For now, we need to see if we can find any more information about the—"

"Vodnyk? Vodnici? Did we decide on a name?" Felix interjects.

"I think any work," Trixie says. "Let's start figuring out what to do about the creature. Whether or not it's Silas, I do think there's one here."

Felix leans forward. "What are we looking for?"

"Any information on how to free the souls." Trixie's eyes are already flying over the page open in front of her.

We pore over the texts in the library, looking for any mention of the vodniks, of their weaknesses, and how to free the souls they've trapped.

By the time my alarm rings on my phone to wake up for school, I might as well be blinking sand from my eyes.

"Anything?" I ask Felix and Trixie.

"Nothing substantial," Felix says as he closes the book in front of him. "A few mentions of them, but most accounts say they're extinct."

"That's about what I found." I reach for another book, but it seems we've gone through them all. "I did see something about needing a mortal form."

Felix perks up. "Now, that's interesting."

"What else did it say?" Trixie asks.

I dig around in the pile of books to my left until I find the one with the marked page. After opening it, I read from the page. "The vodnici are long-lived creatures, able to live for hundreds or even thousands of years based on the number of souls in their collection. Though they rarely age, their lives are tied to the bodies they inhabit. When their current form degrades, the vodnici will abandon the prior body for the body of a soul they recently captured, enabling them to continue to live."

"That would explain how Silas could be one." Felix shrugs.

"Maybe, but who was he inhabiting before? And where'd he get this body?" I ask. Trixie shakes her head and I continue. "Despite previous accounts of vodnici activity, they are believed to be extinct, having been hunted by covens for their murderous appetites."

"And that is less than helpful," Felix says.

"I didn't find anything about how to kill them, just—" Trixie shuffles the loose papers around to uncover an open book. She begins reading from the page. "That 'when they were more populous, their varying lineages favored different types of water: rivers, lakes, springs, et cetera.'"

"Could be helpful."

Trixie sighs. "Nothing about freeing the souls."

"Same," Felix and I say at the same time.

I slam the book in front of me. "I thought figuring out what he was would be the hard part."

"We're still not even positive this is what Silas is."

Felix and I both glare at her.

"I'm just saying," she says, holding up her hands as we stomp upstairs. "We need to exhaust all options."

"This is the only option we've had." I pause at the top of the stairs. "Don't tell Gran. At least not yet."

"Why?" Trixie asks.

"Because she'll take over. And like it or not, this is my burden to bear."

Trixie purses her lips but nods. I look at Felix. He hesitates a moment longer before nodding.

"Fine." He points a finger at me. "I don't like it, but I'll let it go until we're sure. And then we tell her right away. Deal?"

"Deal," I agree. Even though I'm the one who suggested we wait to tell Gran, a part of me still wants nothing more than to run to her for protection.

But she's protected me enough over the years as I wasted my potential within the coven. In this, I will at least make sure I'm not leading them down the wrong path.

Gran's already in the kitchen as we emerge. Breakfast sandwiches are piled on a plate. "What were you three working on?"

We glance at each other before I answer. "History project. It's due today."

"Felix isn't in your history class."

Shit. Sharp as a tack, Gran is. "Yeah, but Trixie and George needed something for their project," Felix says, rescuing us.

"That's awfully nice to come over in the middle of the night for a project you're not a part of."

"Yeah, well," Felix says as he rubs his neck. He's obviously uncomfortable. I send him a silent command to hold it together. "With everything going on, I come whenever George calls."

Part of me hates that he's using my freak-out to lie to Gran, but it seems to work, because she murmurs her agreement.

"Has something else happened?" Gran asks.

"Nope," I say, the lie a bitter taste on my tongue. Gran nods, but her mind is elsewhere. We each grab breakfast sandwiches as we head out the door, even though I'm not sure I could stomach one.

A weariness settles over me as we leave and pile into Felix's car. Maybe it's because part of me knows if I'm right about what Silas is, nothing will ever be the same again.

CHAPTER

30

AS I WALK INTO HISTORY class Monday morning, I sense eyes on me. My skin feels slicked in oil as I scan the room, but no one is paying me any attention. In fact, no one glanced twice at me in the hall. Even Trixie is staring down at her phone.

I was dreading returning to school, both for the reminder of Garrett's death and having to be close to Silas. We may have a guess as to what he is, but we still don't know what to do with that information.

That feeling doesn't go away though. Glancing over my shoulder, I find Silas watching me from where he stands next to Mr. Whitaker's desk. After the looks he was giving me in the library, there's no denying this is intentional.

It's everything I can do to keep my stride steady as I walk to my desk and sit down. Every sense is aware, and I can't help but think of Jack when he raises his hackles at a dog.

I don't think Silas will do anything in school, but nothing about being close to him makes me feel safe.

Silas's gaze is a brand as I start slowly pulling out my books. He only looks away when I pull my phone out, going back to focusing on whatever Mr. Whitaker is saying. But that can't be right either. Mr. Whitaker isn't speaking, just sort of blankly staring ahead.

My fingers fly over the screen.

GEORGE: *don't look up.*

GEORGE: *silas was just staring at me.*

TRIXIE: *i'm going to look up at you but be cool.*

Trixie looks up, smiling and saying hello before her fingers are typing.

TRIXIE: *he's not looking at you now. did he wink again?*

GEORGE: *no, just stared.*

Silas drops into the seat in front of me. I didn't even notice him walk over. My entire body breaks out in a cold sweat, but he doesn't look at me again.

We're given busy work for the period: writing out answers to practice questions for the AP History exam. I try to focus, but I find my eyes flicking up to the back of Silas's head the whole time. He never looks at me, but I swear I can feel his attention. I try to tell myself that I'm just being paranoid, but it's getting harder and harder to believe. My paper barely has ten words on it as the bell rings.

We head out into the hall and something slimy uncurls in my belly. I look up and find Silas watching me from his locker. I drop my gaze.

"He's doing it again," I mumble under my breath.

Out of the corner of my eye, I see Trixie's head whip toward him.

Smooth.

"He definitely is," she says as we walk down the hall. She glances at him again as we turn the corner. "He's still watching you."

I fight the urge to look back at him. "It's creepy."

"It is. Does he know we're on to him?"

"You think?"

Trixie ignores me and continues. "Something's been bothering me for a while now. There could be a million situations where you kill Silas—"

"Hey," I hiss. "People can hear you."

"No one's listening," Trixie says, unfazed. "But what's been bothering me is: why now? If Silas really is that creature, he would have been here all along. Why is it suddenly paying attention to you now?"

"I wondered that too," I say. I hadn't wanted to linger too long on the answer, but it's so blatantly obvious I can't ignore it. "My ascension." I sigh. "I think its interest was piqued the day I touched Silas and saw his death, but it only grew as my power did."

Understanding lights Trixie's face. "Jen's warning came after our Quarterly."

I nod. "And he sought me out after my ascension. Now he hasn't left me alone since I used my gift again to feel Garrett's death, even though it was unwilling."

The warning bell rings as we stop in front of my classroom. She looks torn between being late for class and staying to figure this out.

"Lunch?" she asks.

"Lunch," I confirm as she crosses the hall to her classroom. She gives me one last look before heading inside.

THE DAY IS cold, almost brutally so. No one else is out on the bleachers, which is perfect for what I have planned.

A shadow passes across my face as Felix plops down on the bleachers next to me, Trixie following right after him.

"I never thought we'd get to lunch," he grumbles.

"Tell me about it," Trixie says around a mouthful of apple. She glances at me and chews before speaking again, like she's embarrassed. It's the cutest thing I've ever seen. "I thought high school was terrible enough before we decided one of our classmates was stealing souls from the town."

"Being a teenager sucks," Felix agrees. He looks to me. "What's the next step?"

There was a time when I would look to Felix to make decisions. I've spent my whole life ignoring things, sticking my head in the sand rather than making any substantial choices. Now he's looking to me.

"I have a plan," I say with more confidence than I feel. My eyes catch on something over Trixie's shoulder. "I think this conversation will need to wait for now," I say. "Jen is here, and she looks like she wants to talk."

"You can make her corporeal. No one else is out here to see her."

Trixie bites her bottom lip and it's all I can do to keep myself from wishing I could kiss those lips.

Felix clears his throat, loudly.

It's then that I realize Trixie and I were staring at each other. Even in the middle of trying to figure out how to stop all the deaths in town, I can't keep my eyes off her.

"Why are you two making eyes at each other?" Felix asks, waving his hand to indicate the two of us. "I thought Jen was waiting."

"Never one to beat around the bush," I mutter as my face flames.

"George and I are dating," Trixie says, not a hint of embarrassment in her tone. "If things continue to go well, and I think they will, you will have to see many longing glances."

I snort out of habit, but I'd do anything to kiss her right now.

Felix looks at me, a smile taking over his whole face. "Look at my Georgie, growing up."

"Shut up, Felix."

"Yeah, shut up Felix," Jen says as she sinks down next to him.

Felix narrows his eyes at my smile. "Jen just told me to shut up too, didn't she?"

"She sure did."

"Awesome, so now I'm the third wheel and the odd man out?"

"Yup," Trixie says at the same time Jen does.

Felix rolls his eyes, but he's still smiling. There's something like pride in his face. I don't let myself think about it too long, or my heart might burst.

Making Jen corporeal takes a second of concentration, but my magic is coming more easily now. I feel it all the time, like it's waiting to answer my needs. Now that I'm not avoiding it as much, it's honestly pretty awesome.

"Hey," Jen says, leaning back on her hands. She looks relaxed, but I can feel her joy at being here. "Am I interrupting something? I feel like I'm interrupting something."

"No." Felix's voice is choked when he speaks. He's trying to hide how uncomfortable he is, but his face has turned gray. "We were just talking about weird creatures."

I widen my eyes at Felix, and I can feel Trixie tense next to me, but he ignores us.

"Ew, why?" Jen asks.

"I'm writing a collection of poetry about mythical creatures." Even under duress, he's still got his charm. The color is coming back into his skin and his shoulders are loosening. Seeing Jen may have been a shock, but he's recovering. "I was thinking of writing one about this creature that captures souls and keeps them in water cups."

I will kill him.

Maybe my visions aren't true because I will definitely kill Felix for this. We all agreed not to bring up our suspicions around the ghosts and yet here he is, diving in at the first chance. I try to convey my feeling with a look, but he winks at me. His telltale *trust me* sign.

Jen's brow furrows. "The vodnici?"

Our blinks are audible as we all stare at Jen.

"You know of it?"

"Of course, I do," she says, tucking a strand of hair behind her ear. "My grandmother emigrated from Russia. She used to tell me stories about the evil vodnici who would drown me and capture my soul if I was a bad child."

"Sounds like a peach," Felix says.

"What else did she say about them?" I say.

"Um," she says, thinking. "I know they're supposed to be really ugly. And they keep souls in decorative teapots, which I never understood but whatever."

"And how do you free the souls?" Felix asks.

"Why? Did you meet a vodnici?" Jen says, laughing again. Our silence ends her laughter. "Wait, do you think they're real?"

"No, of course not," Trixie says quickly, adding in a laugh at the end. It still sounds forced.

Jen eyes her for a moment before continuing. "There wasn't a handbook on freeing the souls. I think my grandma just assumed that if your soul was captured, you were a lost cause. Though she did say something about needing to kill the vodnici to free the souls, but it wasn't a task for an ordinary mortal."

Goosebumps cover my arms. If there really is a vodnici in our town, I think for once it might be a good thing I'm not a normal mortal. It takes every bit of restraint I possess not to look at Trixie and Felix. "Huh," I say. "Sounds like a wild story."

"I guess. She had all sorts of stories. Come to think of it, though, they all seemed to involve some type of creature punishing children."

"I repeat my observation about her being a peach," Felix says. He still looks a little gray, but he seems to have regained his composure.

Trixie, on the other hand, looks like she just stepped on a tack. "Can you ask her?" she chokes out. She clears her throat. "You know, for research?"

Jen's face falls. "No. She died when I was ten."

"Bummer," Felix says when neither Trixie nor I respond.

"Yeah." She chews her lower lip again. "I don't know that much. I mean, it was just a children's fairy tale. I wish I could remember anything else about her, but all I have are stories about monsters and flashes of an apartment that was always too dark and too damp."

"Better than nothing," Felix says as he adjusts on the bench. "Both sets of mine died before I was born. I have George's Gran though. She basically adopted me as her other grandchild."

I snort. "You sort of forced her to. You were always at my house."

"I like your gran," Jen says. "She seems like a bad-ass."

Felix laughs. "That's an understatement."

"I like your mom, too."

I don't think Jen realizes the impact of her words as she turns to Trixie and starts talking about how she keeps her curls shiny, but Felix sees the flash of hurt on my face. Jen knows my mom more than I do.

I'm thankful for the roast beef sandwich I can shove into my mouth at that moment. With everything that's been happening, the wound of my parents' death feels fresh. I can feel Felix watching me, even as I try to listen to whatever Trixie and Jen are talking about.

Maybe, when all this is done, I'll have the answer as to why my parents don't show themselves to me, and for now, that hope is enough.

WHEN I FINALLY let Jen's form go, the group is silent. Jen's confirmation that a vodnici needs to be killed to release the souls at least puts a why behind my vision, but it still doesn't mean I'm happy about it.

"I think we need to go to his house," I say finally.

Felix and Trixie turn to me.

"Who is this *we* you're speaking of?" Felix asks.

"You and I," I say to Trixie.

"I'm obviously coming," Felix says.

I snort. "No, you're not."

"You guys are going."

"We're witches," Trixie reminds him. "We have, you know, magic to help us."

"I'm coming," Felix says firmly.

I heave out a heavy sigh. "You don't even know the plan and here you, a mortal, are trying to insert yourself into something that shouldn't have anything to do with you."

"He can be the lookout?" Trixie offers. She shrugs when I gawk at her. "If you can't beat 'em?"

"You're an enabler, you know that?" I say to her. "Fine. Lookout."

"Do you have a plan?" Trixie asks.

"Not completely. But the school play is tomorrow night."

"That's actually kind of genius," Felix says.

Trixie furrows her brow. "And what? Watching a poor showing of *Peter Pan* will suddenly make him confess to being an evil creature?"

"Always with the lip, ye of little faith. No, it's literally the only thing going on in town, so we can assume he'll be there."

Trixie frowns. "What passes for entertainment here is so strange."

I ignore her, pressing on. "Plus, faculty are required to attend, so Mr. Whitaker will be gone too. We could scope out their house."

"Breaking and entering. I like your style," Felix says.

"Got a better suggestion?" I level a glare at him.

Felix holds up his hands. "No, I mean it. I like your style. But I think the play is our best bet."

"So," I say, standing. "We head to his house during the play. We pop in, look around, and pop out. Easy peasy."

Trixie thinks for a second then nods. "We'll have to talk about timing, but I like it. So, tomorrow?"

"Tomorrow," Felix and I say at the same time. I don't know what answers we'll find at Silas's house, but at this point, anything is better than nothing.

CHAPTER

31

WHEN I COME DOWNSTAIRS, I find Gran in the kitchen. She has her back to me, focus set on something in the sink, but I can still feel her attention. Her magic reaches out, prodding me, looking for injury.

Like she used to do when I was little.

"I haven't seen you much," she says, still not looking at me.

Guilt tightens around my heart. I miss her too. Before all this, Gran was my best friend, my confidant. Now the secrets are piling up between us, pushing her further away.

"I've had a lot going on." You know, like figuring out my class-mate is a vicious creature that traps souls. Well, at least I think that's what he is. The words are right there on the tip of my tongue, but they stay behind my lips.

"Like what?"

"School, work, friends."

She turns. "That's no more than normal." Her eyes narrow ever so slightly. If I didn't know her as well as I do, I don't think I'd notice.

"I have one more friend than usual."

"Mm, you do. Are you sure that's it?"

My palms turn slick in my gloves. "Yup. Just a lot going on."

"I thought you might be avoiding me."

"Why would I avoid you?"

Gran pauses a moment before smiling. But it's too wide, too sharp. Then she's facing the sink again. "Never mind, just a twinge of worry."

She's hiding something too. My eyes scan the room, landing on the empty perch. "Where's Benny?"

Gran's shoulders stiffen, but she doesn't turn around. "He's . . . out. He'll be back later."

I watch my grandmother a moment longer, her navy dress as still as she is. Bennington is always by Gran's side, a steady figure in her life, and I almost don't recognize her without his presence.

"Gran," I push.

Her shoulders droop, just a little, and she turns around. "I've been having Bennington connect with other covens, trying to see if there's any additional information about your gift."

"Why?" I say. With her knowledge of my vision with Silas, this seems a weird thing to focus on.

Gran watches Jack prowl into the kitchen before speaking. "Gifts are just that: gifts. You should be able to have control over them. But your touch, you can't control it. It happens with every skin-to-skin contact, regardless of whether you want it to."

"I definitely don't want it to."

"Exactly. Yet it still happens. I thought maybe you just lacked the control to—don't look at me like that, you basically ignored the fact that you were a witch for the past decade; I thought maybe you lacked the control to wield the gift properly."

Gran's words feel like a slap. "You thought it was my lack of control, yet you *let* me ignore my magic."

Gran's lips pull into a thin line. "I did," she says. It feels like there's more she's not saying. "I thought with your ascension that you'd gain that control. And it's clear that even after your ascension, additional power did not grant you freedom from the constant fear of experiencing death. Power may be unskilled and untested, but it should never be unwieldy. You should be able to choose."

My hands ball into fists at my sides. I don't interrupt her, waiting for her to tell me the rest.

"Before, I let myself believe it was a lack of training, but I can't do that any longer. Especially after Silas. Add that with what Renee said the other night." Gran turns, walking to Bennington's empty perch. "That's where Bennington has been. Carrying messages to other Supremes, trying to get any answers."

"And?" I ask, breath caught in my chest.

"And I still haven't found anyone with a gift like yours."

My shoulders fall. "Damn."

"I did find one story of interest. Many years ago, long before covens were as established as they are now, a small gathering of elemental witches were living deep within a forest. One witch was particularly attuned to fire, quite gifted actually. Well, one day, she began lighting fires without meaning to. It didn't always happen, just occasionally at first. The coven could find no ailment or reason this was happening, and at the time, they couldn't find any triggers.

"One night, her magic truly went beyond her control, and hundreds of acres of forest were lost to her flames. There was an unburned circle protecting their houses and the witches within, but the rest of the forest was gone. In the aftermath, they found the remains of a particularly foul creature, one we don't even have a name for anymore. We don't have a clear answer as to what happened, but the witch never lost control of her magic again."

Silence. Utter silence in my head.

"So," I start, "are you saying her proximity to a dangerous creature sent her magic haywire?" If that's true, then the vodnici's presence could be responsible for my lack of control. I still don't understand how Silas could be the vodnici, especially if he just arrived, since there would have had to be one here for over a decade. It's like the answer is hovering just outside my reach.

"It would be possible that the reason you can't control your gift is connected to death though." Her fingers find her brooch and she brushes it gently, like she's looking for some comfort in it. "Honestly, I think it's a combination of a few things. It may be a strange gift, but your connections to the emotions of the dead and your strength as a wielder make me think that maybe this is truly a gift, not a curse."

My heart sinks. "So, there's nothing I can do about it."

"I'm not done." Gran rolls her shoulders back, obviously glad to be able to present something she feels less guilty about. "I don't think the gift itself is a curse. I think your gift presented when you were a child, but your inability to control it, particularly as you got older and especially following your recent control, tells me that something else is going on. Do you remember when your gift got worse?"

"What do you mean, worse? It's been this way since I was little." The only memories I have with my gift are of involuntary visions.

"No, you only experienced imminent deaths when you were little. You could touch people who were not going to die in the near future. You could touch me . . ."

An image of me snuggled into Gran on the couch one night while my parents were out pops into my head. Popcorn and a cheesy Disney movie on the television. For so long, I thought the image was just a hopeful picture I had painted in my mind, but looking back now, I realize it's a memory I had repressed for so long. "I had almost forgotten."

"Of course, because you were so young, and it wasn't long after you experienced your father's death that you lost both parents. And everything changed then. Why would you remember that detail? But you couldn't touch anyone without experiencing their death."

I know it, then. Every piece falls into place. My inability to control my magic is its reaction to a dangerous presence. Whether Silas is the evil or just a pawn in some scheme, that's what I need to find out. But I know I wouldn't kill him unless I had to, unless he were truly dangerous. At least, I hope I'm not the monster I saw in my vision.

Gran doesn't notice my turmoil, her attention on the dishes in her hand. I try to wipe the knowledge from my expression.

"I don't know, Gran. But I think this is worth looking into." I turn, knowing I won't be able to keep the realization from my face if I stay any longer. "But it's a lot to take in. Do you mind if I go lie down before the gathering?"

Gran looks like she wants to argue with me but decides against it, nodding once.

It's an effort to keep my steps steady up the stairs when every piece of me screams to race up to my room, to piece together the final bits of the puzzle, to end this.

--◄◄◆►►--◄◄◆►►--◄◄◆►►--

WITHIN A FEW hours, the basement is filled with coven members. Potluck dishes line one of the tables, their contents already picked over. It's a social gathering tonight, not an official meeting, so it's not mandatory. Still, almost everyone is here just enjoying the chance to see each other.

Someone laughs and it's such a strange sound to me. Coven meetings are always stiff, but this is . . . fun. It's the first time I've been to a true social gathering since I was little. I thought the

Halloween party was a fluke for the holiday, but these people genuinely seem to enjoy each other.

I, though, am not. I'm bouncing on my toes, the information from Gran making me anxious. I just want to be done. I want it to be tomorrow so we can find out if Silas is actually the vodnici and bring in reinforcements.

"What's wrong?" Trixie asks as she hands me a Coke, careful to avoid contact.

"Is my face doing the thing again?" I ask. Trixie nods. "I was just thinking that this is kind of nice."

Trixie looks out across the room. I spot Jack, the traitor, curled in Mistress Rowina's lap. And she's actually petting him.

"What else?" Trixie presses. She knows me too well. I look around, but no one seems to be paying attention to us.

"Nothing," I say finally. "Just anxious for tomorrow." I don't know why, but I don't want to tell Trixie what Gran said. The hope has already started growing in me—I don't want others being disappointed if it doesn't happen.

Trixie frowns. She probably knows there's something I'm not telling her. Thankfully, she lets it go.

"Ready to get out of here?" she asks.

"Sure," I say, adding quickly, "but I don't want you to leave." Trixie's cheeks darken and her smile is nothing short of mischievous.

"I'm not," she says. "At least, I wasn't planning on it. I was thinking I would stay here?" The end of the last word tilts up in question. Unease passes over her face. "My mom already talked to your gran. I figured you'd need some support tonight. I didn't think you'd mind."

"No!" I half yell at her. Trixie takes a step back. "Sorry. No, I don't mind. I've just never had anyone spend the night." I open the door wider, letting her in.

"Never?"

"Nope, never." Not one living friend has spent the night here, not even Felix. And especially not someone I'm dating.

"Well, I'm happy to be your first. And to finally see my girlfriend's room." A thrill runs through me. I don't think I'll ever get tired of hearing that word. Trixie stands awkwardly in the hallway, and I realize I'm supposed to show her where to go. As we start toward the stairs, I pause, turning to her.

"Trix," I say. She waits, letting me process my thoughts. "Thanks for coming. I'm glad you're here."

⫸⫷⫸⫷⫸⫷

MY HANDS ARE near raw from twisting them as I wait for Trixie to emerge from the bathroom. She was only in my room for a minute before disappearing to change, and somehow it feels like she'll be really seeing me for the first time when she comes in.

Gran had already pulled the trundle from under my bed and arranged it. The bed has only been rolled out a handful of times, usually as a second bed for Jack. In fact, he's already made himself comfortable in the fresh sheets. I glance around the room, trying to gauge what level of weird my choices make me.

The wall to the left of me as I sit on my bed is just one solid dark-gray set of bookshelves, each space filled with a book I couldn't put down. The pale pink of the rest of the room seems childish, out of character for how I usually dress and act. The walls are covered in framed sketches of bats and other creatures. The oversized navy velvet chair looks out of place in its spot in the corner.

My desk is littered with papers and notes. I should probably tidy it up, but something keeps me frozen on my black iron bed.

Trixie comes in, door squeaking behind her as she shuts it and climbs into the trundle. She lies down and turns to me.

"It's freezing in here."

"I'm sorry. I keep it cold. I can turn up the heat if you want."

"No, it's fine now that I'm in the bed. I like sleeping in the cold too."

"Only weirdos don't."

She laughs at that. She glances around my room as I hold my breath. "Your room doesn't look like what I thought it would."

"Why?"

"I don't know. I was picturing dark paint and band posters, based on what you wear to school." She nods at my boots in the corner.

My heart sinks. "Is it bad?"

"What? No." Trixie pulls her eyes from her survey of the room to me. "It's actually really nice. It's kind of comforting in here. Cozy."

I look around my room in a new light. "I guess you're right. I spend a lot of time in here."

"Doing what?"

"Writing, playing DnD online, or reading mostly. Sometimes I do homework, but usually I do that at the library with Felix."

Trixie props her head on one elbow as I slide beneath my covers. "Are you going to let me read what you write?"

My eyes flick to my bookshelves, covered in all my favorite fantasy novels, and back. My pulse is an erratic beat in my chest. "Definitely not," I say with a forced chuckle. "Besides, it's mostly fan fiction."

"I like fan fiction." That shy smile is back. Trixie looks at my bookshelves again. "After all this is over, maybe you could show me?"

After. I don't even know what after will look like, but if Trixie's in it, it can't be that bad. "It's a date."

Trixie gives me a sidelong glance. "So, not poetry?"

I snort. "Definitely not poetry. That's Felix's thing. I don't have that kind of emotional depth."

"I don't know if that's true. I think you have it; you just don't want to explore it."

My lips lift in an involuntary smile. "Hm," I muse. "Jen said something similar the other day."

Jen Monroe, my friend. That's a plot twist I never expected.

Trixie punches her pillow to beat it into a more comfortable shape. "What else has she said?" There's a bite to her words. Is she jealous? I stamp the thought down.

"That I was prickly and that's why I didn't make friends, not because I was weird."

"Jen's not as dumb as I thought she was."

"So you think she's right?"

"In part. People would like you, George, if you let them."

I don't answer. I don't know what to say.

"Think about it," Trixie says as she settles onto the pillow. She yawns. "But for now, I think sleep will be good. We should be rested for tomorrow."

I mumble my agreement as I switch off the light and settle us into darkness.

We lie there for a moment, the swirling of the fan the only sound in the room.

Fiddling with the pendant around my neck, I whisper into the dark. "Are you awake?"

"I am now." I hear Trixie shuffling in her bed. "What's up?"

"Is it weird to be a little excited for tomorrow?" Even as the words come out of my mouth, I feel stupid for saying them.

"No," Trixie says quietly. "Where's the excitement coming from?"

"I just . . . I've had so many questions. Not just since I first saw Silas's death, but before that. About my gift and why I have it. Tomorrow feels like I'll finally get answers, at least to some of it."

Trixie rustles again, and I can almost feel her looking at me in the dark. "What will you do, once you have your answers?"

My breath comes out in a long whoosh. "Once we have confirmation, we tell Gran. And the rest of the coven. I'll need their backing." For my vision and everything that will come with it.

Trixie's silent for a long time. Long enough I assume she fell asleep before answering. Finally, she responds. "They'll be behind you, no matter what. We all will."

"What if they're not?" Even though I've tried to avoid it, in gaining their trust, I've started to seek it. The realization that I would be devastated to be ostracized after everything slams into me, stealing my breath. I'm grateful for the darkness that hides the tears pricking my eyes.

"They will be. You'll have proof and they'll support you. You're doing everything you can."

"I just hope it's enough." The words are barely a whisper as they leave my lips, but Trixie hears me.

"It will be enough, George. You're enough."

CHAPTER

32

THE NEXT AFTERNOON, THE DINER is packed. It seems like every student from Windrop Central is here, along with their parents and any other relative who may live in the area. It's tradition, eating at the diner before any major function.

And in a small town, the hastily thrown together school play counts as a major event.

The only ones who aren't here are those involved with the play directly: the actors, stage crew, et cetera. I'm pretty sure the three of us are the only ones without family members here. Gran never comes to town functions, Trixie's mom is working, and Felix's parents are, well, Felix's parents.

A trickle of sweat slips down my temple despite the chill of the diner.

Trixie watches it. "Try not to hold on to your magic so tightly. Think of it more like a caress instead of a grip."

I grit my teeth and exhale, trying to loosen my hold. "It's not that easy. She really wants to be here." I'm doing my best to keep Jen at bay. We don't want her hearing our plans in case she really is connected to Silas and can report back to him. But with this many students here, she really wants to be here too.

"You're doing great," Felix says. He has no idea what I'm actually doing, but it's nice to hear anyway.

Suzy comes by the table. She eyes the basket of fries, barely touched and now cold. "You kids feeling all right tonight?"

I nod and try to swallow past the dryness of my throat to answer her, but Trixie beats me to it. "Just nerves. For the play."

"Oh," she says, obviously surprised. "I didn't think you all were in it."

"We're not." Felix flashes her a smooth smile. "Backstage work, but we're still nervous to see how it's received."

"Well, that makes sense then. I'm sure you kids have nothing to worry about. Fries are on the house then."

We don't even have time to respond before she's turning to another table.

Trixie picks up a cold fry before dropping it back in the basket. "That was nice of her."

"We eat a lot of fries here," Felix explains. "George, you look like you're going to be sick."

In through my nose, out through my mouth. "It'll get better once we leave the diner. Then maybe she won't want to be around so much." I check the time on my phone. Six fifteen. "Everyone should start heading to the school soon. Maybe we should go?"

Trixie shakes her head. "We need to make sure you-know-who doesn't leave early. Better safe than sorry."

I turn to look behind me, trying to look like I'm stretching. Silas is sitting with a group of football players. He should look out of place, considering he's the art nerd, but he looks perfectly at ease.

I still don't understand how someone so handsome, so . . . normal could be this terrible creature. Turning back, I shift in my seat.

"I need to tell you both something before we go." I've been avoiding this conversation, unsure if it would make a difference in the plan tonight. But they need to know, if only so they have all the facts before we head out.

They lean forward, closer to me.

"My gran said something weird last night," I say quietly.

I hadn't told them, even when I called them to tell them this plan. I couldn't process what she said. I don't think I have processed it yet, even though I was up half the night.

Trixie leans forward. "What? Something about . . ." She inclines her eyes toward the table of teachers.

I shake my head. "Something about my gift. She thinks my ability is a gift, but the fact that I can't control it might be a form of protection. She said when I was little, I would only see an imminent death, and it wasn't until my parents died that I could see all death."

"So what? Seeing death is a form of protection? How?" Felix asks.

"Not sure, really. She just said it happened one time and that it might be a possibility."

"It seems like a heavy weight for a child," Felix says softly, lips pulled into a thin line. "Even if it was some way to keep you safe from something."

Trixie's nose wrinkles as she thinks. "Magic is . . . weird. Kind of slippery. Even the Goddess, powerful as she is, can only bestow gifts. She cannot interfere with the lives of the witches she blesses."

Felix frowns at Trixie before looking back to me. "Does this change anything?" Felix asks.

"Other than my feelings toward my magic?" I ask.

"George . . ."

"No. Maybe. I don't know. If *he's* the reason my parents are dead, I certainly want to see him pay for it. Maybe my magic is trying to protect me and the rest of the coven from Silas. There has to be a link somewhere, some bigger reason."

We're silent for a while after that. The buzz of the diner drowns out the roaring of my thoughts.

Finally, Trixie's eyes widen before she speaks. "They're leaving." I don't turn, but a few moments later, I see the table of football players, Silas included, milling about in the parking lot before climbing into their respective cars. The exodus of the football team is some silent symbol to the rest of the diner. They start leaving cash on the tables and tidying up before heading to their cars. In less than ten minutes, we're the last ones here.

The constant push from Jen ebbs as everyone leaves. "Let's go."

CHAPTER

33

WE PARK TWO BLOCKS AWAY from Silas's house. Felix's Jeep is too noticeable to leave in the street, even if it is deserted. Everyone is definitely at the play. Good for us, but really embarrassing for the town as a whole when I think about it for too long.

The house looks just the same as when Mr. Whitaker lived here alone. Just an unassuming Craftsman. The white paint is a little worse for wear, peeling in places, but the house is well-kept and the yard tidy, despite the leaves covering most of the town.

I pull my jacket tighter around me as a chill runs through me. My body has been trembling since we left the diner, either from releasing the magic keeping Jen away or from nerves, there's no way to be sure. Jack weaves between my legs; bringing him wasn't even a question. If something goes south, at least we'll have whatever protection he can provide.

"So, just wait here?" Felix asks, looking at the house.

We've gone over this a dozen times, but I get why he's asking again. I'm nervous too. "Basically. Try not to be too obvious about it. Call us if you see anyone so we can get out."

"Right. I can do that." It sounds like he's trying to convince himself more than us.

"We should go," Trixie says quietly, but even she seems unsure. We're walking toward the house when Felix *pssts* behind me.

"George?" he says as I turn. "Be careful."

I try to smile, but I know it doesn't meet my eyes. "Always am." I turn away from him quickly. If I keep looking at him, I'll lose my nerve, and I can't afford to do that, not with everything at stake.

I walk to the front door out of instinct. Front doors here are never locked. When I grip the handle and try to turn though, nothing happens. "It's locked," I say, more to myself than anyone else.

Looking around, I find Trixie heading to the back gate. "This way," she calls. I follow her and we slip through into the backyard.

"I should have thought of that." Windrop has a few people who lock their front door, but I don't know anyone who locks their back door here.

"Why? I did." I know she's trying to lighten the mood, but her smile looks more like a grimace, which does nothing to calm my nerves. Trixie leads me to the back door. There's no covering in the window on the door, so we peer inside. "Looks empty."

"Try the knob," I say.

She does. It doesn't budge. "Locked."

"Suspicious already."

Trixie glares at me before mumbling under her breath. A spell, if I had to guess. She tries the knob again. "That's weird."

"Did you do it right?"

That earns me another glare. "Of course I did it right. It didn't unlock." She mumbles again, but the knob doesn't budge. "I wasn't creeped out before, but I definitely am now. This should work."

That oily feeling in my gut resurfaces. "Why wouldn't it?" Jack's warmth seeps through the fabric where he's pressed against the leg of my jeans. The hair across his back is raised, stub tail fat.

"There are a couple of reasons why an unlocking spell wouldn't work, but nothing that would be connected to a mortal." She shares a look with me. "I guess we should start trying windows."

"Hold on," I say, digging around in my jacket pocket for the nail file. Pulling it out, I slip it between the door and the frame and work the latch. The door pops open. Jack lets out a low growl before prowling into the house.

"He certainly doesn't like it here. Why do you know how to do that?"

"I used to lock myself out of the house a lot. Like, a lot a lot. Haven't needed to use it in a couple of years but brought it tonight just in case."

I stumble over the words as I step through the doorway and we cross the threshold. A wave of something I can't place passes over me.

Trixie carefully shuts the door behind her, and we take a few tentative steps. "My girlfriend, the lockpick," she muses.

The endearment does little to shake the chill that's settled in me. I listen, but I don't hear anyone inside the house. We're in the kitchen, which is small and cozy. It also looks like it hasn't been updated since the late seventies.

"Do you feel that?" I ask.

"It's weird, but I can't place it. What do you feel?"

Chewing my bottom lip, I search for the right words to describe it. "I don't know, almost heavy. Like there's something pressing down on me. Is that what you feel?"

"Not really," Trixie says in a hushed tone. "It just feels off." She closes her eyes for a moment. "But there's no one here."

At least there's that.

I try to swallow down the lump in my throat. "Look for anything suspicious," I whisper.

Trixie whispers back. "I could've figured that out on my own. I think we should stay together."

I nod. It's a small house. There shouldn't be too much to cover. If there isn't anything here, we should be out in just a few minutes. Before we came, I think I was secretly hoping that all the answers would be here. But now that we're in the house, with the weird weight on my shoulders, I'd give anything to be wrong.

We follow the hallway from the kitchen along the stairs. Another hallway branches out under the stairs, probably leading to the bedrooms. We follow it and find the bedrooms.

The main bedroom is tidy, not an article out of place. No dust either, like someone cleaned before we came over. The guest bedroom is the same way, which I assume is where Silas sleeps. There's no hint of him anywhere though. Even the small bathroom in the hall looks like no one uses it. Trixie shrugs as we head back down to the main hallway, Jack right behind her.

At the front door, the living room is to the left. Once again, it looks like no one even lives here. The furniture is old, probably older than my parents would be, but still looks like it is brand new. We open a few drawers and dig around in the cabinets, but there's still nothing.

Back in the main hallway, Trixie opens the small door under the stairs. There is another set of stairs that leads below the house. "I'll check it out. Stay here."

She's gone only a moment before reappearing. "Just a crawl space. Nothing down there either. Like, nothing. He doesn't even use it for storage."

"Mr. Whitaker must be the biggest neat freak ever." I don't need to finish with what I'm really thinking: Mr. Whitaker may be a neat freak, but there's nothing of Silas anywhere in this house. Even if he isn't the typical messy teenager, something of his would be here. Based on Trixie's weak smile, she's glad I didn't say that part.

"Let's check upstairs and get out of here," I continue. "There doesn't seem to be anything here, but this place is giving me the creeps."

"Right? It's like being in a museum."

The steps to the attic are the only worn part of the house. They look like they've been used multiple times a day, every day, for years. The door at the top of the stairs is locked, and this time, Trixie doesn't even try to open it. She just moves aside and waits, expecting me to pop it with my nail file. It takes a little more work than the back door, but before long, we're in.

I don't know what I am expecting when we open the door to the attic, but it certainly isn't what hits me. The room is light and airy, the streetlights illuminating the room from the window at the front of the house. I turn the switch at the door, and the room is filled with bright, white light. The ceilings aren't quite as high as the rest of the house and they're angled, but it gives the impression of a room much larger than it actually is. The floors are stained a light finish, and the room is also extremely clean. Stacks of canvases are leaned against the wall opposite of the door. Just from the ones visible, there are landscapes and portraits, none of the subjects I recognize, mixed among a few other paintings that I can only categorize as abstract.

Trixie and I move into the room, and I'm pulled closer to the paintings. If anything, the heaviness of the house feels worse in here. When I meet Trixie's gaze, it's obvious she feels the same way. She rubs her arm and shrugs. She doesn't know what it is either.

I kneel in front of the paintings, examining the ones in the front of each pile. They're watercolor. All of them. They're obviously Silas's work. The subjects vary just like his other paintings. Self-portraits, landscapes, abstract, florals, portraits, and everything in between. But every landscape contains a river. Between seeing him painting by the river a few weeks ago and the classes he teaches at school in the evenings, I knew he liked to paint. But by the number of paintings he has here, it's clear that it's an obsession. That, and the fact that the deaths for the past decade have been closer to the river, fills me with dread.

"Trix, come look at these," I say, without turning around.

"I think you should come here first," she says from behind me.

When I turn, I find Trixie staring up at a wall of glasses, Jack next to her. Every hair on Jack's body stands on end. The entire wall is lined with shelves, and each shelf is almost overflowing with glasses of water. Each glass has a different amount of water in it. Some are almost full while others have less than a half inch in the bottom. And they all have lids. But the weird part is the color of the water in each glass. It isn't clear, but rather every shade one can think of. There are reds and oranges, blues and greens, purples and yellows, and every other color in between. As I move toward the wall, I notice that no glass has exactly the same color as another. They're all different, even if it's just a small amount. I step up beside Trixie. "What the hell?"

"Jars of water," Trixie breathes.

I shake my head, some part of me still unwilling to believe that is what they are even as the dread wraps around my heart. "They're paint. He obviously has an obsession with watercolor painting." But even as the words leave my mouth, I hear how ridiculous that sounds. To paint with watercolors, usually one would dip a wet brush into the dry paint. I've never heard of anyone painting with tinted water, but it's not impossible. Better than the alternative.

"George."

"I need a closer look." I take a tentative step toward the wall, then another, until I'm right in front of it. I hold up my hand, hesitating as it hovers in the air in front of the glass. I touch the glass in front of me.

Nothing.

"Gloves," Trixie says.

Right. I tug off the glove on my right hand, then lift it again. The glass in front of me is a light bubblegum pink, almost the same color as Jen's helmet. I don't know why I picked this glass, but I touch my fingers to the side of the glass.

Anguish and loneliness pour into me. Grief over a life too short and a desperate need for freedom. Tears burn my eyes.

I stumble back into Trixie, not even thinking about the risk of experiencing her death. She catches me, the fabric of my jacket a protective layer between us.

"What is it?" she asks.

I'm shaking my head, but no words come out. I can't form them, can't tell her who that is.

"We should go," Trixie says, tugging on the arm of my jacket.

"I can't leave them." My eyes scan the wall again. There must be hundreds of cups here, hundreds of souls trapped on shelves. They land on the bubblegum-pink glass. "I can't leave her here."

"Who? Explain."

My heart constricts as I choke on the words. "Jen. That's Jen's soul in the glass."

Trixie's intake of breath is audible as she studies the wall again.

All of these souls, more than just the ones who have died in town, trapped for who knows how long. The weight I've been feeling since we walked in this house. It's the weight of all their lives, trapped in this small space.

"We need to alert the coven. That was the plan. Find out if we were right, then alert the coven so they can handle it."

I nod, but my feet are still rooted in place. She's right, we need to tell the coven. But I can't leave them trapped, even though I have no idea how to kill a vodnici and free them. The image of myself covered in Silas's blood resurfaces, but even seeing that, there are too many variables. What if I kill him and the souls aren't freed? Or my stabbing spree ends up being ineffective against the creature, and I only kill the body?

And besides, he isn't here, so it's not like it happens now anyway.

I square my shoulders. "Let's go. And get the coven back quickly."

We turn to the door, but two figures now occupy the once empty space.

"I was wondering how long until you made it up here."

C H A P T E R

34

EACH SECOND MIGHT AS WELL be an eternity as I take in the
figures standing in the doorway. A satisfied smirk is plastered on Silas's face, like us being in his attic was his plan all along. His eyes are
fixed on me. Felix stands beside him, face as slack as the arms at his
side. But his eyes . . . his eyes shine panic.

No.

The word courses through me, but the room remains silent as
Silas steps into the space, Felix behind him. Jack hisses at my feet as
they move into the room.

I tell myself to steady my breath. Remain calm. I have my magic
and my familiar.

"I didn't feel him," Trixie whispers under her breath. I can't tell
if it's an admission or an apology. Or maybe both.

Silas turns to close the door and Jack bolts, a flash of black and
orange as he streaks through the room and out the door just before

it shuts behind him. Silas locks the door and turns his gaze back to mine, his smile now predatory.

"Looks like even your familiar knows when to back down."

My heart sinks. Correction, I *had* my familiar. Silas leads Felix farther into the room, stopping in front of the open bathroom door.

Well, at least I have my magic. And Trixie's magic. I catch her gaze out of the corner of my eye. She gives me a small nod.

I asked her once what to do if I ever got into a situation where I needed defensive magic, or even to attack. It had seemed so unlikely, even with the threat of evil in the town. Her response was the same as most of the magic we practiced. There are spells and things a wielder can do specifically, but mostly, defensive magic relies on intent. I draw on that intent now, burrowing deep inside myself, into the well of magic buried within me. No harm will come to Felix; I won't allow it. I take a deep breath, ready to unleash that intent on the creature in front of me.

Nothing.

There's absolutely nothing to unleash. I whip my head to Trixie, but the look of panic on her face confirms she feels the same.

"Naughty children. Those tricks won't work here." Silas smiles. The creature is done hiding. The smile has none of the warmth and friendliness of the act he was putting on before. It's sharp and brittle and hungry.

Silas gestures at one of two chairs along the same wall as the bathroom door and Felix sits. Trixie and I are almost on the other side of the attic, still by the window on the front of the house. There would be no element of surprise if we charged him from here, even if we could move.

"I took precautions." Silas runs a knuckle along Felix's chin. "I wonder what color he will make. I've been wanting a yellow since the last one ran out." Felix's body shivers, despite whatever hold Silas has on him.

"Stop that," I hiss.

"No." Silas—no, I can't think of him that way anymore. I need to see him for what he so obviously is. The vodnici turns to me. For the first time, his eyes shift to Trixie. "You too, come here."

Trixie's body goes rigid before she moves to him. I reach for her wrist with my gloved hand, but she wrenches her arm from my fingers and goes to sit beside Felix. She's staring straight ahead, but that look of terror in her eyes matches Felix's.

I wait for him to summon me, to feel whatever pull he has on my friends, but the vodnici just goes to the small table and easel in the middle of the room. The canvas propped on it is blank. The vodnici unrolls one of the two dark bundles on the small table.

It's an odd time to paint, but some part of me tells me he's going to toy with me. I'm barely breathing as I watch him, trying to figure out his plan. Or maybe it's my plan. My mind swirls as I try to think of anything to do. His movements are unhurried as the contents of the bundle are revealed.

A set of knives, all varying in length and edge, glint in the ever-dimming light of the attic. Flashes of my vision pop into my mind, the rise and fall of the knife. The vodnici notices the darkening of the room and walks back to the attic door. A light flicks on and fills the room with a soft glow, totally unfitting for what is happening. "Can't have you missing anything."

He returns to his knives, running a finger along them. "I'm not one to revel in the brutality of my tasks. My brothers and sisters were more keen on that than I, which is probably what led to their discovery. I like to keep my hands clean." He turns to me, holding up a hand for me. "A little push here, an influence there. Nothing that could ever lead back to me. Quite genius, if you ask me." When I don't respond, he continues, walking to the blank canvas.

"I've known what you are for a long time, Georgiana. I knew there was magic here when I first arrived. There's something so satisfying about living in plain sight. You know that old saying, keep your friends close but your enemies closer? When I got here, there was a magic I've never felt before. So much wild, untrained power. I needed to know where it was coming from.

"I had a hunch when we first met, but you probably don't remember. You'd recognize me better in the body I was in before— Old Mr. Whitaker. But he had aged past his prime and needed to be replaced. I rather like this new form, don't you?"

"How?" The question tumbles from my mouth.

The vodnici doesn't make me specify what I'm asking about, just keeps talking. "When I take a form, the soul remains with me. Usually, it suits me to harvest the soul when I'm done, but when I decided to take the boy," he gestures at his body, "I knew he'd need a caretaker for appearances. And a shell of a person is just so much easier to deal with." He sighs like these are relatable troubles. He turns his eyes on me. "It wasn't until you were older that I truly started to suspect you were the source of the magic. But I knew the moment you touched my skin the first time that things would change, that eventually you'd come to me."

He turns to stare at the blank canvas. If I can get to my friends, maybe I can drag them out of here. I might have to slap them, but we can make it to the door and bolt. If Jack were still here, he could distract the vodnici, but I can't dwell on that.

Gotta work with what I've got.

Ever so slowly, I make my way closer to Silas since he's between me and where my friends sit.

"The little witchling with the touch of death. What a fascinating power you have. I wonder what you saw when you touched me?"

I stop moving.

Either he's toying with me and he knows exactly what I saw, or he has no idea. I wait, the pounding of my heart filling the silence between his words.

He sighs. "Will you tell me, little witchling, what you saw? I would love to know what finally gets me in the end. Is it in this body?" He turns to me, head cocked to the side.

I take a moment to realize he's actually waiting for a response. "I don't know what you're talking about."

He sighs again, this time like he's exhausted by the thought of playing this game with me. "A little liar, too. You'll tell me soon enough." He turns back to his blank canvas. "Will you at least tell me why you're here? It's been so long since anyone truly voiced what I am."

Shifting on my feet, I once again inch forward, this time moving a little to the left to dodge Silas. "A vodnici."

He chuckles and tilts his head back. "Such a beautiful word, don't you think? Though I'm not sure it's entirely accurate. At least not how we've been described over the years. You should know, as the myths about your kind never seem to get it right either."

I stop moving again as he steps away from the canvas. He doesn't turn to me, instead walking to the wall of paintings.

Just a few more feet, and I'll be almost next to Silas. Then I can make a run for Felix. If I can snap him out of it, he can throw Trixie over his shoulder, and we'll make a run for it. I don't let myself think about the fact that I have no idea why he's frozen or how to break him out of it.

One problem at a time.

"The name vodnici might be most popular, but I've been called many things over the centuries." Ice floods my veins. Centuries. My mind can't even comprehend that word, that length of time. Involuntarily, my eyes flick to the wall of souls. He's been doing this for hundreds of years. How many lives were lost because of him?

"Georgiana, come here."

I freeze again, but I don't feel the same compulsion that the others must. It's just a request. He wants me to come of my own volition.

The desire to reach my friends almost wins out, but he turns to me, expectant.

No element of surprise now.

I step to him.

I can dance this dance a little longer.

He smiles at me, then looks down at the paintings. "Is it just me, or aren't these the most beautiful paintings you've ever seen?"

Despite myself, I can't argue that they are beautiful. The work of a true artist. I won't answer him though. Instead, I ask, "Why?"

Again, he doesn't ask me what I mean, but instead tilts his head to the side again, considering. "It just seemed like such a waste, to keep these souls, each their own beautiful color, hidden in jars. Some of my brethren only collected what they needed to survive. Others were gluttons. I think they both were wrong. I think of myself as a collector, a connoisseur of fine life. And since I'm the last of my kind, that entitles me to think whatever I want, don't you agree?"

"I think you're a monster." My jaw is clenched so tight my teeth crack, so my words come out as almost a growl.

"Such a small-minded response. You should know better than anyone that being different doesn't make you a monster. It's what you do with it." Another knowing look. Does he know what I do to him? Maybe he's just referring to my gift. "Look at what I've created." He gestures at his works. "How could a monster make such beauty?"

"How many?"

"How many what? Paintings? Thousands. Most have found other homes throughout the years—museums, personal collections, state buildings. Souls? Too many to count. I tried when I was younger, but as I found an outlet for my collection, I lost any reason to care. The art is the reward, not the number on my shelf. Though I find the two go hand in hand."

"Why are you telling me this?" A bead of sweat rolls down my spine as I fight against whatever invisible hold he has on me. My feet won't budge even an inch.

"Ah, see, that may be a more interesting question to answer. I could give you the simple answer that I am lonely and looking to find solace. I could tell you that this information will never leave this room, so I can tell you whatever I please. But I think, if I were to be truthful with myself, it is both of those things, along with a kinship I feel toward you and your magic."

Disgust turns my stomach. "I am nothing like you."

"Are you not?" He raises a dark brow. "Could have fooled me."

My mouth yearns to ask him what he means, but I force myself silent. Memories of myself in Veritas linger in the back of my mind, the darkness I saw within. I don't want to know what he means. He's trying to distract me.

"Why Windrop?"

"I find I like it here. Originally, I came here on a whim, looking for somewhere new to settle, but once I realized a coven resided here, I think I got a little thrill out of operating under their noses for so long. Even with their Supreme running the show—it's been a long time since I've seen a witch as powerful as she—I stayed. But even that power didn't allow her to see what I was doing."

Gran. I can picture the anger on her face when she realizes this went on in her town, undiscovered by her for so long.

"I didn't think anyone would realize what I was, or what I was doing—that is, until a witch stuck her nose in something she had no business exploring." He glances at me. "I can see the apple didn't fall far from that tree."

My mother.

The realization clangs through me. Gran was right: my mother knew what was happening in the town. And what caused it. She knew, and he killed her for it. It takes everything in me not to turn to the shelf behind me, to scan the wall for the cups that contain my parents' souls. A simmering rage starts deep in my belly, but I push it down. If I let it burn, it'll burn all other thoughts from my mind, and I need to keep my wits about me.

He doesn't seem to notice my anger as he continues. "I was going to leave after I killed her. My secret was once again safe, and I thought it time to move on. I was pretty spent after influencing the death of a powerful witch, so I had to lie low for nearly a year. But once my strength was regained, I thought it time to leave. That is, until I felt you."

My head whips to him. "Me?"

He breathes in deeply, as if smelling the air. "To be fair, I didn't know it was you at first. I only felt hints of the something. It was so infrequent though. It wasn't until a month ago when I felt it again, stronger this time."

The Quarterly. Jen tried to warn me.

"Then on your birthday, the power radiating from you"—he inhales deeply—"was, and is, intoxicating."

"What does my magic have to do with it?" I don't actually want to know. I feel like it makes this worse. But I need him to keep talking. I need time.

His grin turns predatory. "That's the fun part about harvesting, little witchling. When I take a soul, I absorb their strength. It's fleeting but so delicious. When I take the soul of a witch, their magic comes with it. What would I feel when I absorb a witch with the magic of death?"

"You're like a giant cliché." Anger gathers under my skin, growing into a rage so hot I might burst into flame. It burns past my logic. Now I might just as easily piss him off as keep him talking.

"Oh, I'm blessed with the wit of Georgiana Colburn. How delightful." He clasps his hands together. "Yes, I do speak in clichés. Nasty habit to break, I'm afraid."

"How has no one realized what you are? How can you control my friends? Where is our magic?"

"So many questions, little witchling. Now, I can't go revealing all my secrets, can I?"

"Why not? You said we weren't leaving." The words almost choke me. We *are* leaving. We have to. I won't accept any alternative.

"True, but where's the fun in telling you everything?"

My mind races, trying to piece everything together. He's losing interest. Another question falls from my lips. "So you stayed here, all this time, because of me?"

"Yes." He reaches out as if to brush the bangs from my forehead. I rip my head away from him.

"Don't touch me." My heart's a thunderous beat in my chest. I moved, just a bit. Either his control slipped, or I broke it.

He smiles again but drops his hand. "So fiery. Your soul will make the most potent black. It's been so long since I've had one, rare as you are." He turns back to his paintings. "But the works I could create with it. Come now."

CHAPTER

35

THIS TIME, THERE'S A COMMAND in his words. My boots move slowly, but they move all the same to the table where the knives are displayed.

"Wait here. I think you should watch how the process works first."

Then he has the audacity to wink at me. If I didn't want to kill him before, I do now.

He runs his fingers along the knives.

"I don't think I'll use these when I take the boy. The other witchling, maybe."

"I thought you didn't like to get your hands dirty." Bile burns my throat as I speak.

"I don't prefer it. But the more distressed a soul is, the more potent. I think watching me torture your friend is just the suffering you need to be truly delectable." He sighs like this whole process is just too much work for him. "But for now, let me just show you my preferred method." He turns and walks away from me.

My feet are rooted to the spot. I need to move, to tackle him, to make him stop whatever he's about to do, but it's no use. He stops in front of the closed door on the back wall and opens it, revealing a room with a claw-foot tub in the middle. He goes and dips his fingers in. "I like to keep it full, just in case." He shudders. "Might be a bit chilly, but I don't think Felix will mind, will you, Felix?"

Felix's eyes dart around as panic consumes me. I know what he's going to do. He doesn't need to say it, and without my magic, I am powerless to move.

I struggle against the confines of his commands, but nothing happens. I reach out to Gran, trying to call her like Trixie has been teaching me, like I've avoided learning my whole life. But there's nothing, just an empty silence on the other end.

Panic starts to set in. When he was talking, we had time, but now everything is happening too fast. Ragged breathing fills my ears. The warmth from the single light is a mockery of the situation. *My fault. My fault. My fault.*

The words are on repeat in my head, drowning out any other thoughts. All of it, all of them—my fault. He stayed here for me. And now he'll kill my friends because I was too stubborn to involve the coven, because my pride got the best of me.

The creature in Silas's body prowls to where Felix is sitting. He places a finger under Felix's chin and guides him to stand.

"Pity," he tsks. "Shame to lose such a handsome specimen." His eyes cut to me. "Sacrifices must be made."

My cheeks are wet as tears slip down them, the only movement I can make.

"Felix, would you be a dear and wait for me on the edge of the tub?" He says it like a question, but as Felix's feet drag him to the tub, I know it's not.

I can see this playing out in my head, despite this being so different from the death I've seen for him. Maybe this is the part where I learn death isn't as permanent as I've always believed.

I strain against the command of the vodnici.

The creature leans in the bathroom's doorframe. "I can only imagine what a gift it must be to experience a death. Such a lucky girl, and you never even knew. What I would give for a gift like that."

"I'd give it to you if I could."

Surprise lights his features, but it's soon replaced with amusement. "I'm sure you would. Judging by the fact that you found a way to speak, I see I didn't underestimate the power dwelling beneath your skin."

His words catch me off guard. It was me then, not him, loosening his power. My mind races as I try to piece together the bit of information he gave me. I wasn't supposed to be able to speak, but I didn't even think about it, just did it.

"Will you tell me of my death now, little witchling?"

"I don't know what you're talking about," I grind out through clenched teeth. I won't tell him anything, especially since it might be the only way out of here.

The vodnici sighs. "Shame. We both know that is a lie. Let's see if this loosens your tongue."

He remains looking at me as he speaks the next words. "Get into the tub, Felix." His form obstructs most of the doorway, but I can hear water sloshing as Felix obeys.

No. No. No. No. No.

Roaring fills my ears, blocking out all rational thought, followed by a wave of anger. I let it crash into me, consume me. If I'm as powerful as he says I am, why can't I break through his bonds? If I'm as powerful as Gran has always said, I should at least be able to overcome the commands, especially since his focus is spread between three.

Rage pulses through me. My fists clench into tight balls. The first movement since he bade me stay still. I'm vibrating with it.

Tears continue to slip down my cheeks as the festering wounds inside me rip open. He's not the only one I'm angry with. There's anger at myself for ignoring my gifts. Anger at my mother for never coming to me. Anger at the Goddess for what she blessed me with. Anger at the lack of control I feel. Anger at being powerless despite the magic coursing through me. Even now, I've been holding my magic at arm's length, too afraid to accept what I really am.

But I unleash the rage, letting it burn the fear away.

I feel my magic uncoiling inside me, humming under my skin for release. My intent is clear, but I'm still untrained.

Nothing happens as I call on my magic, but the creature's hold on me loosens, like a weight lifting from me. My arm jerks.

The vodnici looks at me, confusion on his face. "Stay still and don't close your eyes," he says.

The weight of the command is laced into his words, but it doesn't feel as heavy as before. I wiggle the toes in my boots, testing. He's not watching me now, rather looking at Felix with something like hunger in his eyes. I dare to lift my heel just the slightest amount. It feels like I'm trying to move my foot through mud, but it moves.

The rage continues to burn through whatever hold he commands. My magic is pulsing now, a steady beat under my skin. It is a wild force within me, begging to be used. But it is *mine* to control. *Mine.*

"Under the water now."

The sound of the vodnici's last command for Felix snaps something deep within me.

I erupt.

A scream fills the room—my scream.

The creature spins toward me, surprise in his features. He lets loose another command to stop, but it slips off me.

Panic fills his eyes as I start moving. He's screaming at me to stop.

I don't even know how the knife ends up in my hand, but it's there as I crash into him.

The icy press of the metal brands the skin of my bare hand.

"Stop," he yells, spittle flying. He's completely focused on me, and water sloshes as Felix breaks the surface and gasps for air. The relief I feel does nothing to dim the rage.

The look on his face as I lift the blade—the shock and surprise —I've seen it before. I know how this ends.

"Stab yourself!" He's desperate now. My smile is as sharp as the blade in my hand. He killed my parents. He killed my neighbors. He killed my classmates.

And then he trapped them. His earlier admission clangs through my head.

You are the reason I truly remained.

"No."

He's still yelling commands at me as I bring the knife down. He finally raises his arms at the last second, trying to fend off the blow.

The knife sinks in. Warmth soaks through the glove of the hand I have pinning his shoulder as I slide it out.

I feel nothing but satisfaction at the pain in his face as I pull my arm back. I plunge it in again. Blood sprays as I rip it out. Again. Blood splashes my face. Again. Coats my mouth. Again. Blurs my eyes. Again.

Someone's screaming. It might be me.

The light in his eyes begins to dim. This is his end. I've felt it. My magic courses through me, keeping me going.

All other thoughts empty from my head. I'm lost in the salt, the copper, the slick feel of blood as it mixes with my tears and slides down my face. Strong hands grip my shoulders. I try to shake them off, to let the knife plunge deeper.

My fault. My fault. My fault.

But the hands are stronger. Bands of ice wrap around me, crushing my arms to my side. Not ice—arms. Wet arms. Felix's arms. Trixie's face appears before me. She grips the sides of my face as she speaks. My choking sobs almost drown out her quiet words.

"George, you're okay. We're okay. He's gone. It's done. Let go of the knife."

I didn't even realize I was still holding it. It clatters to the floor, and I sink into Felix just before the door bursts open.

CHAPTER

36

THERE'S A HEAVY SILENCE BEFORE Gran pushes through the witches standing in the doorway of the attic and takes in the scene before her.

Blood is everywhere, coating every inch of me. I can feel the strands of hair plastered to my face with it, the drops of blood dripping from my hands, the bare one and the gloved one. The room doesn't look any better; it's slicked in the same blood. The metallic smell cloys at my throat.

The members of the coven follow in behind Gran, quietly at first, but then the whispers begin.

Fine, let them talk.

Trixie and Gran speak behind me, their voices barely audible over the murmurs of the coven members. I hope she's filling her in on what happened, if only so I won't have to say the words.

Murderer.

Gran moves to me, kneeling before me. I can't look at her though, can't face what I've done, what I've become now. Instead, I watch as the blood crawls up the silver of her pants.

They'll never be the same. It's a ridiculous thought, but it comes all the same.

"Georgiana." Gran's voice is soft, not the command of the Supreme, but of a grandmother.

I shake my head.

"Georgiana Colburn, you'll look at me right now."

Reluctantly, I drag my eyes up to meet hers.

"I am so proud of you."

Her words are such a shock that I would have fallen back if Felix wasn't still gripping me. "But I'm a . . ." I can't say the last word to voice the monster I've become.

"You are no such thing. That," her eyes flick to the side, but she doesn't turn to see the remains of the vodnici behind her, "is a very dangerous creature who, according to Trixie, has been harming the people of our town for a very long time."

"He stayed because of me." Even now, with his blood cooling on my skin, I still feel the heat of that shame.

"His choices are not a reflection of you," Gran says, resolve clear in her voice.

"This isn't his first town."

She sighs. "I assumed, but you did what very few have been able to do before. The vodnici are powerful creatures, one of the few who can overshadow our magic, but you broke through. And you removed the threat."

I could hug her for just that. For saying removed instead of killed. I finally take in all the coven members gathered in the small attic space.

It's only the elders, but their presence is overwhelming.

"How did you find us?"

"Jack came. I knew when I saw him something was wrong, so I called the council members and followed him here. He brought us right to you."

A sob of relief rips through me. Not a useless bag of fleas after all, it appears. "I thought he left me."

Gran's face crumples. "Dear girl, he was protecting you the best way he knew how. He wasn't strong enough for the vodnici, but you were. And he went to get reinforcements."

Jack meows from the doorway, almost as if he's unsure if he is welcome. But when I open my arms, he runs right into them nuzzling against my chest. He doesn't even seem to mind that he's covered in blood now too. He just starts purring like a chainsaw.

"George . . ." Trixie's voice is nearly a whisper as she stands up from where she was kneeling beside Gran.

I let Jack down as Felix pulls me up and releases me. We turn to follow Trixie's gaze.

The wall of cups remains, but the water in each cup is trembling. No one moves as I step forward, sliding a top off one of the cups. The water drains from the cup as a spirit appears before it. A young woman, dressed for another century, appears before me. She smiles before she fades away.

"Did you see that?" Felix asks from behind me.

I nod. "Did you?"

"I think we all did." Mistress Rowina's voice comes from across the room.

"They want to get out, but the lids are trapping them still. Help me." I pull off another lid. An older gentleman appears as his water fades, and he's gone before I can pull the next lid. My friends step forward, as do the other members of the coven. Given the hundreds of cups—of *souls*—on the shelves, we need to work quickly to free the souls. Hundreds of years. He did this for hundreds of years. If I wasn't sure before, it's obvious by the dress of so many of the spirits.

Somewhere in here, my parents' souls are trapped. I can feel them, but I won't let myself keep the other souls trapped for a moment longer just so I can be the one to find them, to free them. If their souls are no longer trapped, I should be able to call them. Hopefully.

Soon, only the highest shelf remains. Only a few cups have been placed up there. Two chairs are dragged over, and Gran and I stand on top of them. Gran pulls the lid from the one closest to her.

The ghost of Renee appears in the center of the room. Unlike the ones before her, she remains.

"My dear friend." Renee's eyes are lined with silver as she nods to Gran before she turns to me. "You have done well. Never forget the power you wield."

And then she's gone. I turn back to the shelf. Only two cups left. I look to Gran, who reads what I'm thinking in my eyes.

"Together?" she asks.

I nod again as we reach up and slide the tops from the cups.

"My Georgie girl."

I nearly choke on a sob at the voice behind me. I'd know it anywhere.

"Dad," I say as I turn. In the center of the room, behind those gathered behind us, stand my parents.

I clamber from the chair, reaching out to them as I approach. But my arms slip right through their forms.

They may be free, but they're still dead.

"Georgie," my dad says softly. He looks just as I remember. My eyes flick to my mother. Poised royalty in her own right, nothing like the terrified form I saw a few weeks ago when we called her.

"You were so brave," my mom says. There's a waver in her voice. "I am so, so proud of you."

"Was it you?" I ask quietly. Part of me won't be satisfied until I know, but I'm still not sure I want to hear the answer.

My mother quirks her head. "Was what me?"

"Did you curse me with my touch?"

My mother's features fall and her pain barrels into me. "My darling, no. Even if I could, I would never be able to burden you with that."

"Then how?"

My mother looks to Gran then back to me. "Only the Goddess can give gifts, so it would be only fair to assume that she can manipulate them as well." I think of the witch whose magic burned the forest. Maybe I'll become a tale of how magic protected a coven. The thought brings me little comfort.

My dad places his hand on my mother's shoulder. Tears shine in her eyes. "I wish we could hold you."

"There is so much we wanted to show you," Dad says.

A fresh tear slides down my cheek. "I know. But I'm glad I see you now. I'm glad you're free."

Dad looks past me toward something outside of this room. "Monica, it's time."

She follows his gaze, eyes unfocusing for a moment.

"I think we're meant to move on now." There's a fresh wave of anguish that crashes onto me.

I nod, trying to keep my bottom lip from trembling. "Will I see you again?"

Mom shrugs, but there's a smile on her lips. "If you want to, I suppose you will."

"I love you." The words feel too small for what I really want to say, but it's all I can get out.

My dad's eyes crinkle around the edges. His longing and regret crush me, followed by an overwhelming feeling of pride. "We love you too."

Then they're gone. The world feels empty again.

The souls in the cups are free, but the room still feels packed with them. I move to the wall of canvases, Gran close behind me.

"The ones whose water ran out, they remained trapped in the last canvas he used their water on."

Gran sucks her teeth. "That is unfortunate." I whirl to look at her, but she continues before I can say anything. "And something we will figure out how to address. We'll transport them somewhere else for now though. They can't stay here."

Gran places a hand on my shoulder. "We will take care of this. Wait outside with your friends." I turn to leave, but Gran grips my shoulder. "Just a moment." She waves her hand, and the blood disappears from me. I still feel it drying on my skin, but the visible parts are gone. When I look at Jack, the blood is gone from his fur as well. "You'll still need to shower when we get home, but that should disguise it for now."

We clomp downstairs to gather in the backyard. We stand in silence, not sure what to say to one another, as I rip the glove from my hand. It still feels wet and sticky, even though my hands appear clean. I tuck the glove into my back pocket with its twin.

"George?" The sound of the familiar voice makes me jump. Every nerve is so raw that every movement is making me jump.

I turn to find Jen's form a few feet behind me. In the panic, I forgot that she would also be free to go. "Jen." I smile at her. "I'm so glad you're still here. I think I would have been sad if you left before I said goodbye."

Jen smirks. "Grown to like me that much?"

"Despite my best intentions." I try to smile, but my lips still wobble.

"Jen's still here?" Trixie asks from beside me.

"Sure is," I say. I want to give her form, but I don't know that I have the strength. "Thanks for coming to see me before you, you know, move on. I'll miss you."

"Well, that's the thing."

"What's the thing?"

"I don't really want to move on. At least, not right now. With everything that's happened, I kind of feel like that's abandoning you. I was hoping you'd be okay if I stayed?"

Her hope hits me at the same moment as my shock courses through. "Of course." The words are out of my mouth before I have time to think about them.

She smiles, a real one, and steps forward to stand beside Trixie as I turn back to watching the house. The members of the coven emerge as a small flame begins in the kitchen. It doesn't take long for the house, old and wooden as it is, to be consumed by fire. Smoke rises in the air and we're already far down the street by the time the first siren sounds. Even the firefighters were at the play.

As we get to Felix's Jeep, we turn and watch the smoke rising from the house. Trixie reaches for the door handle.

"There's blood on your hands," I say.

She lifts her hands, looking down at them. Blood coats both palms. "I didn't even notice. It must have been from when I . . ." She trails off and looks up at me, eyes wide.

"When you what?" I prod.

"Touched your face."

It comes back to me then, Trixie's hands clutching my face as she tried to calm me down. And the fact that I didn't experience her death.

"I don't know how you die."

Her shoulders sag in what I think is relief.

"It's gone." I stare at my bare hands. I look up to find her still watching me. In a split second, I've made my decision. My hands reach up to cup her face. She must sense what I'm doing, because she meets me halfway, our lips crashing into each other.

I slip into the kiss, forgetting myself. And for the first time in years, death does not greet me.

EPILOGUE

A DUSTING OF SNOW SPRINKLES the parking lot, so at odds with the warm glow from inside Matt's. The windows show perfect little scenes of families enjoying dinner and friends sharing treats.

Felix bumps me with his shoulder. "What's going on in that head of yours?"

"They don't know anything has happened."

"No, I suppose they don't."

"Will it change anything?" I mean it just to ask about the deaths in town, but as it comes out, I realize I'm asking about so much more: my place at school and in the coven, my relationship with my magic, our friendship.

Felix sighs. "It already has." I look up to find him smiling at me. "Just think of why we're here."

Turning back to the windows, I see her inside. Trixie is sitting with a book, smiling at something she just read. Her milkshake sits forgotten in front of her. I reach down to fiddle with my glove, momentarily forgetting that they're not there.

That's a habit that will take a long time to break.

Felix notices my movement. "What are you worried about?"

"Am I making the right decision, bringing Trixie into this?"

"She's safe, George. The whole town's safe. You took care of the threat."

Felix knows better than to say I killed the threat. I'm still not ready to hear that out loud. I'm still not sure what happened to Silas, or rather, the body the vodnici posing as Silas occupied. The coven took care of "cleaning up" after we left. The town knows he left, but that's all. No one asked questions, either because magic encouraged them not to or living in a town filled with death has changed the priorities of the residents of Windrop.

Mr. Whitaker dropped dead at the play. The coroner says of a heart attack, but I know better.

As for the canvases, they're tucked into an alcove of our library, at least until we can figure out how to free the souls trapped in them. And those are the ones we know about. That thing said there were others, scattered throughout the world . . .

One day, I'll set them free too.

It's not the vodnici that worries me about involving Trixie with more of my life. He was here for me. He stayed in Windrop longer than he deemed safe because my magic called to him. How many other creatures may feel the same? And since I ascended so recently, how do I know that my ever-strengthening magic won't call more creatures, and more danger, to me?

That's not to mention other wielders. I may be applying myself and taking a more active role in the coven—hell, I even killed a vodnici that was stealing the souls of townsfolk—but there are many in the coven who still resent me. I feel it in their gazes. Some of them hate me, and as their Rising Supreme, I wonder if any of them will try to change my fate. I wonder what they know about Veritas and the darkness it showed me.

As my friend, Trixie would be at risk for just associating with me, but as my girlfriend . . . I don't even want to think of the target that could paint on her.

I say none of this to Felix though. There's no need to burden him with it. "Right."

"Just take it one day at a time." He offers me his arm, and I loop mine through it, savoring his warmth.

Jack trots in front of us as we walk to the front door, peeling off before we go in. He hasn't left my side since everything happened. He isn't always right next to me like Bennington is with Gran, but he is always nearby. I may not see him all the time, but I know he's watching. Strangely, I find it comforting.

Felix opens the door and the smell of hot grease and cheese floats out with the warmth.

"Got a sec?" a familiar voice calls before I step inside.

A smile tugs at my lips. "You go on ahead. I'll be in shortly."

Felix looks around like he can see her before nodding and heading inside.

I step away from the front door to Felix's Jeep, stopping on the side away from Matt's. We can talk here and it will just look like I forgot something in the car.

"Hey, Jen," I say.

She materializes against the Jeep, leaning on the door. "Hey, George."

"What's up?" She's been around more often since the souls were freed, spending time just quietly sitting with my friends, asking me to make her visible so she can chat with them during my shifts at the library.

"I know the rules about being in public. You know, stay away from you so you don't look crazy?"

"That is important."

"But if I wanted to come into Matt's and just sit, would you send me away?"

Jen's hope blooms in my chest. "I think that would be all right." I can't say no to such a simple request.

Jen beams. "Awesome. Someone has to keep an eye on you, so you don't make a fool of yourself on your date."

My eyes almost roll back in my head. "It's not a date." That would be another day, just Trixie and me. "It's just friends hanging out."

"Uh-huh."

"I'm going inside," I say, waving her off.

Three orders of fries cover the table in addition to the milkshakes now. There are at least eight cups of ranch dressing to go with them, and one sad little container of what appears to be honey mustard. That's probably Trixie's. She's trying to convince us that we can enjoy ranch *and* other sauces. She's wrong.

She spots me as I approach and reaches her hand out to me. I loop my fingers—my bare fingers—through hers and slide into the booth.

I'm staring at our linked hands, trying to ignore the burn in my eyes when she speaks. "Fries are hot, and Suzy was adamant about the ranch. I think she gave us too much though."

"Never," Felix and I say at the same time. Blinking, I look up. "We're going to have to talk about your condiment choice though."

As Trixie laughs, I realize Felix is right. I just have to take this day by day. There might be danger in my life, but right now, sitting at this table, it's worth it.

ACKNOWLEDGMENTS

I TELL MY GIRLS THAT actions mean more than words, but since you've just finished reading a slew of my writing already, I hope these words of thanks will suffice.

To Michael, thank you for your never-ending support. Thank you for picking up the slack so I can meet deadlines, attend writing events, and participate in workshops. For reading my books. For listening to me talk through all my plot ideas. For being the best dad to our little girls.

To my girls, you are the best part of my day. I love you both more than you can ever know.

To my family, who has been steadfast in their support of my dreams. Mom and Dad, you are easily my biggest fans. To Aunt Diane, thank you for being my sounding board and voice of reason, in all life's decisions. To Aunt Vikki and Uncle Karl for your unwavering enthusiasm for my accomplishments. To my sisters (and Homie), you've shaped me for the better more than you know.

To my CP, Aspen, this book would not be here if it weren't for you and your support. This book carries so many pieces of you, and I am so grateful for your support. I can't wait for your debut.

To my friends. Stef and Zac, you gave me a space to talk about some of my favorite things, books, during the dark days of COVID and long after. Thank you for your humor and support, even when I'm chaotic. The group chat keeps me sane, and I am eternally grateful. Sam, you are the most voracious reader I know and having you as a friend, a concert buddy, and a sounding board is the best thing I never knew I needed.

To my editor, Elana Gibson, thank you for helping me shape George into what she is. And to the team at CamCat, thank you for believing in me and helping my story transform into a book.

To all the readers and authors who've cheered on *Touch of Death* with excitement, thank you. I can't wait to share future stories with you.

ABOUT THE AUTHOR

TAYLOR MUNSELL IS A FANTASY and YA author currently reading, writing, and hoarding books. She has a passion for telling magical stories about prickly girls. When she's not writing, you can find Taylor eating a snack, reading a book, or trying to go on an adventure. She lives and writes in the mountains of North Carolina.

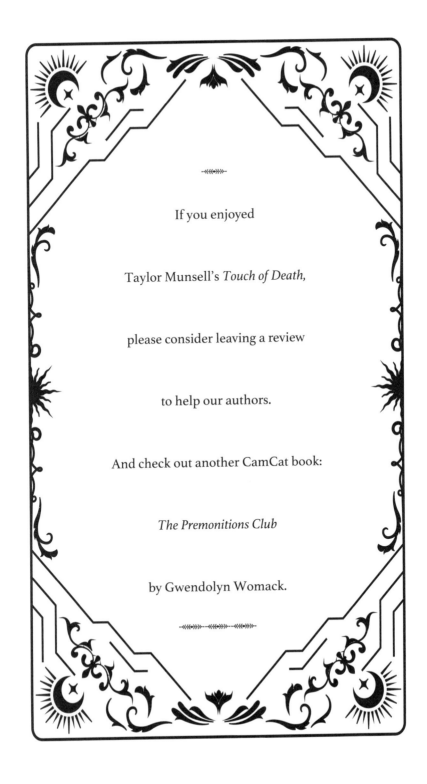

If you enjoyed

Taylor Munsell's *Touch of Death,*

please consider leaving a review

to help our authors.

And check out another CamCat book:

The Premonitions Club

by Gwendolyn Womack.

PRESENT DAY

-⦓⦔⦓⦔- -⦓⦔⦓⦔-

LIV

PREMONITION:

A STRONG FEELING SOMETHING IS ABOUT TO HAPPEN

L IV HALL didn't believe in knowing the future before it happened. If she did, maybe she would have sensed her stepdad had been cheating on her mom all year. Or maybe she
would have known they'd divorce when Bodhi finally confessed so
he could go live with his new girlfriend. Or maybe she could have
foreseen she and her mom—who was busy having a nervous break-
down—would leave New York City to go live with her grandfather
in Hyde Park. And maybe, just maybe, she would have had the inkling to know her grandfather would pass away peacefully in his
sleep two months later, leaving her mom the house and everything
in it.

But life hadn't been predictable. It had come at them full speed,
an eighty-mile-an-hour chain of disasters. They packed their bags in
early spring and came to Hyde Park, where she was forced to finish
out her junior year, all two and half months of it, at Roosevelt High

School as the new girl. "That girl from New York" with the funky jewelry and silver armband.

The night before her first day of school she slapped green dye on her long, auburn hair with a shade appropriately called Manic Panic and wrote "New Girl" on a white T-shirt in black sharpie to make sure everyone knew how she felt about it. The only thing that kept her from completely losing it was at least she had one friend at school, Winnie, the daughter of her mom's old friend.

Growing up, whenever Liv had come to town to visit her grandfather, her mom always signed her up for "summer fun" classes with Winnie. Liv's favorite class had been the baking classes at the Culinary Institute of America, which had its main campus in Hyde Park. To Liv, the building and grounds looked like a magical castle. The Institute was where her mom first met her stepdad. Hazel had come to campus to write a freelance article for a food magazine. Bodhi had fallen hard for the struggling-writer single mom, and they got married by the end of the year. Hazel continued to write articles on food and wine. Over the years, she became the queen of reviews from bean-to-bar chocolate or artisanal cheeses, to gourmet specialty products around the world. Bodhi Hall was a big name in the food industry too, a superstar chef who owned a restaurant in Manhattan.

Liv hadn't talked to her stepdad since he left, and her mother didn't blame her. Bodhi had destroyed their family, as if the last ten years together meant nothing. During the worst of the breakup, at the height of the yelling and her mother's tears, Liv would hide out in her room making jewelry, her longtime hobby. She'd stay up late, bent over her worktable with a soldering iron, as if she could somehow weld her life back together again.

The most intricate piece she made for herself was a silver armband. It looked like braided rope, but really it was a chain of triskelions, an ancient Celtic symbol of three triple spirals joined together.

She found the symbol in a design book, and making the armband had gotten her though that last horrid month of the divorce. Now she never took it off. After the move, her mom barely kept it together. At night, she watched sappy rom-com movies and powered through Kleenex. She retreated into the house in Hyde Park like it was a fortress, locking herself in her bedroom and rarely coming out. Liv's grandfather had welcomed them with open arms, shuttling Liv around town and managing all the cooking. Even with the tragic end of Hazel's marriage, Liv could tell her grandfather was happy to have them come live with him. Clement had been alone, Liv's grandmother having died before Liv was born, and he'd had almost three precious months together with Liv and Hazel before he passed away. Now he was gone, and his house had suddenly become one big ghost of a memory. Her grandfather's estate attorney had called and left several messages that they needed to come and go through some things. Her mom had been putting off returning their calls, saying it was too soon. Liv agreed. She wanted to look through her grandfather's things before a stranger did. She decided to start with the attic, not ready to tackle her grandfather's bedroom or closet yet. Her mother said she was only interested in keeping antiques or family heirlooms and trusted Liv to make the call.

Winnie had come over to help. It was Sunday and they planned to spend most of the day going through boxes. The attic was huge, the kind that could be turned into a spare bedroom or an office loft. It had a pitched-roof ceiling with enough room to stand, and an old-timey circular window looked out onto the street below, and sunlight streamed in through towering oak trees. The house was a two-story Cape Cod and sat in the heart of town. Her grandfather had lived there forever and amassed enough stuff in the attic to prove it.

Liv and Winnie spent all morning opening old boxes and making piles to donate. They laid out old blankets on the floor to sit, and when it got warm around noon, Liv brought up a fan. She was wearing cutoff jeans and a tank top that showed off her armband, and her long hair was up in a hasty twist, secured with a hairclip that liked to slip off every hour. True to form, Winnie was *not* in let's-go-through-the-attic wear. She always wore black skirts, no matter what, and dressed in a unique style that had a vintage Gothic flair. Her hair was the star, a 1920s pageboy blunt cut, dyed jet black with the edges ringed in sapphire blue, framing perfect black eyeliner, siren-red lipstick, and her cat-eyed glasses.

"I think there's more boxes behind this thing." Liv stood on tiptoe and tried to peek over the top of a six-foot wall of wood panels that were tied together and draped with a black tarp. She twisted her falling hair back up and secured it with the clip again.

Winnie fanned herself. "Sorry. I draw the line with heavy lifting. It will completely destroy the manicure I got yesterday." Her nails were painted silver with purple stars and moons stenciled on them. "Maybe Matty could help? He should be here soon."

Liv raised her eyebrows without comment. Matty was Winnie's best friend. He was even shorter and skinnier than she was. He also liked to dress like a fashion designer on *Project Runway* and had already told them he refused to touch anything dusty today.

She looked out the window down below at her neighbor across the street who was washing his car, an old Ford Mustang, in the driveway. He was wearing board shorts, a workout tank, and flip flops. The tank showed off every muscle on his arms.

"I bet he could." Liv nodded to him.

Winnie joined her at the window. "No way. You live across the street from Forester Torres? How did I not know this?" Forester went to their school, but Liv had never talked to him. He had thick, wavy black hair, deep brown eyes, and was ridiculously tan. He reminded Liv a little bit of Bodhi. Maybe that's why she was feeling so fearless and started to open the window.

"What are you doing?" Winnie sounded alarmed.

"Asking for help. He looks like the Hulk down there. He can totally move this thing."

"Wait!" Winnie tried to stop her. "Forester Torres is one of the most popular guys at school. He's captain of the football team."

"So?" Liv turned to Winnie, surprised. "I thought you didn't buy into social cliques."

"I don't. I'm not. But you haven't lived your whole life here going to school with some of these people."

At school, Winnie was a loner and sometimes hung out with the Drama Club along with Matty. Liv didn't know where she fit in the scheme of cliques and cool status, and right now she was beyond caring. All she wanted to do was move this stupid wood.

"Maybe he's really nice and, like you said, we need help." Liv cranked the window open with the handle before Winnie could stop her and called out, "Hey! Hello down there!"

Forester looked up, and Winnie ducked down to hide. "I can't believe you're doing this."

Liv laughed and yelled down, "I'm your new neighbor and clearing out the attic with my friend, and we need help moving some wood panels. Think you can come over for a minute?"

Winnie was laughing now too. "What's he saying?" she whispered.

"He nodded and put down the hose."

"You're kidding me."

"No, he's coming over." Liv grinned and closed the window back up. "See? That was easy."

"I hate you." Winnie picked up the electric fan and blasted her face to cool off. The doorbell rang and Liv ran downstairs, knowing her mother was sound asleep in her room after an all-night Netflix binge. She whipped open the door a little more violently than she intended.

Forester took a step back with a friendly hand up. "Whoa there."

"Sorry." Liv smiled up at him, trying to play it cool. Forester was huge, well over six feet. "Hi. Thanks for coming over. I'm Liv."

"Yeah, I know." Forester gave her an easy grin. "The new girl." He motioned to his T-shirt, mimicking where she'd written it on her shirt that first day.

"That's me." Liv grimaced. "I really appreciate the help."

"No prob. Let's do it." He shrugged off the thanks and followed her up the stairs.

When they got to the attic he gave Winnie a friendly salute. "Yo yo."

Winnie raised her eyebrows in surprise. "Yo yo yourself."

He asked them, "So what are we moving today?"

"That." Liv pointed to the wall of wood.

Forester circled around it. "I see what you mean. Why don't you guys take one end, and we can try and angle it over this way."

"Sorry, team," Winnie announced, shaking her head regretfully. "I gotta sit this one out. My nails." She flashed them to Forester.

"It's fine, Win." Liv rolled her eyes with a smile. "We got it." She and Forester each took a side and tried to lift it together, barely getting it to budge.

They made several attempts until Forester finally said, "I think we need more muscle." He pulled out his cell and speed-dialed someone.

Liv looked to Winnie in alarm. *What* was he doing?

Whoever he called picked up on the first ring. "Yo, dude. You still stopping by? I'm at the house across the street from mine. We need help moving some wood. It'll just take a sec. Think you can come over?"

Winnie was looking at Liv in alarm too. *Who* was he calling?

Forester hesitated, listening to whatever the person was saying. "Seriously? She is? Whatever, man. I don't care. She can come." He sounded annoyed.

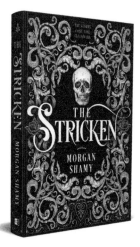
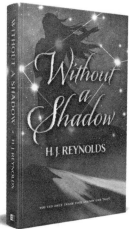

CamCat Books

VISIT US ONLINE FOR MORE BOOKS TO LIVE IN:
CAMCATBOOKS.COM

SIGN UP FOR CAMCAT'S FICTION NEWSLETTER FOR
COVER REVEALS, EBOOK DEALS, AND MORE EXCLUSIVE CONTENT.

CamCatBooks

@CamCatBooks

@CamCat_Books

@CamCatBooks